Relax, Your Life Is Predestined

Relax, Your Life Is Predestined

Raymond H. DuRussel,
D.P.M., A.C.C.P.P.S.

Proctor Publications, LLC • Ann Arbor • Michigan • USA

Copyright © 1997 Raymond H. DuRussel

Published in the USA by
Proctor Publications
PO Box 2498, Ann Arbor, MI 48106

All rights reserved.
No part of this book may by reproduced or utilized
in any form or by any means, electronic or mechanical,
except in the context of reviews, without prior written
permission from the author or publisher.

ISBN 1–882792–43–2
LCCN 97–67281

Cataloging in Publication Data
Prepared by Quality Books

DuRussel, Raymond H.
    Relax, your life is predestined / Raymond H. DuRussel – 1st ed.
    p. cm.
    ISBN: 1–882792–43–2

1. Predestination.   I. Title.

BT810.D87 1997   291.22
                                  QBI97–40660

Acknowledgments

A special thanks to my neighbor, Pat Hintz, for proofreading this work. I appreciate her being there at the right time to supply the expertise I lacked.

Contents

Introduction ix

1. **Your Life is Predestined** 1
2. **All Things Were Created by Him for Him** 7
3. **Lord Jesus Christ has Power Over All Leaders:**
   The Fate of the World is Predestined 16
   - The Devil Is The Original Assassin 16
   - Why Do Terrible Things Happen? 18
   - Why Doesn't God Destroy The Devil And All Evil? 20
   - Why Does God Allow Random Catastrophes?
     (Authority Over the Devil) 22
   - Back To The Thrones, Dominions, Principalities, or Power .. 29
4. **The Realities of Predestination** 35
   - Motivation 36
   - Laws Make Certain A Predictable Outcome 36
   - There Are No Accidents From God's Perspective 37
   - The Concept Of Free Will 38
   - Ahab's Life Ended By God 39
   - The Trials Of Life 40
5. **The Prophet Jonah, Controlling One's Destiny** 44
   - Jonah's Only Path 45
6. **The Life of Joseph** 50
   - Joseph Sent To His Brothers 51
   - Joseph In Egypt As A Slave To Potiphar 53
   - Joseph In Prison 57
   - Joseph Before Pharaoh 58
   - Joseph Made Governor Of Egypt 60
   - Joseph As Governor Of Egypt 60
   - Diverging From Joseph For Awhile 64
   - Joseph And His Family Connections 68
   - God's Plans For Joseph's Sons 70
   - Joseph Suffers By The Will Of God 71
   - Joseph's Brothers Changed By Suffering 72
   - Sin Is Sin 74
7. **The Life of Samson** 77
   - Your Plans May Not Be His Plans 79
   - Two Kingdoms 80
   - Samson's Marriage Falls Apart 81

	Samson's Wife Given To Another	87
	Samson Takes Revenge For His Despair	89
	The Results Of Samson's Actions	91
8.	**The Life of Nebuchadnezzar**	**93**
	Jesus Christ Came To Save Sinners	97
	We All Serve God	97
	Nebuchadnezzar Exalts Himself And Fails To Honor God	99
9.	**The Pharaoh**	**104**
	Back To God's Original Declaration	105
	Who Is The Lord?	106
	The Correct Attitude (Diverging From Pharaoh)	108
	The Power Of Blessing And The Power Of Cursing	109
	Back To The Pahraoh	111
	The Red Sea Experience	113
10.	**The Lord Jesus Christ**	**116**
	Abel's Revelation	118
	Some Important Differences Between The Elect And Non-Elect	120
	Ordained To Be Crucified Two Positions	122
	Everything About The Lord Jesus Christ Is Foretold In The Scriptures	124
	Revelations	125
	Lamb Slain From The Foundation To The World	130
	Abraham's Symbolic Sacrifice Of Issac	131
	The Sacrifice Of Jesus Established In The Law	133
	Jesus Sacrificed In The Law	135
	Resurrection	136
	Upon This Rock I Will Build My Church	139
	I Am The Alpha And The Omega	140
	Jesus' Suffering And Ours Is According To The Will Of The Father	142
	Jesus, The Name The Father Is Exalting	146
11.	**Prayer: Its Nature, Purpose, and Place in Our Lives**	**151**
	Jehovah's Will Is Immutable	151
	Agreement With God As A Way Of Life	152
	Selective Sight	155
	Why Do We Pray?	157
	The Comfort Of Understanding	159
	Miraculous Prayer	163

	Misguided Prayer	170
	Other Avenues Of Prayer	171
12.	**Heaven and Hell**	**172**
	Judas	174
	You Must Be Born Again	176
	When Life Is Death	179
	Of His Own Will Begot He Us (James 1:8)	181
	The Thieves On The Cross	184
	Nebuchadnezzar	185
	Jabez's Prayer	188
	"I Form Light, And Create Darkness"	190
	Others, Turning Away Or Toward The Light	192
	The Quality Of Choice	193
	Other Sheep I Have, Not Of This Fold	195
	My Own Thoughts	197
	The Final Word	203

Introduction

Relax, your life is predestined. This title sums up my goal, to bring you rest. It is a matter of faith. If you believe that everything around you hinges upon your own efforts, you will never have any rest. However, if you discover the truth, you can enter into a deep understanding of life, and rest.

Knowledge and faith go hand in hand. The more you know about everything, the greater becomes your faith. You no longer have superstition and speculation, but understanding. You have more confidence because your faith becomes an inward assurance that things are so. If your faith is weak and imperfect, it is because you have little understanding and knowledge. The weaker your faith, the more you are reduced to guessing. A guess can never give much peace and assurance, but knowledge does.

Let me take you through the steps and foundations of predestination to give you new found confidence and assurance. I felt deeply inspired, daily, to write this book. Because of that inspiration, I believe it will help to greatly deepen your faith and peace.

There is a lot of controversy surrounding the topic of predestination. This book will challenge you. I have endeavored to be as factual as possible. I do not see how it is possible to refute what I have written. Without a doubt, this book will stimulate a great deal of thought and discussion.

I hope you will enjoy reading this book as much as I enjoyed writing it. If so, I will have been successful in adding a small amount of joy to your life; for that, I would be eternally thankful.

1
Your Life is Predestined

If you have ever wondered about things which seem to occur for a reason, then what you are about to read is for you. Many of us struggle with the concept of our own free will. Are the events in our lives, the people we meet, the path we have taken, and things that occur in the world around us beyond a matter of coincidence and pure chance? Does everything unfold within an elaborate scheme of destiny? We have all wanted something or someone with great desire, but because of factors beyond our control, this desire or person was beyond our reach. Depending upon how much experience we have had with living, we may be retrospectively glad that things did not work out the way we had hoped. In other cases, we may be left with a lingering regret or a lack of understanding of why things went the way they did. To be sure, everything that occurs, has occurred or will occur, has profound effect on the type of people we become. In a sense, we are formed and reformed by the events within our own little universe. Just as our conception and birth was beyond our personal control, other events around us birth us into a more complete definition of who we are and who we are to become.

I, at one time, believed strongly in the concept of chance and thought that I was master of my own destiny. Gradually, as my faith in God and the Lord Jesus Christ increased and the circumstances in my life began to take shape, I began to realize that God intervened providentially, saving me from time to time. As I developed my understanding, so did my realization that I could not take just any path I chose, but could successfully go in only a specific direction regardless of the amount of effort I exerted; this discovery has been demonstrated to me over and over again in the numerous enthusiastic adventures I have attempted to undertake. In each case, success or lack of success has been the reward and outcome of each venture. Not one venture was a complete waste; each experience reinforced the truth that my life, like your life, is not under our full control. We, like Pavlov's dog, are manipulated by the treats we receive as motivations to encourage or discourage us along a path. None of us exist without the concept of reward and motivation. It is the driving force of our universe. With this in mind, we must understand that this concept of motivation and reward is not only for the behavior of man and lower animals, but also for the actions of Devils or angels.

I have chosen to open with the following scripture from the Psalms as a truth which can only be accepted by faith, however, the evidence of this truth is all around us. Ps. 37:23 *The steps of a good man are "ordered" by the LORD: and He delighteth in his way.*[1] First of all, notice that it does not say "some of the steps" are ordered, but that "the steps" of a good man are ordered by the Lord. It may be hard to comprehend, but this scripture means just what it says; all your steps are "ordered." The original word for "ordered" in the original Hebrew is 3559h. kun – a primary, primitive root; to be firm.[2] Translations from other scriptures help us grasp the full meaning of this word: appointed, confirm, direct, carried out, certain, definitely, determined, directed, established, fashioned, installed, make ready, prepared, strengthen, took, firmly established, formed, made preparations, made provision, ordained, provided, right.

As you can see by these strong words, we are being told that it is God Himself who directs our path. Your path, like my path is not left to chance. It may seem so at times from our own perspective, but this is only because of our limited understanding of what goes on around us.

For years, we have been sold the concept of random chance. There is nothing random about life or matter in this universe. Point

---

[1] All scriptures in this text used with permission from The King James Version Bible and the New American Standard Bible, Copyright 1988, The Lockeman Foundation.
[2] All route word definitions in this text used from the same source with permission.

to anything and there are laws which govern it, reasons for where it is, how it got there, and everything else about it. From our vantage point, because we do not know all the factors involved, it may appear random chance. However, what we are calling random chance is not random chance at all, but many complex factors of which we are ignorant. If we knew these factors, they would explain a thing, where it is, how it got there, and everything else about it.

Let me give you an example. We see a bird land on a particular tree, on a particular branch. Someone may say that everything we have just observed is random chance. Again, there is nothing random about what we have observed at all; we simply do not know all the factors. The tree grew in the spot it did because of events which led to where the seed was placed into the soil. The tree grew because of its genetic program and because of correct environmental conditions. The branch developed because of the genetic program and may have been modified by other very exact factors exposed to it. The bird chose the branch because it met its criteria. The bird thus was motivated to choose this branch; the bird likewise may be motivated not to remain on this branch. In each case, there are reasons connected to reasons and nothing happens for no reason at all. From our vantage point, it may seem meaningless. Nevertheless, if you go up or down the scale, we ourselves are supported by a very large foundation of very small reasons.

I would like to cite more examples before we proceed to refute some of the thinking we have about random chance. A very good foundation is important in order for us to draw the same conclusions and feel comfortable with them. If we drop a ball from the same height repeatedly, it will take the exact amount of time for that ball to hit the earth each and every time we drop it. Why? Because the forces acting on the ball are determined and precise; they are not random. When the ball hits the ground, it may bounce, but the bounce also is not random. It has an exact trajectory which occurs because of exact forces propelling it in the direction it travels. If all the factors and forces were known, we would be able to determine exactly how the ball would bounce and account for every detail of that bounce. If we do not know all the factors, we may call it random, but there is nothing random about it. We are simply unable to predict what will happen because of our relative ignorance of all the factors.

Let's look at something more complex. If you were to hurl an uncooked egg against a wall to splatter it, it would leave a pattern that some may claim is a random pattern. The pattern itself, if repeated by another egg being hurled, would show a variable pattern of staining the wall. These two patterns would seem on the surface to establish the concept of being purely random. If we look closely at each and every factor and property of the egg, the surface of the wall, the velocity and angle of the collision, the temperature, and every detail of which we can account, we would come to the conclusion that this information would be insufficient to predict the pattern of the splatter. However, it should be clear to us that it is because of the complexity and our lack of knowing everything about all the interactions that we are unable to predict the pattern. With the simple ball, we are able to predict its course, but the egg splatter is far too complex. We can appreciate the fact that it would only be possible to predict if we were endowed with much greater ability or knowledge than we currently possess. Therefore, from our vantage point, things unknown and too complex for us to understand are defined as purely random chance. Nevertheless, we must appreciate the fact that there is an exact reason behind every occurrence in which, if we had sufficient understanding, would be predictable. This is the way we interact in life. Understanding everything is beyond our comprehension; nothing occurs without a reason or a purpose.

Yet, the concept of randomness is valid to the observer. It does not mean that there are no reasons. It means only that from the vantage point of the observer, things appear to be random. To illustrate further this concept, let me cite an example I noticed while walking through the woods. On the side of the trail was a tree with hundreds of very small holes in the bark created by a woodpecker. Some of the holes were aligned in a pattern; others were scattered diffusely. Overall, there was no predictable pattern in the bark. From my vantage point, it was an excellent display of a random pattern created by a little creature. The entire tree was covered by the small indentations placed at nonspecific intervals.

I reasoned that this pattern is basically random from visual observation. However, the little bird had a deliberate reason for making each hole! In the bird's mind, it was not making random holes. It was searching for food in the most appropriate spots. Each hole was a decision! Even the insect had specific reasons for choosing this portion of this bark on this tree. Thus the concept of random holds true only from the vantage point of the casual observer.

Eccl. 3:11 *He has made everything appropriate in its time. He has also set eternity in their heart, yet so that man will not find out the work which God has done from the beginning even to the end.* Every one of us can appreciate in our imaginations the concept of infinity or extremely vast periods of time, distance, and events beyond our grasp. This is the part of us that makes us special. This ability to appreciate things beyond our grasp makes us reach to understand and grow more. This is one of our finest attributes. With this attribute, to appreciate and imagine thoughts of things beyond our ability, comes the understanding that we do not possess the faculties to fully comprehend them. We each grow continually toward that end, but with each plateau comes a greater understanding that we have just begun to understand. It seems that the less we know, the more we think we understand. The more we learn about what the Lord has created, about life, and all that is about us, the more humbled we become of its vastness and complexity and our own feeble grasp of everything. The older we get, the more we understand about all things. Yet, we become humbler because we are more aware of our own limitations and smallness in this vast ocean. The apostle Paul wrote 1 Cor. 8:2 *And if any man think that he knoweth any thing, he knoweth nothing yet as he ought to know.*

I want to go back to Eccl. 3:11 and look at the word "everything." We are faced with accepting what this scripture states or failing to grasp the significance. "Everything" means all things unless we adopt the idea that it really doesn't mean "everything," but "something." By changing this word, we would change the meaning and significance of what God is communicating to us. By substituting "something" or "most things" for "everything," we can allow for things outside of the Lord's control. This would give space for the idea of chance. It would also give credence to the notion that God does not have His hand in everything that occurs, but that some things occur outside of that which He has determined. The notion that anything occurs outside of the plans and purposes of God is not supported by the scriptures. The Lord does not run around like a firefighter putting out fires started by rowdy forces acting outside of His control. It takes faith to believe what Eccl. 3:11 tells us. When we are young and less experienced in life, it is more difficult to grasp the concept of predestination because so much of what goes on around us seems by chance. There are those who never see or understand almost anything that occurs in this world. Jesus referred to these people as spiritually blind. Matt. 15:14 *Let them alone: they be blind leaders of the blind. And if the blind lead the blind, both shall fall into the ditch.*

2
All Things were Created by Him and for Him

I want to start with a statement to help us examine the validity of our mind set. Everything is interrelated and connected from the beginning of time. These interactions influence each other and therefore continue to be related, such as cause and effect. Nothing exists without a reason and nothing stands alone. Because something exists (or has existed), it effects other things around it.

We can think of this interrelation like a ripple effect of a stone thrown into a still pool of water. The wave that spreads outward from the epicenter is part of the effect of the stone. Even things at rest, seeming to do nothing, exert their effect by simply being there. The stone, for instance, after causing the wave ripple, now sits in the bottom of the pool, changing the shape of the floor of that pool. Furthermore, stationary objects in the pool, which seem to be doing nothing, influence the shape and direction of the wave ripple. The wave is disturbed by the presence of the stationary object. Thus, the stationary object, seemingly doing nothing, influences the ripple wave minimally or greatly by its mere presence. Everything in the universe is similarly interrelated from the beginning of time unto now and will be so in the future. Similarly, natural boundaries as things just sitting there, exert their influence. In the social realm, parents may act as natural boundaries controlling things that may influence their children.

Whether we are in motion or at rest, each of is influenced by things in which we come into contact. We, by our very existence, influence the people and the world around us. We influence cause and effect, whether doing nothing at all or by being very active. Each of us changes and adapts as the result of all these interactions. Furthermore, we make decisions motivated by influences that formed us internally and externally. It is important to understand that decisions are not random, nor are they by chance. There are reasons for what each of us chooses. If you control what influences people, your control is what motivates them. Influence, control, and motivation are key factors which are constantly at work and are key players in destiny and predestination. This is the work of God which He does by His very nature. Ps. 24:1 (A Psalm of David) *The earth is the Lord's, and all it contains, The world, and those who dwell in it.*

I am laying a foundation. There is nothing in this universe that can escape the laws of God. Everything from the beginning is governed by precise laws. That is why we live in a universe of order and not random chance. The foundation of the universe was order and that order continues today. We may not understand what we see, but that does not change the facts. A newborn baby does not understand very much either, and one may think a lot of things are by chance and random, but as the baby learns, order is discovered and put to use. Consider what the Holy Spirit said through the apostle John: John 1:1 *In the beginning was the Word, and the Word was with God, and the Word was God.* John 1:2 *The same was in the beginning with God.* John 1:3 *All things were made (created) by Him; and without Him was not any thing made that was made.*

If we look at the New American Standard version of John 1:3, it states the same thing but substitutes the word "made" for "came into being." John 1:3 *All things came into being by Him and apart from Him nothing came into being that has come into being.*

This being true in the beginning, where did the notion originate that God somehow lost control? This same scripture also states "apart from Him nothing came into being." The Word of God is alive and active. It is not a dead statement of history no longer pertaining to us. Being that the Word of God is "alive," this Living Word is active and forceful. Heb. 4:12 *For the word of God is living and active and sharper than any two-edged sword, and piercing as far as the division of soul and spirit, of both joints and marrow, and able to judge the thoughts and intentions of the heart.*

Note what the Lord Jesus said to communicate that God the

Father is active in everything: Matt. 10:29 *Are not two sparrows sold for a farthing? and one of them shall not fall on the ground without your father.* Matt. 10:30 *But the very hairs of your head are numbered.* The Lord more than knows what is happening in this world, He is active in everything; not even a sparrow can die without His consent. We may not understand God's reasoning in the events that occur around us but those of us who are called to be part of His elect through the Lord Jesus Christ are instructed to have faith in God. Faith transcends our understanding and knowledge, filling us with an assurance in all circumstances.

The crucifixion of the Lord Jesus Christ appeared to be a terrible event to the believing people witnessing this event. They wondered how such a thing could have happened. It appeared that the whole situation got out of God's control. This is witnessed by the following scriptures: Luke 23:48 *And all the multitudes who came together for this spectacle, when they observed what had happened, [began] to return, beating their breasts.* These people were feeling deep sorrow for their great loss. They had no idea of the plan and purpose of God through the violent death of the Lord Jesus. We can see other examples of the inability of the people to see God's purpose in this tragedy. Luke 24:18 *And the one of them, whose name was Cleopas, answering said unto him, Art thou only a stranger in Jerusalem, and hast not known the things which are come to pass there in these days?* Luke 24:19 *And he said unto them, What things? And they said unto him, Concerning Jesus of Nazareth, which was a prophet mighty in deed and word before God and all the people:* Luke 24:20 *And how the chief priests and our rulers delivered him to be condemned to death, and have crucified him.* Luke 24:21 *But we trusted that it had been he which should have redeemed Israel: and beside all this, today is the third day since these things were done.*

But Jesus' crucifixion was the Father's plan from the foundation of the world. Gen. 4:4 *And Abel, on his part also brought of the firstlings of his flock and of their fat portions. And the Lord had regard for Abel and for his offering;* Gen. 4:5 *but for Cain and for his offering He had no regard. So Cain became very angry and his countenance fell.* This sacrificial death carried out by Abel in the offering up to God the "firstlings of his flock" was a type and shadow of the Father's future plan in the sacrifice of the Lord Jesus Christ; the innocent dying in place of the guilty. Thus, Jesus was crucified from the foundation of the world in God's thinking. Although all this was true, no one understood the plan. For those standing around who loved Jesus, it was a heartrending tragedy because the only thing they could see was the loss. To us, the crucifixion of the Lord Jesus Christ was a blood sacrifice that set us free from certain and righteous damnation because of our disgustingly sinful nature. It was the Father's plan to kill the Lord Jesus Christ as a sacrifice for our sins long before the Devil thought about killing Him.

God's purposes in the death of the Lord Jesus Christ was revealed to us. It was His plan too, for this to be revealed, otherwise His death would have been like all others. Jesus' death was predestined and so are all others. With most other seemingly untimely deaths, we do not understand the reason. There are many things around us that we do not understand. It is not God's plan to reveal all things to us at this time.

Take for example what was spoken to the Apostle John in the Book of Revelation: Rev. 10:4 *And when the seven thunders had uttered their voices, I was about to write: and I heard a voice from heaven saying unto me, Seal up those things which the seven thunders uttered, and write them not.* It is clear that the Lord did not want those things revealed. Be certain that everything prophesied in the Book of Revelation will come true at the precise time ordained; not as man interprets them, but as the Lord intends. It will not come true because God looks into the future and predicts these events, but because the Lord God Almighty creates the future. The future is set and cannot be altered by Devil, man or angel; it is immutable.

There are some examples of people whose deaths were clearly ordained as revealed by the scriptures. You may at this point of your spiritual development, believe that some things and some deaths are predestined, but not all. We will explore the inconsistency of occasional predestination as we examine the depths, widths, and heights of what the scriptures boldly declare.

Going back to the Gospel of John, we read again: John 1:3 *All things were made (created) by Him; and without Him was not any thing made that was made.* Thus all things came into being by Him and through Him (the Word of God incarnate in the Lord Jesus Christ) via very precise order and direction. This order is displayed in Laws which God set into motion when He ordered everything in the universe, both visible and invisible. Nothing exists outside of the bounds and confines of God's Laws.

The laws which God set into being in the beginning are still in force. That is why it was written that "All things came into being by Him." There exists nothing in this universe that can function free from the constricts of the very exacting Laws established by and through the Word of God; it was true in the beginning; it is true today; it will be true in the future. These Laws never cease to function. They are an extension of God Himself. Not one of us can do anything that escapes the scrutiny of His Law. If we do or say something kind, it will have a ripple effect; it does not lie alone. If we do some cruel and heartless act, it also will have an effect. There is no such thing as an act having no effect on anyone but ourselves. There are no private sins of which we can say, "they are okay because they only effect me." What we think and do effects our behavior and how we interact with those around us. These effects may not be immediately noticeable to ourselves. Man and angels are all inescapably subject to those laws. Physical creation is also governed by this body of God's law whether it be visible or invisible.

One law may supersede another law, such as the law of Faith (Jesus walking on the water not being subject to the laws which would have made Him sink) but such laws also display God ordained guidelines.

The idea of luck, random misfortune, and chance have their roots in a darkened understanding of the presence and knowledge of God. We grope along as blind men. What we don't understand, we call luck. The wise accept the guidance which comes from God

Himself. **John 9 41** J*esus said unto them if you were blind you should have no sin: but now you say We see therefore your sin remains.* True spiritual understanding is a gift to us by the Holy Spirit. God reveals Himself and His plans to those who diligently seek Him. To those who seek Him, He takes great pleasure in rewarding them for their attention.

Col. 1:16 *For by him were all things created that are in heaven, and that are in earth, visible and invisible, whether they be thrones, or dominions, or principalities, or powers: all things were created by him and for him...* In this scripture, we again come face to face with the statement "all things" were created by Him. This is not, however, what we all read. Some of us read "some things" were created by Him and the thought continues that the Devil created a lot of things also. "All things" has a very different meaning than to say "some things." At this point is where some people want to go off on a tangent and say, "What about all the evil in the world?"

Is. 45:7 *I form the light, and create darkness: I make peace, and create evil: I the LORD do all these things.* The Devil cannot do a thing which is not ordained to occur by the Lord. Look at what Satan said to God regarding Job. Satan had, at an earlier time, tried to hurt Job but was prevented until the time God ordained. Satan was then ordained to afflict Job with the guidelines the Lord dictated. **Job 1:8** *And the Lord said to Satan, "Have you considered My servant Job? For there is no one like him on the earth, a blameless and upright man, fearing God and turning away from evil."* **Job 1:9** *Then Satan answered the Lord, "Does Job fear God for nothing?"* **Job 1:10** *"Hast Thou not made a hedge about him and his house and all that he has on every side? Thou hast blessed the work of his hands, and his possessions have increased in the land."* **Job 1:11** *"But put forth Thy hand now and touch all that he has; he will surely curse Thee to Thy face."* **Job 1:12** *Then the Lord said to Satan, "Behold all that he has is in your power, only do not put forth your hand on him." So Satan departed from the presence of the Lord.*

Job's troubles, although terrible, were ordained by God, not the Devil. It is true that the Devil was enthusiastic to carry out this dictate; but it could not happen until the Lord had issued a decree for this to occur. What did he lose? Job lost the children he loved and nurtured to violent deaths; most of his servants were murdered; his wife had turned against him; much of his labors and wealth were taken away from him by thieves; natural forces destroyed much of what belonged to him; he contracted a terrible disease that made him a social outcast; lastly, his close friends instead of comforting him, accused him of evil. Everything I have stated here was ordained and planned; chance had nothing to do with any of Job's troubles. Job is a good example for anyone who wants to say that life's ups and downs are just random chance. Job's experiences were predestined to occur. His life serves as an ensign to every one of us who experiences difficulties, personal loss or tragedy in our lives. What Job experienced effected changes in him. Painful though they were, they deepened his faith and broadened his personal testimony eternally.

There is another issue in the experience of Job that translates into our own lives. Some of us want to think of ourselves as being master of our destinies. Job, when he was going through the tribulation of his life, was unable to prevent these things from happening. There are times when we can change what we are doing or an attitude. When this is possible, we must take action. There are other occasions ordained by God that we can only endure with patience, as did Job. Some things are beyond our control. If we understand that we can do nothing, it comes down to an issue of faith.

In Job's life, he experienced great success to become one of the wealthiest men alive in the then known world. With all the array of accomplishments he experienced, it would have seemed easy for him to get the idea that he was a superior individual. This was not Job's attitude. He acknowledged the Lord every day. Job 1:5 *And it was so, when the days of their feasting [referring to Job's children] were gone about, that Job sent and sanctified them, and rose up early in the morning and offered burnt offerings according to the number of them all: for Job said, It may be that my sons have sinned, and cursed God in their hearts. Thus did Job continually. . .* Job was concerned about losing God's blessings in his life and the lives of his children. It is obvious from his actions that he did not take what God had given him for granted. We do not see arrogance or self conceit in Job. Job was aware that his blessings came from the Lord. Satan confirmed this, where we read: Job 1:9 *Then Satan answered the Lord, "Does Job fear God for nothing?"* Job 1:10 *"Hast Thou not made a hedge about him and his house and all that he has, on every side? Thou hast blessed the work of his hands, and his possessions have increased in the land."*

The blessings of Job were orchestrated by God. Job worked and planned, but it was the Lord who established the things he attempted to accomplish. Job's position in the world in which he lived was secured by God. Job's life had a purpose similar to the lives of each and every one of us. As humbling as this thought may be, with our finite abilities, we are not able to comprehend all the complexities of life and their purpose. There are some things and some issues beyond our ability to grasp. It is our own blindness that prevents us to fully acknowledge the glory of God in our own destiny. For us, perhaps, it is enough to have faith in God; however, increasing our knowledge of Him brings great satisfaction. It brings us comfort to know that God is active in every area of our lives. Phil. 2:13 *For it is God which worketh in you both to will and to do of his good pleasure.* This scripture speaks warmly to us as Christians, but it also speaks to the non-Christian with equal but more somber consequences.

If God is "working in us," then destiny is at work and we accomplish what we are predestined to achieve. The apostle Paul states clearly in Philippians that it is God working in Christians both to "will" and to "do" what He desires. This statement stands in counter distinction to the notion that the life of a Christian is random and by chance. God's work does not produce random chance. You may think you are bumbling through life, but you are not. Your experiences, acquaintances, accomplishments, failures, successes, communications, postponements, and gratification are all part of the web of life. In the life of the elect, all things work together for the good because the Lord is in control. The apostle Paul understood this very profoundly: Rom. 8:28 *And we know that God causes all things to work together for good to those who love God, to those who are called according to His purpose.* If what I have written were not true, then this statement in Romans could not possibly be reliable.

All that occurs to us and to the world around us is an extension to the statement we read at the beginning of the Gospel of John. John 1:3 *All things were made by him; and without him was not any thing made that was made.* What we read here is the living and active Word of God. Without Him, nothing will ever be made. In this world, even suffering is not without purpose.

It is impossible to oppose God. Every act plays into His plans. Take for example the crucifixion of the Lord Jesus. The Devil thought that by killing Jesus, he would thwart the plans of the Father; but in so doing, he fulfilled them. Anyone, man or angel, who thinks that they can successfully oppose God is blindly deceived. Ps. 59:7 *Behold, they belch out with their mouth: swords are in their lips: for who, say they, doth hear?* Ps. 59:8 *But thou, O Lord, shalt laugh at them; thou shalt have all the heathen in derision.*

3
Lord Jesus Christ Has Power Over All Leaders: The Fate Of The World Is Predestined

Col. 1:15 *And He (the Lord Jesus Christ) is the image of the invisible God, the firstborn of all creation.* Col. 1:16 *For by him were all things created, that are in heaven, and that are in earth, visible and invisible, whether they be thrones, or dominions, or principalities, or powers: all things were created by him, and for him:...*

You may ask yourself, "How is this possible?" What a mystery that authorities who would seem to be in opposition to the Lord Jesus Christ were created by Him! It is important to see that these four classifications of authority in this world did not come into being on their own accord. Also note that the Devil is not credited with their creation. Satan, as a prowling lion, roams around God's earthly creation fulfilling the desires of his nature in all areas the Lord allows. As in the account of Job, Satan cannot do whatever he pleases. The Lord keeps him in check so that his bounds are maintained. If he is allowed to do anything, it is to fulfill the plans or purposes of the Lord. An example of the Devil in action by permission of God was the attempted destruction of the Lord Jesus Christ at His birth in Bethlehem. This action fulfilled prophecy but Jesus was kept safe. It should be abundantly clear that the Devil would have destroyed all of creation, including you and me if he had free rein. Everything which occurs is by the council of God; not a thing occurs outside of that council; all is predestined.

The Devil is the Original Assassin

You might say, "If Jesus rules over all powers and rulers, how did the Devil muster forces to attempt to kill Him?" Two things should be clear to you. First, true leaders are not always revered by those subject to their authority. This is true of Satan. He is the pattern usurper of authority and is an assassin at heart. He is subject to Jesus only out of compulsion. His idea of an ideal world is with himself in command with no regard for the plans of God. Note what the scriptures say of the Devil's thoughts about himself: Is. 14:13 *For thou hast said in thine heart, I will ascend into heaven, I will exalt my throne above the stars of God: I will sit also upon the mount of the congregation, in the sides of the north:* Is. 14:14 *I will ascend above the heights of the clouds; I will be like the most High.*

Assassins are opportunists. They can only dream of their plans until an opportunity arises that makes it possible to fulfill their desires. This brings us to the second thing we need to see clearly. Before the Word of God (who became Jesus) took flesh and blood to be fashioned in the form of a man, He had no weakness. Satan previously, before Jesus was a man, had no opportunity to destroy Him. He was not even a close match for Jesus prior to His incarnation! When Jesus took on weakness, so that like ourselves He could suffer and experience death, He took on vulnerability; Jesus took on mortality so that He could taste death. During the time Jesus left His place to become our Savior, His place of authority was left vacant to be watched over by God the Father and all the Father's angels. While Jesus humbled Himself, it was up to the Father and His angels to keep this schemer under control. After His resurrection, the Lord Jesus received back His power and authority with one important difference; now He was a resurrected man, the first born of many of a totally New Creation. (Jn. 1:1, Phil. 2:6-8, 2 Cor. 13:14, Heb. 2:9, Heb. 5:7, Matt. 28:18, 1 Tim. 2:5)

Satan's plans were known from start to finish. His failure was predestined from the foundation of the world and is clearly declared in prophecy. Satan's failure and doom are ordained by the power of God. When I say ordained I do not mean that his failure has been predicted. Prophecy is not a prediction like the statements of a fortune-teller, but a statement of fact. Prophecy is a declaration of a planned event which cannot be altered. There exists no power which can alter or nullify what God has planned. It is impossible for God to fail at anything. (Matt. 2:12-13, 19, 12; Jer. 31:15; Matt. 2:15; Heb. 6:18)

There is a third point we need to consider when discussing all the apparent rebellion in the power and authority structure which, according to the scriptures, was all made "by Him and for Him." It is obvious that there is a lot of non Christian activity going on in the world today, as has been the picture from its foundation. Jesus Himself commented on the world authority structure when He said: Luke 22:25 *And He said to them, "The kings of the Gentiles lord it over them; and those who have authority over them are called 'Benefactors.'* Luke 22:26 *"But not so with you, but let him who is the greatest among you become as the youngest, and the leader as the servant.*

Why Do Terrible Things Happen?

We all need understanding. Have you ever heard someone say, "Why did God let this terrible thing happen?" The statement is usually uttered in response to a tragic death or violent event. People have different reasons for asking this question. Some say this more out of a challenge than an honest desire to understand. Trying to communicate with someone who has no desire to know the truth is a waste of time. They want a quick and simple answer to one of the great mysteries of life. However, there are reasons for what occurs in our world. We need to acknowledge that with many things, it may be beyond our faculties to understand completely, but we can understand in part. When we come to the end of our abilities, our faith in God fills in the gaps. It is to those who want understanding that I wish to communicate the truth behind this apparent paradox of evil in the presence of a Holy God.

1 Cor. 15:55 *O death, where is thy sting? O grave, where is thy victory?* 1 Cor. 15:56 *The sting of death is sin; and the strength of sin is the law.* 1 Cor. 15:26 *The last enemy that shall be destroyed is death.* Sin must be eradicated before death can be destroyed. The predilection to sin was passed on to all mankind from the foun-

dation of the world through Adam's self willed actions. The heritage of the world through Adam is a nature and mind set opposed to submission to God and His ways. Previously, we discussed that everything in this universe functions subject to very exact laws. The apostle Paul discusses two spiritual laws at work in the world today. Rom. 8:2 *For the law of the Spirit of life in Christ Jesus hath made me free from the law of sin and death.* It is the law of sin and death that we are examining. This law is active today, bringing forth fruit for mankind to taste and behold. The fruit of sin is not pleasant. Take a look around you. How can this world be perfect as long as the law of sin is so active? Who does not suffer because of the fruit of sin? Even the innocent are impacted by the ripple wave effect of sin.

Why do bad things happen? Why do you do bad things? Anytime any of us participates in something contrary to the Spirit of life in Christ Jesus, we release consequences which enforce everything we see in this world today. Why did God allow you to sin? Do you expect Him to physically prevent you from doing these things? God will indeed prevent you from sinning, but you must first understand that it is Him that makes you righteous through the Lord Jesus Christ, and that this is not of yourself. If you rely upon God and His grace to deliver you from the clutches of sin, then He will deliver you from committing sin.

Think for one moment of the arrogance of mankind. If all people were prevented from committing sinful acts, we would get the impression that we were all a bunch of wonderful people, because everything on the outside was forcefully contained by the power of God. God would be active every moment containing some evil or another by preventing the expression of an ugly or violent thought. Why would any of us care? Why would any of us ever see the need to change? We would be living in a perfect world, contained and maintained by the power of God. God would intercede to prevent people from doing bad things for eternity; what's more, none of us would care. Everything about us would be a lie. The world we live in would be perfect, although we would be corrupt on the inside. Does that appeal to you? It is not God's plan.

The presence of sin makes all of creation suffer, not just mankind, but the entire planet. God's plan is not to hide sin, but to expose it and eradicate it. Rom. 8:19 *For the earnest expectation of the creature waiteth for the manifestation of the sons of God.* Rom. 8:20 *For the creature was made subject to vanity, not willingly, but by reason of him who hath subjected the same in hope,* Rom. 8:21 *Because the creature itself also shall be delivered from the bondage of corruption into the glorious liberty of the children of God.* Rom. 8:22 *For we know that the whole creation groaneth and travaileth in vain together until now.* God's entire creation is suffering because of sin. It is not logical for you to think that you or anyone else will escape suffering because of it.

God's plan is to create a New World in which dwells righteousness. This righteousness will not be just some outside manifestation with evil lurking behind the scenes. This is to be a world filled with pure people freed of sinful nature. This new world will not come about by random chance, but by the forceful intent of the Lord.

Think of the most vile and violent person that you can imagine. This person is defined by his actions in this world. The deeds he committed and the stands he took were but an outward manifestation of what was within him. If the Lord were to give this person resurrection angelic power, and remove his restraints, he would cause hell in paradise. Furthermore, as terrible as were the deeds of this person in his life, if the Lord had not restrained him from doing some of what he imagined, he would have done far worse. What is true for the vilest is also true for others whose deeds were less extreme and less noteworthy. It is necessary for a tree to grow and fall where it is destined and so help purge the universe by defining itself. Eccl. 11:3 *If the clouds be full of rain, they empty themselves upon the earth: and if the tree falls toward the south, or toward the north, in the place where the tree falleth, there it shall be.*

Why Doesn't God Destroy the Devil and All Evil?

Next, someone may say, "If God is omnipotent, why doesn't He destroy the Devil, wicked angels, and evil people?" For much the same reason as we have previously discussed. Allowing evil to grow and develop serves a very necessary function. Evil must be purged from every one of us. Show me someone who does not realize that he is capable of sin, and I will show you someone who has deceived himself. God has a plan for ridding the world of sin; this plan is the Lord Jesus Christ. God does not need multiple plans to purge the world of sin; He just needs one. If there were multiple plans to deal with evil, there would be multiple standards for judging mankind and angels. There is just one standard for all judgment. He who receives the Lord Jesus Christ as his Lord, receives the Father's plan for the future. He who rejects Jesus Christ, rejects fellowship with Father God because he rejects His plans for them in Christ Jesus. The destiny of the rejectees is spiritual prison forever – a place for the lawless, or in other words, a special place for those who live by their own standards.

If there were more than one standard, there would be people of different quality. There would be no justice if a consistent standard was not upheld. God is just; therefore there is one standard, the Lord Jesus Christ. By faith we accept this standard. God, through the Holy Spirit, recreates us to conform to the image of Christ. If God were to destroy anyone manifesting evil behavior, He would need to destroy everyone except the Lord Jesus Christ. If He allowed one person to do some evil sinful deeds, but destroyed someone else committing the same deeds, that would be tantamount to two standards. I am not saying that God does not bring judgment into the life of a sinful individual. God's plan is not to hide sin, but to expose it. The best way for all to see and understand that the wages of sin are death is to allow the fruits of sin to come to maturity. Those who love sin must be given a chance to embrace it, to become one with it, while at the same time allowing others to learn to hate the ravages of sin by gaining understanding and insight into its destructive effects. Some people discover that they cannot live without fellowship with the Lord, while others discover that they have no desire for His companionship.

If Lucifer would have been destroyed before he was allowed to develop into Satan, there would have been no rebellion of angels and no revelation of sin. Sin would have lurked in the minds of these magnificent beings tainting their actions and personalities, never to be effectively confronted. The revelation of sin is important in God's plan for the future. How could He have fellowship with a destructive mind set? God is a god of order. Sin, by its very nature, is erosive and destructive. The heavens themselves must be purged of the desire to sin. To instantly destroy anyone who sins is possible, but this is the solution of the feeble minded. Such actions would have grave consequences. Do you destroy those whom you love because they displease you? It is superior to bring forth those who, with conviction, eschew evil. Jesus put things this way:

Matt. 13:24 *Another parable put he forth unto them, saying, The kingdom of heaven is likened unto a man which sowed good seed in his field:* Matt. 13:25 *But while men slept, his enemy came and sowed tares among the wheat, and went his way.* Matt. 13:26 *But when the blade was sprung up, and brought forth fruits then appeared the tares also.* Matt. 13:27 *So the servants of the householder came and said unto him, Sir, didst not thou sow good seed in thy field? from whence then hath it tares?* Matt. 13:28 *He said unto them, An enemy hath done this. The servants said unto him, Wilt thou then that we go and gather them up?* Matt. 13:29 *But he said, Nay; lest while ye gather up the tares, ye root up also the wheat with them.* Matt. 13:30 *Let both grow together until the harvest: and in the time of harvest I will say to the reapers, Gather ye together first the tares, and bind them in bundles to burn them: but gather the wheat into my barn.* If God vaporized everyone who did evil, you and I would have ceased to exist before we could appreciate the Lord Jesus Christ.

Why Does God Allow Random Catastrophes? (Authority Over The Devil)

Why does God allow random catastrophes? If Jesus has all this power, then how do you explain these and all the accidents?

First of all, just because all authority and power was reinstated to the Lord Jesus at His resurrection is not the same as to say He is fully manifesting it to the world. Note what it says in the book of Revelation: Rev. 11:15 *And the seventh angel sounded; and there were great voices in heaven, saying, "The kingdoms of this world are become the kingdoms of our Lord, and of his Christ; and he shall reign for ever and ever."* Rev. 11:16 *And the twenty-four elders, who sit on their thrones before God, fell on their faces and worshipped God,* Rev. 11:17 *saying, "We give Thee thanks, O Lord God, the Almighty, who art and who wast, because Thou hast taken Thy great power and hast begun to reign.* Rev. 11:18 *"And the nations were enraged, and Thy wrath came, and the time came for the dead to be judged, and the time to give their reward to Thy bond-servants the prophets and to the saints and to those who fear Thy name, the small and the great, and to destroy those who destroy the earth."*

Having power is not the same thing as using it. The Father has already given all power and authority to Jesus. However, Jesus with all this authority does not use it to negate the plans of the Father. Remember the parable we read just a little earlier. The servants asked, "Lord, shall we gather up all the tares (weeds) from among the good wheat?" The Lord answered, "No." Power to order this accomplished is with the Lord. He explained that everything must be allowed to mature. The fruits of both must become manifest. Jesus is no rogue. He is fully submitted to the plans of the Father. John 5:30 *I can of mine own self do nothing: as I hear, I judge: and my judgment is just; because I seek not mine own will, but the will of the Father which hath sent me.*

Let's look at another example. The bible teaches that by faith in Jesus Christ, we have authority to heal the sick. This statement is true. However, this authority does not function apart from the plans and intents of the Lord. If a Christian were allowed to work all these works apart from the direction of the Lord, they by their actions would negate the future God had determined for this world system. Let's look partially at how this would occur. You know in your heart that healing is promised in the scripture and believe it is true (it is true). Therefore, you take it upon yourself to go to the local hospital and empty it by miraculously healing every person in it by your prayer of faith. Think of the commotion that this would cause. Think of the amount of publicity such a display would generate. Your actions would dramatically alter the future events in the entire area and would spill over on the rest of the world. If this same action were done in hospitals around the world, it would change the destiny of the world and the way all things culminate. Future prophecy would be negated, because you, by your actions, would alter the future. People who were to die would not die. People in outward opposition to the plans of God would no longer manifest this stand. God would no longer be in control, His plans altered by the actions of individual Christians. Does that sound like confusion?

If we ask anything according to His will, He will grant it. 1 John 5:14 *And this is the confidence that we have in him! that, if we ask anything according to his will, he heareth us. . .* Why? Because the future and everything about it is predestined by God Himself. If God granted prayers according to needs as we perceive them, we would have the future as we desired, and not as He has ordained. It should be clear that what we receive in prayer has an effect on future events in our own lives and the lives of others that our life impacts.

Let's take a closer look at the authority the Lord has given to those who belong to Him. Luke 10:19 *Behold, I give unto you power (authority) to tread on serpents and scorpions, and over all the power of the enemy: and nothing shall by any means hurt you.* This decree is to us, to be used in our lives and the lives of those around us in service to the Lord. Anyone who has served the Lord very long will confess that they have seen some remarkable things. Evil has its day, but the knowledge of the Lord Jesus Christ keeps expanding in this world and triumphs in every life truly committed to the Lord Jesus Christ. However, there are again limits to the use of this authority over Satan and those in his dark kingdom. This is the key, this power functions expressly "in the lives of everyone truly committed to the Lord Jesus Christ." It is God's purpose to expose sin. A Christian has the authority over all the power of the enemy as an Ambassador of Christ, not as an independent party acting outside of the will of God.

Take for example the binding or ordering the Devil so that he is to refrain from doing anymore evil in this world. You will quickly discover that you do not have this authority. This dispensation of "authority over all the power of the enemy" is factual only as it abides in the will of the Father God and is related to the Ambassadorship of the believer in service to the Lord Jesus Christ. The Lord has not granted you authority to function outside of what He has planned because it would change what He has predestined. Each one of us would act in such a manner as we saw fit for correcting things as we thought appropriate. I can promise you, God's ways are not our ways and what He has planned is superior to anything we could imagine. Our authority over evil is restricted to our ambassadorship as ordained by God because even the actions of the Devil have a purpose in fulfilling what God has predestined to occur.

The Lord Jesus Christ has infinite power over Satan and all those who follow in Satan's steps, but the Lord will not fully display this authority until the proper time. Until then, many catastrophes will continue to occur around the world, claiming lives and causing mayhem. Jesus himself prophesied that toward the end of the age, calamities would increase in frequency. Luke 21:9 *"And when you hear of wars and disturbances, do not be terrified; for these things must take place first, but the end does not follow immediately."* Luke 21:10 *Then He continued by saying to them, "Nation will rise against nation, and kingdom against kingdom,* Luke 21:11 *and there will be great earthquakes and in various places plagues and famines; and there will be terrors and great signs from heaven.*

Why are all these thing happening? Why does the intensity increase at the close of the age (it is not the end of the world)? Rev. 12:10 *And I heard a loud voice saying in heaven, "Now is come salvation, and strength, and the kingdom of our God, and the power of his Christ: for the accuser of our brethren is cast down, which accused them before our God day and night."* Rev. 12:12 *"Therefore rejoice, ye heavens, and ye that dwell in them. Woe to the inhibitors of the earth and of the sea! for the Devil is come down unto you, having great wrath, because he knoweth that he hath but a short time. . ."* It is difficult for any of us who has a scientific education to think of evil spiritual forces causing natural calamities. It is a matter of faith to accept these things. Even though we understand something by faith, we can examine these ideas very closely. Any diligent person, when they want to understand something they believe (or possibly don't believe), will look at all the information at hand to determine if there is any substance to the statement. We can do the same thing with truth as it is revealed to us in the scriptures.

Natural calamities are what we are considering. Are they all just random occurrences? I say no. If we look at what Jesus spoke as quoted in two paragraphs above, we see that at the close of the age, there will be an increase in "wars and disturbances" and also an increase in the occurrence of "kingdom rising against kingdom and nation against nation." When we compare these scriptures with those quoted from the Book of Revelation in the preceding paragraph, it is easy to conclude that it is the Devil and his dark kingdom which is the cause of all the increased violence. Note the statement in the latter half of Rev. 12:12 *"Woe to the inhibitors of the earth and of the sea! for the Devil is come down unto you, having great wrath, because he knoweth that he hath but a short time. . ."* There is a one to one correlation between the shortness of time Satan and his kingdom have left and the increase in violence. This increase in calamity is not natural nor is it a random occurrence.

Let's also look at some scriptures from the Book of Daniel. Dan. 10:12 *Then said he unto me, Fear not, Daniel: for from the first day that thou didst set thine heart to understand, and to chasten thyself before thy God, thy words were heard, and I am come for thy words.* Dan. 10:13 *But the prince of the kingdom of Persia withstood me one and twenty days: but, Lo, Michael, one of the chief princes, came to help me; and I remained there with the kings of Persia.* Dan. 10:20 *Then said he, Knowest thou wherefore I come unto thee? and now will I return to fight with the prince of Persia: and when I am gone forth, lo, the prince of Grecia shall come.* Dan. 10:21 *But I will show thee that which is noted in the scripture of truth: and there is none that holdeth with me in these things, but Michael your prince.* It is the archangel Gabriel who is being "withstood by the prince of Persia." No man has the spiritual or physical strength to withstand an angel of God. Note 2 Kin. 19:35, one angel killed 185,000 soldiers in a single night! If one angel could kill that many men with no apparent struggle, it can be stated with certainty that the "prince of Persia" was no man. Indeed, the "prince of Persia" is one of the angels who left the place the Father had ordained for him to join the ranks of Satan. This dark angel ruled over the kingdom of Persia. You will also note that Gabriel told Daniel that the "prince of Grecia" would come as soon as he left speaking with him (Dan 10:20). This "prince of Grecia" is another dark angel who ruled over Grecia (Greece). These dark angels are alive and ruling in their kingdoms today. They wrestle with each other for dominance and power, resulting in wars and disturbances.

Accepting that war and disturbances are caused from dark forces is easier to grasp than natural disasters. Natural disasters and the forces of nature are discussed in the scriptures as being controlled by spiritual forces. Look what Jesus did to a tempestuous storm: Luke 8:24 *And, they came to him, and awoke him, saying, Master, Master, we perish. Then He arose, and rebuked the wind and the raging of the water: and they ceased, and there was a calm.* Luke 8:25 *And he said unto them, "Where is your faith?" And they being afraid wondered, saying one to another, "What manner of man is this for he commandeth even the winds and water, and they obey him."* If the wind and the raging water can be commanded to stop, they can also be commanded to do the opposite. To everyone on the surrounding shores, the calm which followed seemed like a natural occurrence. Only Jesus' disciples knew the truth.

If we look at nine of the ten plagues which the Lord brought upon Egypt, they all had to do with Spirit over natural forces. To the natural man, it took convincing that these were not natural occurrences. We have not changed very much in our thinking compared to the Egyptians; they did not understand that the natural calamities which overtook them were not random chance. There are many other examples in the scripture of the forces of nature being controlled by Spirit. There are also some examples of the forces of nature being controlled by Satan.

Note that wind of sufficient force destroyed the house of Job's eldest son, killing this son as well as the rest of Job's children. Job 1:19 *And, behold there came a Great wind from the wilderness, and smote the four corners of the house, and it fell upon the young men, and they are dead: and I only am escaped alone to tell thee. . .* This destructive force was the action of Satan's spiritual power being manifest. We also read in Job that Satan manifested other destructive uses of the forces of nature – lightning! Job 1:16 *While he was yet speaking, there came also another, and said, The fire of God is fallen from heaven, and hath burned up the sheep and the servants, and consumed them; and I only am escaped alone to tell thee.* In this case, it was not the fire of God. It was lightning utilized by the Devil to destroy. The Devil had been given broad authority by the Lord to test Job; his only restriction in this authority was that he was forbidden to kill Job. Job's account is quite clear that it was the Devil who was doing this. Before this time, Job had been protected from the Devil by God. Job 1:9 *Then Satan answered the Lord, and said, "Doth Job fear God for nought?"* Job 1:10 *"Hast not thou made an hedge about him, and about his house, and about all that he hath on every side? thou hast blessed the work of his hands, and his substance is increased in the land. . ."* When the protection was lifted, natural calamities befell Job on every side; the same natural calamities which are common to befall all mankind.

I want to point out that although evil forces cause terrible calamities in this earth, they do not act without restraint from the Lord. By this restraint, the Lord controls all things and orders the future. The future is not random chance, but predetermined, because the Lord controls the bounds, and by so doing, keeps everything going exactly as He desires.

There are many other examples in the scriptures of extreme forces of nature being controlled by spiritual authority. I will close on this topic with the words of the Lord Jesus Christ and a list of some other scriptural sources showing what I have stated. Matt. 5:45 *That ye may be the children of your Father which is in heaven: for he maketh his sun to rise on the evil and on the good, and sendeth rain on the just and on the unjust.* Jesus did not consider the weather to be simple providence! If you meditate on the following scriptures, you will gain a deeper insight into what these men of God came to understand: Gen. 19:24, 1 Kin. 18:38, 2 Kin. 1:10-14, Ex. 14:16, Ex. 11:31, Josh. 10:13, Ex. 23:28, Jon. 1:14, Acts 27:22-24, Matt. 7:27, 2 Sam. 18:9, Is. 29:6, Num. 16:32, Rev. 6:8, Ezek. 20:47, Gen. 41:25, Gen. 7:4, Ezek. 38:22, 2 Kin. 8:1, Duet. 11:14, Zech. 14:17, Rev. 8:5, Duet. 11:17, Rev. 11:6, 1 Chr. 21:12, Jer. 24:10, Duet. 28:12, Jer. 29:17, Jer. 44:13, Ezek. 5:17, 1 Sam. 12:18, 1 Kin. 17:1, 1 Kin. 18:1, Amos 4:7.

Back to the Thrones, Dominions, Principalities or Powers

Col. 1:16 *"For by him were all things created, that are in heaven, and that are in earth, visible and invisible, whether they be thrones, or dominions, or principalities, or powers: all things were created by him, and for him:"* In our world, we see that there exists a struggle for authority. This is true even though the Lord Jesus Christ is above all and has power over all created seats of authority. Understanding this in our present world is not difficult because we can see the scenario being enacted over and over at almost every level. The opposition to leadership and the opposition of one leader to another does not nullify or negate the fact that there is someone with greater authority. Leaders sometime ignore opposition waiting for the proper timing to correct the situation. This is the picture with the Lord Jesus Christ.

As I have stated, it is impossible to oppose God. All opposition to any of His plans is only apparent because the opposition itself plays into His plans. Remember talking about Satan opposing Jesus by crucifying Him. This action only fulfilled Mosaic law for the blood sacrificial requirements for the forgiveness of sin. The Father then raised Jesus from the dead to fulfill more of His own plan which required opposition. All opposition in leadership is ordained by God to fulfill His plans, and is ordained to bring about a predetermined ending; the ending is just the beginning for what He has planned next.

There are some instances where God will directly and consistently oppose someone. Let's read the following passages about Moses on Mt. Nebo: Deut. 34:4 *Then the Lord said to him, "This is the land which I swore to Abraham, Isaac, and Jacob, saying, 'I will give it to your descendants'; I have let you see it with your eyes, but you shall not go over there."* Deut. 34:5 *So Moses the servant of the Lord died there in the land of Moab, according to the word of the Lord.* Deut. 34:6 *And He buried him in the valley in the land of Moab, opposite Beth-peor; but no man knows his burial place to this day.* Deut. 34:7 *Although Moses was one hundred and twenty years old when he died, his eye was not dim, nor his vigor abated.* Jude 1:9 *Yet Michael the archangel, when contending with the Devil he disputed about the body of Moses, durst not bring against him a railing accusation, but said, The Lord rebuke thee.*

Satan wanted the body of Moses for his own plans. This body did not die of natural causes and was in fine condition. The spirit of Moses had simply left the body to be with the Lord. All the Devil needed to do was to enter this body, because the body without the spirit is dead. The deception he then could orchestrate would have monumental effects on everything God had planned for future generations. He was opposed by direct confrontation because this act of evil did not fit into the scheme of things God had planned, otherwise the Lord would have allowed him to proceed. This scheme of Satan's needed to be opposed for a second, less obvious reason.

Moses symbolically represents the law, the school master, and the Old Covenant. God, in setting up everything in the Old Covenant worship rituals, did so with reference to the death, burial, and resurrection of the Lord Jesus Christ. Moses represented the forethought of God in the flesh and blood. However, flesh and blood cannot inherit the Kingdom of God; it can only be symbolically representative; therefore Moses could not enter into the Promised Land. (The reason given to Moses was his failure to sanctify the Lord in the eyes of the people at the water of Meribah, but the full implication of what was told him could not be understood except from hindsight.) It was the Lord's intention that the symbolism He had carefully developed be preserved. If Satan would have been permitted to enter Moses' body, the symbolism God was developing would have been destroyed. God had predestined the future crucifixion of the Lord Jesus Christ and the New Covenant to follow. He exerted whatever power was necessary to accomplish exactly what He had ordained; this will always be the case because the future is not a result of random occurrences, but of precise certainty.

The thrones, dominions, principalities or powers that rule in the heavens surrounding this world are not in voluntary submission to Jesus Christ. 1 Cor. 15:24 *Then cometh the end, when he shall have delivered up the kingdom to God, even the Father: when he shall have put down all rule and all authority and power.* 1 Cor. 15:25 *For he must reign, till he hath put all enemies under his feet.* 1 Cor. 15:27 *For he hath put all things under his feet. But when he saith all things are put under him, it is manifest that he is excepted, which did put all things under him. . .* These authorities, although ordained of God for order on the earth, are in opposition to the Lord Jesus. They oppose Him as leader and do not embrace his ideology. In this present age, they serve a purpose, as we shall see in the following scriptures. If the Lord were to rid himself of all of these foes immediately, chaos would ensue on the earth because of anarchy. It is necessary to replace these authorities, not just eliminate them.

Rom. 13:1 *Let every soul be subject unto the higher powers. For there is no power but of God: the powers that be are ordained of God.* Rom. 13:2 *Whosoever therefore resisteth the power, resisteth the ordinance of God: and they that resist shall receive to themselves damnation.* Rom. 13:3 *For rulers are not a terror to good works, but to the evil. Wilt thou then not be afraid of the power? Do that which is good, and thou shalt have praise of the same:* Rom.

13:4 *For he is the minister of God to thee for good. But if thou do that which is evil, be afraid; for he beareth not the sword in vain: for he is the minister of God, a revenger to execute wrath upon him that doeth evil...* It may seem like a contradiction to state that the leadership in this world is ordained by God yet opposes the Lord Jesus Christ, but this is the reality of the world in which we live. Both are true. The opposition we see serves the purposes of the Father to expose and separate sin. The whole process is similar to separating the wheat from the chaff and weeds, or fishing with a net and keeping some of what the net captures while throwing away everything else.

God rules in all the affairs of men. It may not be apparent because there seems to be so much evil occurring in the world. However, the evil you see is a manifestation of His plan to expose sin and not conceal it. It is not just a few rebellious angels who are filled with evil inclinations, but mankind also. Whether we like it or not, God will not change His plans to rid this sphere of evil in a way in which it will be revealed to all that His judgment is correct and just. Jer. 27:6 *"And now have I given all these lands into the hand of Nebuchadnezzar the king of Babylon, my servant; and the beasts of the field have I given him also to serve him."* Jer. 43:10 *And say unto them, Thus saith the Lord of hosts, the God of Israel; "Behold, I will send and take Nebuchadnezzar the king of Babylon, my servant and will set his throne upon these stones that I have hid; and he shall spread his royal pavilion over them."* We therefore see that Nebuchadnezzar, although violent and evil in his actions, was called by God His servant because all that he was doing was ordained by God, even though Nebuchadnezzar at that time did not know God or acknowledge Him in any way. Many people suffered greatly because of this man's actions. To those who lived at that time, with the exception of Jeremiah and those who believed his prophecies, it may have seemed like the Devil had thrown off God's restraint and caused all this destruction. Undoubtedly, the Devil and his forces were very active; however, the authority ordaining their actions and setting bounds to what they did was Father God.

Ps. 75:6 *For promotion cometh neither from the east, nor from the west, nor from the south.* Ps. 75:7 *But God is the judge: he putteth down one, and setteth up another.* Ps. 75:8 *For in the hand of the Lord there is a cup, and the wine is red; it is full of mixture; and he poureth out of the same: but the dregs thereof, all the wicked of the earth shall wring them out, and drink them. . .* 'The working of God is not contingent on man acknowledging His presence or approving His actions. God is active in the lives of all people – those who know Him and those who do not. In most instances, He does not reveal Himself directly in the things He is doing; there may be a perception, even a shadow of His presence noted. There are times that the Lord chooses to reveal Himself directly in a matter; this is especially true in the lives of those who love Him. These scriptures in the Psalms are not directed just to believers. They are a blanket statement of authority in the operation of all things. No person, angel or spirit can remain in any position or advance apart from God's determination. Directly or indirectly, knowingly or unknowingly, all people serve the Lord in the purposes He has determined.

Dan. 4:28 *All this came upon the King Nebuchadnezzar.* Dan. 4:29 *At the end of twelve months he walked in the palace of the kingdom of Babylon.* Dan. 4:30 *The king spake, and said, Is not this great Babylon, that I have built for the house of the kingdom by the might of my power, and for the honour of my majesty?* Dan. 4:31 *While the word was in the king's mouth, there fell a voice from heaven, saving, O King Nebuchadnezzar, to thee it is spoken; The kingdom is departed from thee.* Dan. 4:32 *And they shall drive thee from men, and thy dwelling shall be with the beasts of the field: they shall make thee to eat grass as oxen, and seven times shall pass over thee, until thou know that the most High ruleth in the kingdom of men, and giveth it to whomsoever he will.* Dan. 4:33 *The same hour was the thing fulfilled upon Nebuchadnezzar: and he was driven from men, and did eat grass as oxen, and his body was wet with the dew of heaven, till his hairs were grown like eagles' feathers, and his nails like birds' claws.* Dan. 4:34 *And at the end of the days, I, Nebuchadnezzar lifted up mine eyes unto heaven, and mine understanding returned unto me, and I blessed the most High, and I praised and honored him that liveth for ever, whose dominion is an everlasting dominion, and his kingdom is from generation to generation:* Dan. 4:35 *And all the inhabitants of the earth are reputed as nothing: and he doeth according to his will in the army of heaven, and among the inhabitants of the earth: and none can stay his hand, or say unto him, What doest thou?* Dan. 4:36 *At the same time my reason returned unto me; and for the glory of my kingdom, mine honour and brightness returned unto me; and my counselors and my lords sought unto me; and I was established in my kingdom, and excellent majesty was added unto me.* Dan. 4:37 *Now I Nebuchadnezzar praise and extol and honour the King of heaven, all whose works are truths and his ways judgment: and those that walk in pride he is able to abase.*

Rank or position are from God, whether you are a man or angel. In the above scriptures about the great King Nebuchadnezzar, it is easy to see how a person of great wealth, power, and high position may think they possess their place by their own actions and efforts. Nebuchadnezzar was made a king of the Lord God even though this man did not know or acknowledge Him. This prideful king did many terrible things to the people he conquered and to the people over whom he ruled. It was not a prerequisite that he know the Lord or be a good man; he was chosen to fulfill God's purposes in this world. The scriptures do not say that Satan gave him this authority. The authority and position was the Lord's to give, the Lord's to establish, and the Lord's to take away as was clearly demonstrated in these scriptures in the Book of Daniel. A person may have many plans and ideas in their imagination. However, it is the Lord who will establish the chosen path or let it come to naught; this truth applies to all people or angelic powers. Prov. 19:21 *There are many devices (plans) in a man's heart; nevertheless the counsel of the Lord, that shall stand. . .* Think what you wish; make whatever plans you choose; only those devices which go along with God's program for your life and the rest of the world will be sanctioned to stand.

4
Realities of Predestination

After saying all this, there are still some who reject the realities of predestination. I have used the scriptures as the basis for what I write as the only truly reliable source tried and proven from the foundation of the world. I would encourage all readers to examine your own lives for evidence of the providence of God at work, in what you have experienced in your life, and in the things in which you have not been permitted to experience. The truth of predestination is not based upon the necessity of faith. It has as much to do with the positions of the stars and inanimate objects in this universe, as well as all sanctioned life, and everything in between. It is not necessary to believe in the concept of predestination for the effects of destiny to manipulate your path. Rev. 3:7 *"And to the angel of the church in Philadelphia write: He who is holy, who is true, who has the key of David, who opens and no one will shut, and who shuts and no one opens, says this:* Rev. 3:8 *'I know your deeds. Behold, I have put before you an open door which no one can shut, because you have a little power, and have kept My word, and have not denied My name. . .* There is nothing passive about "opening doors which no one can shut" or "closing doors which no one can open."

How can there be argument against the actual power of God being involved in destiny and controlling the direction of things? "Opening" or "closing" doors controls the path that one is able to take; this, in essence, controls one's destiny and manipulates what will occur as a result of taking that direction. You might argue, "But I chose to do what I do." Yes, that is true. However, if you are not permitted to do everything you attempt because it does not work out for reasons beyond your control, your choice then is limited. Many times it appears that you have only "one" choice and you are blind to any other.

Motivation

There is also another element in controlling your destiny – motivation. Motivation is a primal force in the life of man, angel or Devil, and is at the root of all your actions. If you control what motivates people, then you influence their thoughts, actions, and desires. Since God has no boundaries except those which He sets for Himself, He has no boundaries on what He will use to motivate you.

You may argue that some behavior is instinctual and not regulated by higher cortical functions. This is also true. Nonetheless, even instinctual behavior is in some ways triggered by motivational forces. We may not understand the intensities of cause and effect, but we can appreciate that they exist. Therefore, environment itself is, in essence, a powerful motivational force.

Let's look at the biological creation from an educated and scientific point of view. Some would argue that all we see in life forms on this planet are as a result of the evolution of each species by random chance. The ability to adapt is also a factor. As the environment changed, certain members with special attributes, which occurred randomly, were better able to make the needed adjustments, and therefore thrive while others died out.

Laws Make Certain A Predictable Outcome

The physical universe is a place governed by precise laws that can be expressed mathematically. Nothing occurs which escapes these laws, but merely demonstrates other laws. There are laws for the micro universe as well as the macro universe; for example, when two objects collide, the collision is predictable if we know enough about the objects. They may stick together, they may bounce off in a different direction, they may fuse, they may partially fuse, they may assume a different shape, they may change in their basic nature, they may give off heat, sound or some other energy or they may splatter. All these possibilities would be predictable if we knew enough about these objects. However, the complexities involved may go beyond our ability to comprehend and therefore our ability to predict. There are, for instance, forces and laws beyond our ability to measure. These interact with the physical universe, influencing what we observe. Some of these forces and laws are spiritual in nature and lie at the very foundation of every cause and effect. God's Spirit flows into all creation to guide it, influence it, and maintain it. Gen. 1:1 *In the beginning God created the heaven and the earth.* Gen. 1:2 *And the earth was without form, and void; and darkness was upon the face of the deep. And the Spirit of God moved upon the face of the waters.*

There Are No Accidents From God's Perspective

Therefore, God's Spirit interacts with the whole of the visible and invisible universe. Evidence exists that life evolves, but God's Spirit is creatively behind the development of all life. The development of the dinosaurs was not an accident and neither was their demise; all was planned, carefully watched over, and had nothing to do with blind, random chance. If you have a mind for calculating the odds of life randomly occurring in this world, you would have to take into account the enormity of variation of species we see today; each of these varied life forms has its own story with the development of all its various complex systems and interactions. You would also need to take into account all the possibilities of life taking every wrong dead end path so that it would have failed and died out countless times. It would then need to restart over and over again with the same possibility of failure until it randomly succeeded. This possibility of failure would need to be taken into account for each life form which has been presented on this planet (even viruses and other virus-like structures). I am confident that we lack the mental capacity to comprehend all the possibilities and factors needed to arrive at the true odds. However, we can use our reasoning abilities coupled with our ability to appreciate that which is beyond our grasp and come to conclusions. The odds for this to occur randomly approach infinity to one. Furthermore, if you then want to calculate the number of years that would be required for this to occur and the precise conditions which would have to reoccur over and over again, you should realize that it is impossible for life to have occurred on its own (the odds are incalculable).

The Concept of Free Will

Since God controlled all things in the beginning, why would He cease to do so now? He wouldn't. God does not change just because He has brought man into this world. The world and all things in it change according to His desires and plans. Is it so hard to grasp that God Who created the entire universe before your existence, then brought you into being, would not allow you by your "free will" to alter the determined course of humanity and this world? It is true that you cause change by your actions. The actions you take are all part of the interactions of life. Each of us needs to think, plan, and act. By our actions, or lack of actions, we interact with our environment and bring about minute changes. If we do nothing, we may have regrets which linger in our thoughts, effecting our action in the future. If we refrain from action, we may yet be brought to act based upon the motivational forces which come to bear on the situation. If we act, we may regret our actions, which will effect our actions in the future; or conversely, we may be pleased with the outcome, encouraging us to take more action. Everything we do, or refrain from doing, has an effect on who we become and the world around us.

The things you "will" are all part of God's plan. Phil. 2:13 *For it is God which worketh in You both to will and to do of His good pleasure...* This scripture clearly states that believers in the Lord Jesus Christ are being influenced by God to "will" and to "do" according to the dictates of God. You do make choices and those choices are by your own choosing. However, it is apparent by this scripture that although you exercise your "free will," the path and actions you choose are determined by God. The Lord motivates your choices, supplying you with whatever you need to make the "right" choices.

If we examine this concept further, we find that even those who do not know the Lord are likewise influenced to make decisions based upon His will. Prov. 21:1 *The king's heart is in the hand of the Lord, as the rivers of water: He turneth it whithersoever*

He will. It is not just kings who the Lord influences for His purposes. Note what God does to those who do not love the truth: 2 Thess. 2:10 *. . .because they received not the love of the truth, that they might be saved.* 2 Thess. 2:11 *And for this cause God shall send them strong delusion, that they should believe a lie. . .* This delusion is believable and designed to carry people away. It is not the Devil who is sending "them" a strong delusion; it is God. God does not lie; however, He has at His disposal those who love lying. It is God Who rules the earth, the sea, the sky, the heavens, and every other realm. Absolutely nothing happens without His plan. Matt. 10:29 *Are not two sparrows sold for a farthing? and one of them shall not fall on the ground without your Father.* Nothing can happen even to a sparrow without the Father being somehow involved. Every one of us is of far greater value than a sparrow. What is true for the lowly sparrow is true for every person alive today. God loves everyone in His creation, yet He chooses to give each being a life which is best suited for what it is ultimately going to evolve. Sending a "strong delusion" upon those who do not "love the truth" is, in fact, an act of love and mercy. We will explore this concept fully later.

Ahab's Life Ended by God

2 Chr. 18:19 *And the Lord said, Who shall entice Ahab king of Israel, that he may go up and fall at Ramothgilead? And one spake saying after this manner, and another saying after that manner.* 2 Chr. 18:20 *Then there came out a spirit, and stood before the Lord, and said, I will entice him. And the Lord said unto him, Wherewith?* 2 Chr. 18:21 *And he said, I will go out, and be a lying spirit in the mouth of all his prophets. And the Lord said, Thou shalt entice him and thou shalt also prevail: go out and do even so.* 2 Chr. 18:22 *Now therefore, behold, the Lord hath put a lying spirit in the mouth of these thy prophets, and the Lord hath spoken evil against thee.* 2 Chr. 18:33 *And a certain man drew a bow at a venture, and smote the king of Israel between the joints of the harness: therefore he said to his chariot man, Turn thine hand, that thou mayest carry me out of the host; for I am wounded.* 2 Chr.

18:34 And the battle increased that day: howbeit the king of Israel stayed himself up in his chariot against the Syrians until the evening: and about the time of the sun going down he died.

Usually, you do not know the details behind the scenes that precipitate events we observe in the world. The death of King Ahab was just as newsworthy in its time as any event today. Ahab did not die as a result of bad luck or the misfortune of being at the wrong place at the right time. His death was orchestrated by God. The man drawing his bow "at a venture," trying to make an unlikely shot, was ordained to be successful by God. King Ahab's death, like every other death, serves a purpose. Often we do not understand the reasons for an untimely death, but like the sparrow, no one falls to the ground without the Father's involvement. It is only God who ultimately has power over life and death, not the Devil.

The Trials of Life

Ps. 37:23 *The steps of a good man are ordered by the Lord: and he delighteth in his way...* The fact that the Lord orders your steps indicates that your direction is planned. An ancient historian once said, "Circumstances rule men; men do not rule circumstances." While it is true that each one of us is thrust into unavoidable circumstances, how we react is a gift from God. The things we do or do not do, have a direct bearing on most of the circumstances we encounter. The forces and pressures encountered in each scenario force us to make judgments based upon what is inside of us and respond to what is around us. In essence, each one of us is formed by forces beyond our control. These circumstances give us motivation to use our free will. We act according to what is in us and the stimulus at hand. In each encounter, we get some type of feedback from which we learn, develop, and grow. It is possible to do the right thing or wrong thing, under-react or overreact. In each instance, our future behavior can be modified by what we experience as a result of our actions.

Some of us are purified by our suffering from wrong behavior while others seem not to learn anything or simply seem to get away with things. Prov. 24:16 *For a just man falleth seven times, and riseth up again: but the wicked shall fall into mischief.* . . . There is a reason for encountering circumstances in which we can make wrong decisions or carry out inappropriate fantasies. Some of us will suffer terribly for these actions or fantasies while others will be established in them. Each experience is designed to form you into what you are destined to become. Dan. 11:35 *And some of them of understanding shall fall, to try them, and to purge, and to make them white, even to the time of the end: because it is yet for a time appointed.*

With those who have a spark of desire to know the truth, God will deal with them in such a way to cultivate that desire, or, to bring them to the place where they turn away from the truth to discover that they hate it. Those who God finds worthy to be brought into a covenant relationship with Him, He disciplines to conform them into the image of Christ. Heb. 12:6 *For whom the Lord loveth he chasteneth, and scourgeth every son whom he receiveth.* Heb. 12:7 *If ye endure chastening, God dealeth with you as with sons; for what son is he whom the father chasteneth not?* Heb. 12:8 *But if ye be without chastisement, whereof all are partakers, then are ye bastards, and not sons.* Heb. 12:9 *Furthermore we have had fathers of our flesh which corrected us, and we gave them reverence: shall we not much rather be in subjection unto the Father of spirits, and live?* Heb. 12:10 *For they verily for a few days chastened us after their own pleasure; but he for our profit, that we might be partakers of his holiness.* Heb. 12:11 *Now no chastening for the present seemeth to be joyous, but grievous: nevertheless afterward it yieldeth the peaceable fruit of righteousness unto them which are exercised thereby.*

Prov. 16:4 *The Lord hath made all things for himself: yea, even the wicked for the day of evil.* . . . You can twist the scriptures any way you want. This scripture is clear. It is much easier to accept what it says and endeavor to understand than to skip over it and pretend it doesn't say what it does. Just as it is God's creative power in us which imparts the nature of the Lord Jesus Christ until we become His express image, this same God will make those outside of Jesus wicked. Is. 45:7 *I form the fight, and create darkness: I* make peace, and create evil: I the Lord do all these things... For far too long, everything has been blamed on a renegade Devil. What we observe in the world today is the creative work of God. Matt. 6:22 *"The lamp of the body is the eye; if therefore your eye is clear, your whole body will be full of light.* Matt. 6:23 *"But if your eye is bad, your whole body will be full of darkness. If therefore the light that is in you is darkness, how great is the darkness...* If the eyes of a man's understanding are darkened, instead of seeing the hand of God working everywhere, he will instead see the Devil. There is no other reality but that God rules, always, all the time.

King David, because of the notable way the Lord dealt with him and delivered him time and again, understood that the things which occurred to him and around him were ordained by the Lord. It is very clear how strongly David believed that the things which touched his life were from the Lord, as is seen in the account of the day Shimei cursed him. 2 Sam. 16:7 *And thus said Shimei when he cursed, Come out, come out, thou bloody man, and thou man of Belial:* 2 Sam. 16:8 *The Lord hath returned upon thee all the blood of the house of Saul, in whose stead thou hast reigned; and the Lord hath delivered the kingdom into the hand of Absalom thy son: and, behold, thou art taken in thy mischief, because thou art a bloody man.* 2 Sam. 16:9 *Then said Abishai the son of Zeruiah unto the king, Why should this dead dog curse my lord the king? let me go over, I pray thee, and take off his head.* 2 Sam. 16:10 *And the king said, What have I to do with you, ye sons of Zeruiah? so let him curse, because the Lord hath said unto him, Curse David. Who shall then say, Wherefore hast thou done so?* 2 Sam. 16:11 *And David said to Abishai, and to all his servants, Beholds my son, which came forth of my bowels, seeketh my life: how much more now may this Benjamite do it? let him alone, and let him curse; for the Lord hath bidden him.* 2 Sam. 16:12 *It may be that the Lord will look on mine affliction, and that the Lord will requite me good for his cursing this day.* 2 Sam. 16:13 *And as David and his men went by the way, Shimei went along on the hill's side over against him, and cursed as he went, and threw stones at him, and cast dust.*

If we experience humbling situations, it is God doing a work in us to improve our character. It is not easy to endure, but when the work is complete, the situation will be eliminated. If we fail to recognize the Lord's hand and refuse to be humbled, then difficulties of greater magnitude will develop to bring us to the place we feel humbled from within. What painful situations, but what beautiful results. Those who cannot be humbled are not suitable to have eternal fellowship with those who are.

Any system left to run helter-skelter, randomly bumping along by chance, goes from order to disorder in a predictable linear manner. The concept of "free will" is a romantic notion. However, people or angels expressing the wiles of their uncontrolled " free wills" would be like uncontrolled fires breaking out everywhere. Fire proceeds unstopped. If there is no barrier, it continues to consume everything in its path until there is nothing left. Then the fire itself dies. Life and society would fail if God did not control or intercede. Like the fire, "free will" must also be controlled. People and angels left totally to themselves would lend a new meaning to the word chaos.

5
The Prophet Jonah
Controlling One's Destiny

There is a certain amount of arrogance in the statement, "I am master of my own destiny." Such thinking is devoid of the knowledge of the prescience of God and comes from a darkened understanding of everything that is going on around them. From time to time, we hear remarkable stories of people who have planned out every step of the carrier and life, which according to them, has gone just about the way they have planned. These stories are exceedingly rare. When we look at these lives closely, they are not on line as much as the person reports them to be. There is a universe of details of occurrences that transpire around them beyond their personal input, making their success possible of which they had little or nothing to do. It is rather like failing to acknowledge everything that made you what you are today.

None of us is an island unto ourselves. Even if we should attempt to isolate ourselves from all other people, we are not beyond the influence of past experiences and nonhuman influences that control our ultimate destiny. Controlling your own destiny is only a relative thing and is true only when you choose the right path. Prov. 19:21 *There are many devices in a man's heart; nevertheless the counsel of the Lord, that shall stand.* Prov. 19:21 *Many are the plans in a man's heart, But the counsel of the Lord, it will stand.*

Therefore, plan what you want. Only that which goes along with the thoughts of the Lord will be allowed to last; this is true for every person on this planet; it is true even for the Devil. God rules in the affairs of men, angels, and the rest of creation. Anything that will be, will be only if He says it will be. If you have good fortune come into your life, acknowledge the Lord. If trouble assails you, overcome the difficulty in the way that God gives you to deal with it, understanding that there is a reason for everything.

Jonah's Only Path

We read in the Book of Jonah three themes: the prophecy God gave him to deliver to Nineveh, the extraordinary manner God dealt with this man on a personal level, and the symbolism of what the Lord Jesus was to experience. On every level, the foreknowledge of God is manifest, not passively, but with power and force to accomplish exactly what He had planned.

Jon. 1:1 *Now the word of the Lord came unto Jonah the son of Amittai, saying,* Jon. 1:2 *Arise, go to Nineveh, that great city, and cry against it; for their wickedness is come up before me.* Jon. 1:3 *But Jonah rose up to flee unto Tarshish from the presence of the Lord, and went down to Joppa; and he found a ship going to Tarshish: so he paid the fare thereof, and went down into it, to go with them unto Tarshish from the presence of the Lord. . .* We see Jonah, a man chosen by God but endeavoring to choose his own path in life. The scriptures do not go into detail about Jonah's life and God's relationship with him prior to this word, saying that he simply fled. Without a doubt, Jonah did a lot of thinking before he made a run for it.

Jonah had anticipated everything that might befall him in Nineveh and God's reaction to these people if they listened to his message. Some of his forethought is recorded at the end of the Book of Jonah. Jon. 3:10 *And God saw their works [the people of Nineveh], that they turned from their evil way; and God repented of the evil, that he had said that he would do unto them; and he did it not.* Jon. 4:1 *But it displeased Jonah exceedingly, and he was very angry.* Jon. 4:2 *And he prayed unto the Lord, and said, I pray these O Lord, was not this my saying, when I was yet in my country? Therefore I fled before unto Tarshish: for I knew that thou art a gracious God, and merciful, slow to anger, and of great kindness, and repentest thee of the evil.* Jon. 4:11 *And should not I spare Nineveh, that great city, wherein are more than six score thousand persons that cannot discern between their right hand and their left hand; and also much cattle?*

It is important that you see that Jonah did do a lot of thinking about whether he was going to go to Nineveh, because God influences our thoughts. If a man is hungry, he has thoughts of food; if he is thirsty, he has thoughts of water; if he is lonely, he has thoughts about companionship. Since God has control over all influences that come into each of our lives, He has the ability to stimulate our thoughts. This does not mean that you do not have your own thoughts – you do; but your thoughts from those influences stimulate your behavior and bring out what is lurking within you. Your behavior is perfectly predictable to God to such an extent that He is never wrong. Jonah is an example of this. His behavior was predicted, even planned.

Instead of going to Nineveh, Jonah made a run for it. He had decided that he did not want to go and prophecy to these people. He thought that if he got far enough away for the place God had called him, that possibly God would let him live the life he wanted without requesting such uncomfortable things. So he set it into his heart to move to a different location and put some distance between where he presently lived and Nineveh. God could have prevented Jonah from getting to Joppa; He could have stopped him from even leaving his own home or land, but He didn't for a very specific reason. The experience Jonah was about to have was planned to be recorded for future generations. Jonah, even in his disobedience, played into the blueprint of the Lord. This blueprint is not haphazardly put together moment by moment as some would suppose. The End is known from the Beginning.

Predictably, (as planned) Jonah set out on this ship to Tarshish with his thoughts of his future life in a distant land. Is. 55:8 *For my thoughts are not your thoughts, neither are your ways my ways, saith the Lord.* Is. 55:9 *For as the heavens are higher than the earth, so are my ways higher than your ways, and my thoughts than your thoughts. . .* God's thoughts were that Jonah not get to Tarshish. It was in God's plan for Jonah to get as far as the ship on the sea and that is where He met him. Jon. 1:4 *But the Lord sent out a great wind into the sea, and there was a mighty tempest in the sea, so that the ship was like to be broken.* Jon. 1:8 *Then said they unto him, "Tell us, we pray these for whose cause this evil is upon us; What is thine occupation? and whence comest thou? What is thy country? And of what people art thou?"* Jon. 1:10 *Then were the men exceedingly afraid, and said unto him, Why hast thou done this? For the men knew that he fled from the presence of the Lord, because he had told them.* Jon. 1:11 *Then said they unto him, "What shall we do unto thee, that the sea may be calm unto us?" For the sea wrought, and was tempestuous.* Jon. 1:12 *And he said unto them, "Take me up, and cast me forth into the sea; so shall the sea be calm unto you: for I know that for my sake this great tempest is upon you."* Jon. 1:14 *Wherefore they cried unto the Lord, and said, "We beseech thee, O Lord, we beseech thee, let us not perish for this man's life, and lay not upon us innocent blood: for thou, O Lord, hast done as it pleased thee."* Jon. 1:15 *So they took up Jonah, and cast him forth into the sea: and the sea ceased from her raging.* Jon. 1:16 *Then the men feared the Lord exceedingly, and offered a sacrifice unto the Lord and made vows.*

It could be argued that Jonah still had a free will in this matter. He could have refrained from telling these men the truth when "the lot" fell on him. He could also have refrained from telling them to throw him into the sea. But he didn't! He chose to tell the mariners to throw him overboard. Jonah felt responsible for the ill fate that these men were suffering for his own waywardness. Jonah was fated not to make it to Tarshish. This opposition was not a last minute decision on the part of the Lord. He had made plans to deliver him from the situation He had brought upon him to deal with his rebellious nature. Jon. 1:17 *Now the Lord had prepared a great fish to swallow up Jonah. And Jonah was in the belly of the fish three days and three nights.* Jon. 2:1 *Then Jonah prayed unto the Lord his God out of the fish's belly,...*

Note that it says that "the Lord prepared a great fish." This was not a spontaneous decision. This fish had to be present at the exact place in the raging sea to get to Jonah before he drowned. The fish needed to be extremely large and would need to swallow him whole without crushing him in its jaws (the Great White Shark has been known to swallow prey the size of man in like manner and is known to frequent the Mediterranean Sea). I hope you can see that the power of God was present and active to insure this incident occurred exactly as planned; none of this was accident or coincidental.

You could argue that any large fish could have swallowed him. The decision could have been a simple response to the situation and that God's salvation was reactionary to save him, as a moment by moment decision process. However, that is not exactly the way things were. Jon. 1:17 *Now the Lord had prepared a great fish to swallow up Jonah...* "Preparation" implies forethought and design. We have already expressed the thought that this fish had to be exactly at the right spot to have gotten to Jonah before he drowned. This fact in itself would state that God would have had to know that Jonah was to be thrown into the sea. But there is a more startling demonstration of the preparation the Lord had made for this moment.

Jon. 1:17 ...A*nd Jonah was in the belly of the fish three days and three nights.* In any ordinary fish, he would have died within minutes of entering this extraordinary stomach; but he didn't, as is evidenced by the thoughts and prayer he expressed to God while there. Jon. 2:1 *Then Jonah prayed unto the Lord his God out of the fish's belly,* Jon. 2:2 *And said, I cried by reason of mine affliction unto the Lord, and he heard me; out of the belly of hell cried I, and thou heardest my voice.* Jon. 2:5 *The waters compassed me about, even to the soul: the depth closed me round about, the weeds were wrapped about my head.* Jon. 2:7 *When my soul fainted within me I remembered the Lord: and my prayer came in unto thee, into thine holy temple.* Jon. 2:9 *But I will sacrifice unto thee with the voice of thanksgiving; I will pay that I have vowed. Salvation is of the Lord...* Even if you take the position that Jonah did die in this experience and was brought back to life, things still point to a planned event. Jonah, in an ordinary stomach, would have been well on his way toward being digested by this fish during the three days. It takes an enormous amount of energy to maintain the muscular activity of such a large creature to propel its way in the seas. An inefficient digestive system would not sustain its life. This stomach had been prepared so that Jonah's body would not be destroyed. God could have neutralized all the acids and enzymes in its stomach and prevented it from producing more digestive enzymes while Jonah was there. Regardless, God had planned for Jonah to survive, a fact that was made evident three days later. Jon. 2:10 *And the Lord spake unto the fish, and it vomited out Jonah upon the dry land.*

The forethought of the Lord is further demonstrated in the amount of time Jonah spent in the belly of this fish. Matt. 12:40 *For as Jonah was three days and three nights in the whale's belly* [sea monster: 2785g. ke_tos: a primary, primitive word; a huge fish]; *so shall the Son of man be three days and three nights in the heart of the earth.* Matt. 16:4 *A wicked and adulterous generation seeketh after a sign; and there shall no sign be given unto it, but the sign of the prophet Jonas. And he left them, and departed. . .* Jonah's experience was a sign to future generations which the Lord Jesus Christ would use to depict future events occurring in His own life. Jonah was in this fish for three days because God the Father had already planned the amount of time the Lord Jesus Christ would remain in the grave and declared this clearly in the experience of Jonah. It should also be clear that Jesus also declared openly the amount of time He was predestined to spend in the grave in His reference to Jonah. The fact that Jesus was to spend three days in the grave was not a matter of just seeing into the future and declaring what He saw. The three days was a planned event! Jesus also gives credence to the prophet Jonah, that his experience was not a fable, being that Jonah's experience was in reference to Him.

6
The Life of Joseph

Gen. 37:4 *And when his brethren saw that their father loved him more than all his brethren, they hated him, and could not speak peaceably unto him.* Gen. 37:5 *And Joseph dreamed a dream, and he told it his brethren: and they hated him yet the more.* Gen. 37:6 *And he said unto them, Hear, I pray you, this dream which I have dreamed:* Gen. 37:7 *For, behold, we were binding sheaves in the field, and, lo, my sheaf arose, and also stood upright; and, behold, your sheaves stood round about, and made obeisance to my sheaf.* Gen. 37:8 *And his brethren said to him, Shalt thou indeed reign over us? or shalt thou indeed have dominion over us? And they hated him yet the more for his dreams, and for his words.* Gen. 37:9 *And he dreamed yet another dream, and told it his brethren, and said, Behold, I have dreamed a dream more; and, behold, the sun and the moon and the eleven stars made obeisance to me.* Gen. 37:10 *And he told it to his father, and to his brethren: and his father rebuked him, and said unto him, What is this dream that thou hast dreamed? Shall I and thy mother and thy brethren indeed come to bow down ourselves to thee to the earth?* Gen. 37:11 *And his brethren envied him; but his father observed the saying.*

In this account of the dream of Joseph, son of Jacob, he is a young teenager of about seventeen years old. In his mind, he is innocent of any plans or plots of his own intention to make himself a renowned figure. He has heard of the promises of God, the visitations and dreams of Abraham, Isaac, and his father Jacob, and is somewhat excited at the possibilities that God has revealed something of importance to him, therefore he shares these dreams with his family. For reasons beyond his control, Joseph is envied and hated by his brothers. He is in a position that he is without power to change or correct; if he is civil, they are uncivil, if he is cordial, they are aloof. Joseph, except for the affections of his father, is somewhat isolated even in his own home. This entire situation was by the plan and purposes of God, like a master chess player arranging His pieces. The dreams given to Joseph were reassurances to him from the Lord that He had a plan in all that he was suffering. Contained in these dreams were the seeds of faith which were to develop in his imagination and help sustain him through difficult times to come.

These dreams were more than looking into the future; they were divinely revealed plans. The symbolism is not the actual future, but a shadow of the substance of the future. There was nothing that Joseph could do to influence the timetable of these future events to speed them up, slow them down or, by his own planning, make them happen. The things which were to occur to him were beyond his control. Furthermore, even as great as Jacob was in the purposes of God, he was not given understanding into what God was doing except a slight glimpse by believing the dreams of Joseph. God's purposes do not require our understanding for their success.

Joseph Sent to his Brothers

Gen. 37:13 *And Israel said unto Joseph, "Do not thy brethren feed the flock in Shechem? come, and I will send thee unto them." And he said to him, "Here am I."* Gen. 37:18 *And when they saw him afar off, even before he came near unto them, they conspired against him to slay him.* Gen. 37:20 *Come now therefore, and let us slay him, and cast him into some pit, and we will say, "Some evil beast hath devoured him:" and we shall see what will become of his dreams.* Gen. 37:21 *And Reuben heard it, and he delivered him out of their hands; and said, "Let us not kill him."* Gen. 37:22 *And Reuben said unto them, "Shed no blood, but cast him into this pit that is in the wilderness, and lay no hand upon him;" that he might rid him out of their hands, to deliver him to his father again.* Gen. 37:23 *And it came to pass, when Joseph was come unto his brethren, that they stripped Joseph out of his coat, his coat of many colors that was on him;* Gen. 37:24 *And they took him, and cast him into a pit: and the pit was empty, there was no water in it.* Gen. 37:25 *And they sat down to eat bread: and they lifted up their eyes* and looked, and, behold, a company of Ishmeelites came from Gilead with their camels bearing spicery and balm and myrrh, going to carry it down to Egypt. Gen. 37:26 And Judah said unto his brethren, "What profit is it if we slay our brother, and conceal his blood?" Gen. 37:27 "Come, and let us sell him to the Ishmeelites, and let not our hand be upon him; for he is our brother and our flesh." And his brethren were content. Gen. 37:28 Then there passed by Midianite merchant men; and they drew and lifted up Joseph out of the pit, and sold Joseph to the Ishmeelites for twenty pieces of silver: and they brought Joseph into Egypt. Gen. 37:29 And Reuben returned unto the pit; and, behold, Joseph was not in the pit; and he rent his clothes. Gen. 37:30 And he returned unto his brethren, and said, "The child is not; and I, whither shall I go?" Gen. 37:31 And they took Joseph's coat, and killed a kid of the goats, and dipped the coat in the blood; Gen. 37:32 And they sent the coat of many colors, and they brought it to their father; and said, "This have we found: know now whether it be thy son's coat or no." Gen. 37:33 And he knew it, and said, "It is my son's coat; an evil beast hath devoured him; Joseph is without doubt rent in pieces."

The above passages from the book of Genesis display Joseph caught in a web of circumstances that ultimately brought him to Egypt. The only choice he is given in the above account is his obedience to his father in going to check up on his brothers and father's herds. He has no control over the events which followed. His brothers, being cognizant of his dreams, relish the idea of preventing them from ever happening (Gen. 37:20). They are aware that their father Jacob ended up with the blessings of Isaac instead of Esau, they wonder, given Jacob's fondness of Joseph, that the dreams point to him inheriting his fathers blessing. Reuben is more confident in these things, being Jacob's firstborn, and wants to be pleasing to his father in all things, and so remains in his favor. Therefore, Reuben wants to protect Joseph from the harm his other brothers have planned for him. Plans and good intentions are not enough to change what God has ordained.

Reuben is not permitted to save Joseph from the fate of being sold into slavery. He is instrumental in preventing his death, which is as far as his kind thoughts will allow him. This brief intervention was all that was required to fulfill the plan of God, which would have been derailed if Joseph would have been murdered. Reuben was prevented by circumstances from completely delivering Joseph from his brothers because Joseph had to go to Egypt.

Look at the hatred and envy among these brothers directed toward Joseph (Gen. 37:4). There is no record of them hating each other, only Joseph. There is no record of hatred toward Joseph's younger brother Benjamin; if it were to be argued that this condition resulted from Joseph being born of Rachel, Jacob's favorite wife, we still have the issue of the intensity of the hatred and why it was not directed toward Benjamin. These brothers had four different mothers, sharing only the same father, Jacob. Joseph was set apart by God to be hated for a reason. The reason for this hatred was not apparent to Joseph, nor any family member. No number of family discussions could have corrected this situation because this animosity is with purpose; it was destined to separate Joseph from his father. Without this hatred, Joseph's brothers would not have sold him into slavery and Joseph would have remained with his father.

It was not enough that Joseph could have been sent to Egypt. He had to be in the right place at the right time. The following scriptures will illustrate Joseph's plight, a path beyond his control, from great suffering to glory.

Joseph in Egypt as a Slave to Potiphar

Gen. 37:36 *And the Midianites sold him into Egypt unto Potiphar, an officer of Pharaoh's, and captain of the guard.* Gen. 39:2 *And the Lord was with Joseph, and he was a prosperous man; and he was in the house of his master the Egyptian.* Gen. 39:3 *And his master saw that the Lord was with him, and that the Lord made all that he did to prosper in his hand.* Gen. 39:4 *And Joseph found grace in his sight, and he served him: and he made him overseer over his house, and all that he had he put into his hand.* Gen. 39:7 *And it came to pass after these things, that his master's wife cast her eyes upon Joseph; and she said, Lie with me. Gen. 39:8 But he refused and said to his master's wife, "Behold, with me, my master does not concern himself with anything in the house, and he has put all that he owns in my charge. Gen. 39:9 There is none greater in this house than I; neither hath he kept back any thing from me but thee, because thou art his wife: how then can I do this great wickedness, and sin against God? Gen. 39:10 And it came to pass, as she spake to Joseph day by day, that he hearkened not unto her, to lie by her, or to be with her. Gen. 39:11 And it came to pass about this time, that Joseph went into the house to do his business; and there was none of the men of the house there within. Gen. 39:12 And she caught him by his garment, saying, Lie with me: and he left his garment in her hand, and fled, and got him out. Gen. 39:14 That she called unto the men of her house, and spake unto them, saying, See, he hath brought in an Hebrew unto us to mock us; he came in unto me to lie with me, and I cried with a loud voice: Gen. 39:16 And she laid up his garment by her, until his lord came home. Gen. 39:19 And it came to pass, when his master heard the words of his wife, which she spake unto him, saying, After this manner did thy servant to me; that his wrath was kindled. Gen. 39:20 And Joseph's master took him, and put him into the prison, a place where the king's prisoners were bound: and he was there in the prison. Gen. 39:21 But the Lord was with Joseph, and showed him mercy, and gave him favor in the sight of the keeper of the prison. Gen. 40:1 And it came to pass after these things, that the butler of the king of Egypt and his baker had offended their lord the king of Egypt. Gen. 40:5 And they dreamed a dream both of them, each man his dream in one night, each man according to the interpretation of his dream, the butler and the baker of the king of Egypt, which were bound in the prison. Gen. 40:8 And they said unto him, We have dreamed a dream, and there is no interpreter of it. And Joseph said unto them, Do not interpretations belong to God? tell me them, I pray you. Gen. 40:9-13 Joseph then made known to each man the interpretation of his dream. Gen. 40:14 But think on me when it shall be well with thee, and show kindness, I pray thee, unto me, and make mention of me unto Pharaoh, and bring me out of this house:* Gen. 40:23 *Yet did not the chief butler remember Joseph, but forgat him.* Gen. 41:1 *And it came to pass at the end of two full years, that Pharaoh dreamed: and, behold, he stood by the river.* Gen. 41:8 *And it came to pass in the morning that his spirit was troubled; and he sent and called for all the magicians of Egypt, and all the wise men thereof: and Pharaoh told them his dream; but there was none that could interpret them unto Pharaoh.* Gen. 41:9 *Then spake the chief butler unto Pharaoh, saying, I do remember my faults this day:* Gen. 41:12 *And there was there with us a young man, an Hebrew, servant to the captain of the guard; and we told him, and he interpreted to us our dreams; to each man according to his dream he did interpret.* Gen. 41:14 *Then Pharaoh sent and called Joseph, and they brought him hastily out of the dungeon: and he shaved himself, and changed his raiment, and came in unto Pharaoh.* Gen. 41:15 *And Pharaoh said unto Joseph, I have dreamed a dream, and there is none that can interpret it: and I have heard say of these that thou canst understand a dream to interpret it.* Gen. 41:16 *And Joseph answered Pharaoh, saying, It is not in me: God shall give Pharaoh an answer of peace.* Gen. 41:25 *And Joseph said unto Pharaoh, The dream of Pharaoh is one: God hath showed Pharaoh what he is about to do.* Gen. 41:29 *Behold, there come seven years of great plenty throughout all the land of Egypt:* Gen. 41:30 *And there shall arise after them seven years of famine; and all the plenty shall be forgotten in the land of Egypt; and the famine shall consume the land;* Gen 41:33 *Now therefore lit the Pharaoh look out a man discreet and wise, and set him over the land of Egypt,* (to store up food from the years of plenty against the years of famine). Gen. 41:38 *And Pharaoh said unto his servants, Can we find such a one as this is, a man in whom the Spirit of God is?* Gen. 41:40 *Thou shalt be over my house, and according unto thy word shall all my people be ruled: only in the throne will I be greater than thou.* Gen. 41:41 *And Pharaoh said unto Joseph, See, I have set thee over all the land of Egypt.*

One can only imagine the depth of despair of young Joseph. He was seventeen years old and sold into slavery by his own brothers. He had pleaded with them earnestly not to do this to him, but his pleas fell on deaf ears. Even the Midianites hearts were hardened. They undoubtedly were told the story by Joseph, but ignored what they were told. It was God's will to get Joseph away from Jacob and into close proximity to the Pharaoh. Joseph could not understand what was happening. It seemed to him that this great evil was coming upon him to destroy his life. Indeed, the evil did destroy his life with his father and his family in order to create a new life with a special destiny.

Incredibly, the Midianites sold Joseph to Potiphar, an officer in Pharaoh's army and the captain of the guard. Here, he flourished. His fastidious nature and ability to organize won him the respect of his master, who appreciated these qualities, being a military officer. Potiphar liked Joseph. It can be assumed with great certainty that Joseph had told him about his own family and the circumstances which lead to him being a slave in his service. Potiphar wanted to make Joseph's life as pleasant as possible and help him forget the pain of his captivity. Therefore, he gave him as much authority as he felt the young man could handle. This position helped Joseph to develop skills in dealing with other people and helped shape his way of thinking. Joseph thought highly of Potiphar and did everything he could to please him. He became to Joseph almost an extension of his own father.

This relationship between Joseph and Potiphar continued for a number of years, in which time Joseph gained recognition even among some of Potiphar's acquaintances. But this relationship was destined to come to end. Potiphar was a man of some substance, evidenced by the size of his household and the need for Joseph to oversee his affairs. With the relative wealth and authority he possessed, it would put him in a position to have a beautiful wife whose relationship with him had nothing to do with mental and physical attraction. Because of the strong relationship between Joseph and Potiphar, little could be done to separate them except in the case of a great offense. Potiphar's weakness was his wife, whom he cherished and provided for. The weakness in this marriage was her carnal needs and her attraction to Joseph. The fact that this woman cast her eyes upon Joseph was no accident. Joseph was put in a situation in which there was no escape for the very purpose of moving him out of this household.

It made no difference whether Joseph would have slept with this woman or not (except to Joseph in his own integrity). She was chosen as the instrument to separate. Joseph could not run from this situation, because he was a slave, even though he was highly exalted. He attempted being up front with this woman and appealed to logic. Just as he could do nothing to correct the hatred and envy of his brothers, he was also powerless to control the dangerous attraction this woman had for him. Though Joseph was innocent of wrongdoing, the outcome would be the same as if he were guilty. There were higher purposes at work which needed him to be thrown into prison. Potiphar was not just any man; and Joseph was not just anywhere in Egypt. Potiphar had the authority to throw him into prison and the prison was close in proximity to the Pharaoh.

Joseph in Prison

To Joseph, his life seemed one terrible circumstance after another. How could this have happened? He had heard the stories of all the blessings of his father, all the way back to Abraham. Nothing like this had ever happened to any of them. The Lord seemed to bless them on every side. What about the dreams he had? Joseph again knew deep despair as the conditions of circumstances beyond his control carried him along like a leaf being carried by the wind. But his life was more than just fertilizer for the ground; it had a purpose, as did the leaf to the tree.

While in prison for accusations of which he was innocent, Joseph again began to shine. He was a trustworthy man with the ability to organize, quickly recognized by the jailer. Again, Joseph was elevated in his circumstance to help run the jail. He was not free to come and go, but this position helped take his mind off his captivity, afforded him a few privileges, and further prepared him for future events yet to unfold. In each circumstance, the Lord made his situation as easy as possible, short of removing him from it. It was the Lord Who had put him there for His own purposes, purposes yet to be revealed. The dreams the Lord gave to Joseph earlier were with him through each ordeal as beacons of faith to help sustain him through the darkness of his experiences. Joseph would find out the purpose in his suffering, but not immediately.

How many years passed is not clear. It can be ascertained that he was around seventeen when he was sold as a slave by the Midianites. It also would have taken some time for Potiphar to have recognized his abilities in order to elevate him to head steward of his household. It is also clear that Joseph was in prison until the age of thirty (Gen. 41:46). Thus, it would have taken some time to gain the attention of the jailer to prove himself and gain his trust that he might elevate him to stewardship over the other prisoners. It is possible after looking at all these factors that he may have been in prison for up to nine years!

What a time of darkness and despair! It would be one thing if Joseph were guilty of some heinous crime, but to be innocent and suffer such things would be very difficult to bear emotionally. Joseph was a victim of circumstances. His dreams were his only hope, which gave him faith. He understood the meaning of dreams and that some were from God; a communication which helps us prepare or comfort us. It was with this understanding well entrenched within Joseph that Pharaoh's butler and baker told him their dreams while incarcerated for offensive behavior. The fact that these men were put in contact with Joseph and that they dreamed meaningful dreams while with him was no accident. This seemingly uneventful encounter lead him to being brought before the Pharaoh. Without this experience, Joseph would have remained unanimous to the opportunity to speak to the Pharaoh about his dream.

Joseph Before Pharaoh

It was well understood in the ancient world that dreams were important. The fact that there was no one around the Pharaoh who understood this dream was orchestrated by God. The Holy Spirit richly dwelt with Joseph to comfort him in his lowly state. The spiritual side of his nature was the only sector of his life in which he had any freedom. When Joseph is brought in before Pharaoh, it is this quality which impresses him. Joseph is quick to point out that meaningful dreams are from God, who also can supply the correct meaning. He takes no credit for the moment, but sees that it is the Lord who has brought him to hear the Pharaoh's dream.

Joseph, even after all the difficult things he has endured thus far, has begun to grasp that the Lord rules all things and controls the future. After he has heard the two dreams of Pharaoh, his reply expresses these thoughts. Gen. 41:25 *And Joseph said unto Pharaoh, The dream of Pharaoh is one: God hath showed Pharaoh what he is about to do. . .* Joseph does not say, "God has showed Pharaoh the future." This is because Joseph recognized that the future belongs to the Lord; it is not a result of random occurrences which bring forth an uncertain end. As God orchestrated all things in the beginning, He has never stopped along the way. Thus His predictions of the future are not really predictions, but plans! The seven years of plenty were by the power of God and the Seven years of famine were also by God.

How can a righteous God do such things and bring a famine upon the land? The apostle Paul answered this question best when he cited God's choice of Jacob over Esau. Rom. 9:11 *For the children being not yet born, neither having done any good or evil, that the purpose of God according to election might stand. not of works. but of him that calleth:. . .* Therefore the "purposes of God according to election" must be fulfilled. The apostle Paul goes on in his expository expressing the understanding which God had given him. Rom. 9:19 *Thou wilt say then unto me, Why doth he yet find fault? For who hath resisted his will?* (No one!) Rom. 9:20 *Nay but, O man, who art thou that readiest against God? Shall the thing formed say to him that formed it, Why hast thou made me thus?* Rom. 9:21 *Hath not the potter power over the clay, of the same lump to make one vessel unto honour, and another unto dishonor?* But some have a very weak understanding of the Lord. They see Him in a similitude to a fireman, who runs around all day putting out fires that the Devil started. The Lord does not predict the future, He creates it.

I am only expostulating upon that which is clearly written. I am making no effort to explain away what is stated. I am however, in an effort to reason and see things as put forth, taking a very close, methodical, and thoughtful look at what God is telling us in these scriptures.

Joseph Made Governor of Egypt

Gen. 41:38 *And Pharaoh said unto his servants, Can we find such a one as this is, a man in whom the Spirit of God is?* Gen. 41:40 *Thou shalt be over my house, and according unto thy word shall all my people be ruled: only in the throne will I be greater than thou.* Gen. 41:41 *And Pharaoh said unto Joseph, See, I have set thee over all the land of Egypt...* It is obvious that the Pharaoh had a strong belief that the things which occurred in this world were under divine control by his acceptance of Joseph. Joseph made no attempt to impress this man with psychic abilities or himself. It was the spiritual qualities of Joseph and his acknowledgment that God was in control which held his attention. This acknowledgment from Joseph had developed through the years and was very firmly rooted in him from the things he had suffered in his own life. This was an understanding which grew with experience. He was now ready to assume the position God had ordained from the beginning; a position that the power and workings of God had predestined him to occupy. It was not chance or accident occurrence that brought him to this place. He suffered each day, wrestling with the circumstances of his life versus the faith imparted to him by his dreams and the comfort of the overshadowing presence of the Holy Spirit.

How could Joseph have foreseen such a change in his circumstances, from bondage and anonymity to power and glory? The things he suffered did not destroy his life, but opened the door for its very expression. What a preparation! What a leader! His experiences had given him a firm knowledge that the power behind his authority is the Lord. It would be wonderful if all leaders understood the power behind their power.

Joseph as Governor of Egypt

The following scriptures deal with the next stage of Joseph's life. I have chosen key phrases to give a general overview and illuminate the issue of destiny and fulfillment. You may want to read this account in its complete form in the Bible.

Gen. 41:57 *And all countries came into Egypt to Joseph for to buy corn; because that the famine was so sore in all lands.* Gen. 42:5 *And the sons of Israel came to buy corn among those that came: for the famine was in the land of Canaan.* Gen. 42:6 *And Joseph was the governor over the land, and he it was that sold to all the people of the land: and Joseph's brethren came, and bowed down themselves before him with their faces to the earth.* Gen. 42:9 *And Joseph remembered the dreams which he dreamed of them and said unto them, "Ye are spies; to see the nakedness of the land ye are come."* Gen. 42:10 *And they said unto him, "Nay, my lord, but to buy food are thy servants come."* Gen. 42:19 *"If ye be true men, let one of your brethren be bound in the house of your prison: go ye, carry corn for the famine of your houses:* Gen. 42:20 *But bring your youngest brother unto me; so shall your words be verified, and ye shall not die." And they did so.* Gen. 42:21 *And they said one to another, "We are verily guilty concerning our brother, in that we saw the anguish of his soul, when he besought us, and we would not hear; therefore is this distress come upon us."* Gen. 42:22 *And Reuben answered them, saying, "Spake I not unto you, saying, Do not sin against the child; and ye would not hear? therefore, behold, also his blood is required."* Gen. 42:25 *Then Joseph commanded to fill their sacks with corn, and to restore every man's money into his sack, and to give them provision for the way: and thus did he unto them.* Gen. 43:13 *Take also your brother, and arise, go again unto the man:* Gen. 43:24 *And the man brought the men into Joseph's house, and gave them water, and they washed their feet; and he gave their asses provender.* Gen. 43:27 *And he asked them of their welfare, and said, "Is your father well, the old man of whom ye spake? Is he yet alive?"* Gen. 43:28 *And they answered, "Thy servant our father is in good health, he is yet alive." And they bowed down their heads, and made obeisance.* Gen. 45:1 *Then Joseph could not refrain himself before all them that stood by him; and he cried, "Cause every man to go out from me." And there stood no man with him, while Joseph made himself known unto his brethren.* Gen. 45:2 *And he wept aloud: and the Egyptians and the house of Pharaoh heard.* Gen. 45:3 *And Joseph said unto his brethren, "I am Joseph; doth my father yet live?" And his brethren could not answer him; for they were troubled at his presence.* Gen. 45:4 *And Joseph said unto his brethren, "Come near to me, I pray you." And they came near. And he said, "I am Joseph your brother, whom ye sold into Egypt.* Gen. 45:5 *Now therefore be not grieved, nor angry with yourselves, that ye sold me hither: for God did send me before you to preserve life.* Gen. 45:6 *For these two years hath the famine been in the land: and yet there are five years, in the which there shall neither be earing nor harvest.* Gen. 45:7 *And God sent me before you to preserve you a posterity in the earth, and to save your lives by a great deliverance.* Gen. 45:8 *So now it was not you that sent me hither, but God: and he hath made me a father to Pharaoh, and lord of all his house! and a ruler throughout all the land of Egypt.* Gen. 45:9 *Haste ye, and go up to my father, and say unto him, 'Thus saith thy son Joseph, God hath made me lord of all Egypt: come down unto me, tarry not:* Gen. 45:10 *And thou shalt dwell in the land of Goshen, and thou shalt be near unto me, thou, and thy children, and thy children's children, and thy flocks, and thy herds, and all that thou hast:* Gen. 45:11 *And there will I nourish thee; for yet there are five years of famine; lest thou, and thy household, and all that thou hast, come to poverty.'"* Gen. 46:2 *And God spake unto Israel in the visions of the night, and said, "Jacob, Jacob." And he said, "Here am I."* Gen. 46:3 *And he said, "I am God, the God of thy father: fear not to go down into Egypt; for I will there make of thee a great nation:* Gen. 46:4 *I will go down with thee into Egypt; and I will also surely bring thee up again: and Joseph shall put his hand upon thine eyes."* Gen. 46:31 *And Joseph said unto his brethren, and unto his father's house, "I will go up, and show Pharaoh, and say unto him, My brethren, and my father's house, which were in the land of Canaan, are come unto me;* Gen. 46:33 *And it shall come to pass, when Pharaoh shall call you, and shall say, What is your occupation?* Gen. 46:34 *That ye shall say, Thy servants' trade* hath been about cattle from our youth even until now, both we, and also our fathers: that ye may dwell in the land of Goshen; for every shepherd is an abomination unto the Egyptians." Gen. 47:3 And Pharaoh said unto his brethren, "What is your occupation?" And they said unto Pharaohs "Thy servants are shepherds, both we, and also our fathers." Gen. 47:6 "The land of Egypt is before thee; in the best of the land make thy father and brethren to dwell; in the land of Goshen let them dwell: and if thou knowest any men of activity among them, then make them rulers over my cattle." Gen. 47:20 And Joseph bought all the land of Egypt for Pharaoh; for the Egyptians sold every man his field, because the famine prevailed over them: so the land became Pharaoh's. Gen. 47:21 And as for the people, he removed them to cities from one end of the borders of Egypt even to the other end thereof. Gen. 47:24 And it shall come to pass in the increase, that ye shall give the fifth part unto Pharaoh, and four parts shall be your own, for seed of the field, and for your food, and for them of your households, and for food for your little ones. Gen. 47:26 And Joseph made it a law over the land of Egypt unto this day, that Pharaoh should have the fifth part; except the land of the priests only, which became not Pharaoh's. Gen. 50:15 And when Joseph's brethren saw that their father was dead, they said, Joseph will peradventure hate us, and will certainly requite us all the evil which we did unto him. Gen. 50:16 And they sent a messenger unto Joseph, saying, Thy father did command before he died, saying, Gen. 50:17 So shall ye say unto Joseph, Forgive, I pray thee now, the trespass of thy brethren, and their sin; for they did unto thee evil: and now, we pray thee, forgive the trespass of the servants of the God of thy father. And Joseph wept when they spake unto him. Gen. 50:18 And his brethren also went and fell down before his face; and they said, "Behold, we be thy servants." Gen. 50:19 And Joseph said unto them, "Fear not: for am I in the place of God? Gen. 50:20 But as for you, ye thought evil against me; but God meant it unto good, to bring to pass, as it is this day, to save much people alive. Gen. 50:21 Now therefore fear ye not: I will nourish you, and your little ones." And he comforted them, and spake kindly unto them.

Joseph is an example of being in the right place at the right time. Other people have received great opportunities because, coincidentally, they knew certain people or certain things had happened to them. You can imagine his joy. Yet, even with this new found position he did not know the reasons for all he had suffered.

If God is good, how could He do such terrible things? How could a good God hurt so many innocent people by bringing famine? These are good questions but reflect short-term goals and a lack of understanding. With the Lord, the end is justified by the means. This in not to say that the Lord has no mercy. Joseph, in all the things he suffered, was put in positions to lighten the impact of the circumstance. He could not change his circumstances because, unbeknown to him, the Lord had already determined his future and the course he must take to get there. The future, contrary to some people's understanding, is not malleable with multiple possibilities. We, like Joseph, are often fraught with anxiety of the possibilities of wrong decisions. However, our Creator is the Lord, who will also fully guide our path. It is only in our own eyes that we, at times, seem to loose sight of Him. Do not fear but give thanks. 1 Thess. 5:18 *In every thing give thanks: for this is the will of God in Christ Jesus concerning you. . .*

A Diversion from Joseph

Some people want to argue against what they call Darwinism. On one hand, they state that God created all things according to His own will by His direct actions; then in direct contradiction to themselves, they argue that we all do our own thing with our glorified free. We create our own future. These people want you to believe that once everything was created, God simply let things go their merry way. How myopic an understanding! Who said that God has ever stopped creating? John 5:16 *And for this reason the Jews were persecuting Jesus, because He was doing these things on the Sabbath.* John 5:17 *But He answered them, "My Father is working until now, and I Myself am working.".* . . Jesus understood that "creation" was an ongoing process. God created the beginning; He creates the present; and He will create the future.

Gen. 2:2 *And by the seventh day God completed His work which He had done; and He rested on the seventh day from all His work which He had done.* Gen. 2:3 *Then God blessed the seventh day and sanctified it, because in it He rested from all His work which God had created and made...* This scripture does not mean what many people report it to mean. It does not mean that God made all the physical things in the past and now does nothing. Jesus said, "My Father is working until now." What the Lord is communicating is that creation in His eyes is complete, the past, the present, and the future. In God's eyes, it is all created; that is why we are admonished to enter into His rest. You, by your worrying, will not alter the future. Enter into the Lord Jesus Christ and live your life with the understanding that the end is fixed (determined) from the beginning of time. God is creating today, and tomorrow, and so forth to bring about the end He has predetermined. Let me cite an example from the Book of Daniel, in which an angel is speaking with him. Dan. 8:19 *And he said, "Behold. I am going to let you know what will occur at the final period of the indignation, for [it] pertains to the appointed time of the end...*

God does not predict the future. He creates it. Therefore we can know it by statements of facts He has provided for us in the scriptures. What a contradiction in reasoning to say, "God created everything in the beginning, but now He lets things bump along being directed by (uninfluenced) free will! If you recant, and say "free will is influenced by God," then you admit that God does indeed manipulate all things for His purposes. The apostle Paul writes, Heb. 4:3 *For we which have believed do enter into rest, as he said, "As I have sworn in my wrath, if they shall enter into my rest:" although the works were finished from the foundation of the world...* Why are the "works finished" if "My Father is working still"? Because everything is destined from the beginning to occur with a determined outcome; that is why the works were finished. The Lord works because everything is not running itself. We "enter into rest" when we realize that everything is finished. The outcome of all things is already determined. When you accept this, you rest.

What must I do to work the works of God? Believe. John 6:28 *Then said they unto him, What shall we do, that we might work the works of God?* John 6:29 *Jesus answered and said unto them, This is the work of God, that ye believe on him whom he hath sent...* Jesus Christ is the beginning and the end of the plan of God with regard to us. Rev. 21:6 *And He said to me, "It is done. I am the Alpha and the Omega, the beginning and the end. I will give to the one who thirsts from the spring of the water of life without cost...* This is a declaration of present truth or reality. The fact that Jesus is the Omega is not a prediction. It is truth based upon that which is already established. For us, everything is based upon faith; for God the Father, what is to be, will be, because He has determined the future.

So many scriptures recognize the contingency of the will of God regarding prayers of faith to change a circumstance because God will not answer prayers according to our desire, but rather according to His divine plan for our life and all things. Rom. 1:10 *Making request, if by any means now at length I might have a prosperous journey by the will of God to come unto you...* The apostle Paul understood that though he was the Lord's servant in the preaching of the gospel, it was God who directed his steps. He could not go wherever he wanted. The will of God has everything to do with what each one of us experiences along the way. Rom. 8:27 *And he that searcheth the hearts knoweth what is the mind of the Spirit, because he maketh intercession for the saints according to the will of God...* We see again that the Lord does not simply make intercession for his elect in an aimless fashion; He is careful to make intercession only according to the will of God. There is no intercession for any of us which is contrary to the plans and purposes of God. Almost without exception, the Lord does not make intercession for us according to our own desires.

Note, for example, the Lord Jesus Christ in the garden before His crucifixion. He knew what death lay before Him and prayed for intercession according the will to His Father, not according to the weakness of His own desire. In this instance, we see how we can want to be delivered from our circumstances because they are painful to us. However, we need to be armed with the knowledge that there may be higher purposes at work that necessitate our suffering. 1 Pet. 4:1 *Forasmuch then as Christ hath suffered for us in the flesh, arm yourselves likewise with the same mind: for he that hath suffered in the flesh hath ceased from sin;...* The apostle Paul also recognized that it was sometimes necessary to suffer. Some of this suffering is according to the purposes of the Father. Col. 1:24 *Who now rejoice in my sufferings for you, and fill up that which is behind of the afflictions of Christ in my flesh for his body's sake, which is the church...* If this apostle understood that it may be required for him to suffer at times for Christ's sake, is it not true, that each one of us will also be called upon to suffer at times according to the will of God?

Yet some oppose the concept of predestination on the sole premise that it would mean that suffering was the will of God. The notion of a good God causing suffering is too much to fathom. I have discussed earlier how the Lord does not cause misfortune to come upon anyone directly, but uses forces which He refuses to completely restrain to do His will. We make the judgment as to this being "good or evil," which has been our problem since the Garden of Eden. Gen. 2:9 *And out of the ground made the Lord God to grow every tree that is pleasant to the sight, and good for food; the tree of life also in the midst of the garden, and the tree of knowledge of good and evil* Gen. 2:17 *But of the tree of the knowledge of good and evil, thou shalt not eat of it: for in the day that thou eatest thereof thou shalt surely die...* The apostle Paul put it a slightly different way. Titus 1:15 *Unto the pure all things are pure: but unto them that are defiled and unbelieving is nothing pure; but even their mind and conscience is defiled...* To the defiled mind it is sometimes impossible to reason with it. Even the logic of the simple flow of an explanation would be interrupted so that the idea you are trying to communicate will be disrupted. These people oppose themselves.

Look at the example of the blind man who Jesus healed as an example of suffering. Is there anyone who will argue that blindness in any society will not bring with it a considerable amount of suffering? John 9:2 *And his disciples asked him, saying, Masters who did sin, this man, or his parents, that he was born blind?* John 9:3 *Jesus answered, "Neither hath this man sinned, nor his parents: but that the works of God should be made manifest in him."* John 9:6 *When he had thus spoken, he spat on the ground, and made clay of the spittle, and he anointed the eyes of the blind man with the clay,* John 9:7 *And said unto him, Go, wash in the pool of Siloam, (which is by interpretation, Sent.) He went his way therefore, and washed, and came seeing...* This man was blind, that God could demonstrate His miraculous power to restore through faith in the Lord Jesus Christ. His life and what happened, still speaks to us today, each time this portion of the gospel is meditated upon or read. The suffering this man experienced in his life before being touched by the Lord Jesus Christ was swallowed up by the joy of seeing; a simple faculty which each one of us possesses, but takes somewhat for granted. In some cases, the purposes of the will of God in suffering is revealed, in others it is not. That which we change, we change; that which we cannot change, we cannot change.

Joseph and His Family Connections

It should be clear that it was the Lord that put Joseph in the position of authority. The Lord also strengthened this position by his marriage to Asenath. She was the daughter of a member of the high society, her father being priest of the Egyptian god On. Gen. 41:45 *And Pharaoh called Joseph's name Zaphnathpaaneah; and he gave him to wife Asenath the daughter of Potipherah priest of On. And Joseph went out over all the land of Egypt.* Without this marriage, Joseph would have had to make his own roads into Egyptian higher society. Without the support from this sector of society, he would have had many difficulties with his new authority. But, the Lord does all things well. Joseph's needs and the desires of the Lord were fulfilled at the same time. You can also believe, based upon everything else, that this young woman Asenath was prepared, physically, emotionally, and intellectually, to be the right force in Joseph's life to assist him in all things he was destined to fulfill.

The birth of Joseph's two sons further strengthened his place in Egyptian society. Potipherah was given a vested interest in Joseph's success because of the sons he received by his daughter. In Potipherah's eyes, they would be Egyptian, while in Joseph's eyes, Hebrew. This was a further strong advantage to Joseph in that it more securely cemented him into Egyptian high society. With his wife and children as Egyptian, the power of Joseph was in Potipherah's eyes an extension of the power of his own house. He would do nothing to oppose Joseph, but support him.

The Lord however, had different designs for the sons of Joseph. Joseph had suffered greatly in his preparation to assume the role the Lord had set aside for him. But God is able to make people forget their sorrows and disappointments. The birth of Joseph's sons would expand his heart so that he would be able to comprehend that these sons would not exist if he were not in Egypt. Joseph's love for these sons helped him heal part of his grief. By loving his sons, which came forth from his union in Egypt, he saw the joy they brought him.

Gen. 41:50 *And unto Joseph were born two sons before the years of famine came, which Asenath the daughter of Potipherah priest of On bare unto him.* Gen. 41:51 *And Joseph called the name of the firstborn Manasseh: For God said he, hath made me forget all my toil and all my father's house.* Gen. 41:52 *And the name of the second called he Ephraim: For God hath caused me to be fruitful in the land of my affliction. . .* Joseph's sons, though, were not destined to become the son's of Egypt. Joseph's favorite son was Manasseh, his firstborn. This is demonstrated by Joseph's insistence that his father, Jacob, bless his firstborn with a special blessing; a request that was rejected by Jacob. Gen. 48:1 *And it came to pass after these things, that one told Joseph, "Behold, thy father is sick:" and he took with him his two sons, Manasseh and Ephraim.* Gen. 48:5 *"And now thy two sons, Ephraim and Manasseh, which were born unto thee in the land of Egypt before I came unto thee into Egypt, are mine; as Reuben and Simeon, they shall be mine."* Gen. 48:14 *And Israel stretched out his right hand, and laid it upon*

Ephraim's head, who was the younger, and his left hand upon Manasseh's head, guiding his hands wittingly; for Manasseh was the firstborn. Gen. 48:17 And when Joseph saw that his father laid his right hand upon the head of Ephraim, it displeased him: and he held up his father's hand, to remove it from Ephraim's head unto Manasseh's head. Gen. 48:18 And Joseph said unto his father, "Not so, my father: for this is the firstborn; put thy right hand upon his head." Gen. 48:19 And his father refused, and said, "I know it, my son, I know it: he also shall become a people, and he also shall be great: but truly his younger brother shall be greater than he, and his seed shall become a multitude of nations." Gen. 48:20 And he blessed them that day, saying, "In thee shall Israel bless, saying, God make thee as Ephraim and as Manasseh:" and he set Ephraim before Manasseh. Gen. 48:1 And it came to pass after these things, that one told Joseph, behold, thy father is sick:" and he took with him his two sons, Manasseh and Ephraim. . .

God's Plans for Joseph's Sons

Several things become evident in the preceding scriptures. God has intentions of saving Joseph's sons from the judgment that is to come upon Egypt, in that they are being fully embraced by Jacob as one of his own sons. These "sons" are chosen to become tribes in Israel. There is no tribe of Joseph. In every other instance, the sons of the other eleven sons of Jacob were not named as separate tribes, but are included in the tribe designated by the name and blessing of their father. This is significant in understanding the covenant of adoption and the blessing passed on those who enter into Israel by the Lord Jesus Christ through His bride the Church.

We see that, at the time, Jacob utters the blessing over Ephraim and Manasseh, that to those observing, these seem like simple poetic words. You see two young boys with strong Egyptian ties standing before their dying grandfather in the very bud of their lives. Yet, from a retrospective observation, everything Jacob stated about them came to pass. Was this an example of random chance, that two boys became great tribes in Israel instead of Egypt, or was this an example of the power of God at work to bring this about? To be certain, the boys would make many "free will" choices throughout their lives. The end result of all these "free will" choices was the exact end that fulfilled Jacob's imparted blessing. If these blessings were not fulfilled exactly as prophesied, the history of Israel would have been different. If the history of Israel could be altered, the Devil would have influenced its change a long time ago. But what we do see is everything unfolding according to divine plan. We also see Ephraim as greater than Manasseh, as Jacob hundreds of years earlier had stated.

Joseph Suffers by the Will of God

1 John 5:14 *And this is the confidence that we have in him, that, if we ask any thing according to his will, he heareth us. . .* We can ask whatever we desire. However, only those requests which line up with the future which the Lord has planned will be answered. This may seem frustrating to some, but to those who have faith, it is a great assurance of confidence, peace, and safety. You see that it is not a simple matter of you making your choices that determine your future, because you cannot have everything you choose. Like Joseph, you cannot deliver yourself from every circumstance, even though you may so desire. The things you can change will be changed according to the will of God.

1 Pet. 4:19 *Wherefore let them that suffer according to the will of God commit the keeping of their souls to him in well doing, as unto a faithful Creator. . .* All things are for a purpose. We cannot, from our prospective, understand all things. But by faith, we can come to an understanding that our lives, like everything in this universe, are ordered by God; this is true for those who choose to do God's will and for those who do His will without their knowledge because of providential circumstances and forces which are acting within and upon them. An example of someone doing God's will "without their knowledge" is the Pharaoh whom the Lord used at the time of the exodus of the children of Israel from Egypt. Ex. 4:21 *And the Lord said unto Moses, "When thou goest to return into Egypt, see that thou do all those wonders before Pharaoh, which I have put in thine hand: but I will harden his heart, that he*

shall not let the people go. Ex. 7:3 *And I will harden Pharaoh's heart, and multiply my signs and my wonders in the land of Egypt.* Ex. 14:4 *And I will harden Pharaoh's heart, that he shall follow after them; and I will be honoured upon Pharaoh, and upon all his host; that the Egyptians may know that I am the Lord."* And they did so. Ex. 14:17 *And "I, behold, I will harden the hearts of the Egyptians, and they shall follow them: and I will get me honour upon Pharaoh, and upon all his host, upon his chariots, and upon his horsemen..."* There is suffering, which is the will of God, that we eliminate or overcome. This type suffering is not immutable. There is a solution in the prayer of faith, by actions, by remedies or by change of attitude. Examples of this type of suffering are all around us.

Joseph suffered according to the will of God. The circumstances thrust upon him were immutable. Even the woman he ultimately wed was orchestrated by the Lord. He could fantasize about having a special young lady in his life and envy those who seemed to have a wonderful intimate relationship, but he was powerless to bring this about until the time ordained by the Lord. What he wanted, no matter how strong his desire, would not be within his grasp until the time ordained by the Lord. In retrospect, we can see how God directed his path, but in Joseph's eyes, it was all by faith; faith that the Lord had not forgotten him; faith that God had a purpose in all this; faith that he would have happiness; faith that God had a purpose for his life. Joseph would fulfill the purpose for which he was called. Like a race horse brought to the starting gate, he really had only one direction to run.

Joseph's Brothers Changed by Suffering

After he had lived long enough to develop a history of experiences and after the Lord had brought him into some of the blessings of the purpose of his life, Joseph began to see that the things which befell him were directed by the Lord. Gen. 50:17 (a messenger is sent to Joseph from his brothers after his father, Jacob died) *So shall ye say unto Joseph, "Forgive, I pray thee now, the trespass of thy brethren, and their sin; for they did unto thee evil: and* now, we pray thee, forgive the trespass of the servants of the God of thy father." And Joseph wept when they spake unto him. Gen. 50:19 And Joseph said unto them, "Fear not: for am I in the place of God? Gen. 50:20 But as for you, ye thought evil against me; but God meant it unto good, to bring to pass, as it is this day, to save much people alive. Gen. 50:21 Now therefore fear ye not: I will nourish you, and your little ones." And he comforted them, and spake kindly unto them. . .*

We see several important thoughts communicated to us in the preceding scriptures. Joseph's brothers acknowledge their sin of hatred and malice toward him in their actions for which he suffered greatly. These men acted from what they understood to be their "free will." It is also true that they suffered each day that he was separated from them with the consequences of their actions. They had to live with the guilt of such a terrible lie; the thoughts that they had wanted to kill him. They also had to face the suffering of their father, Jacob, in the unrelenting grief he suffered with Joseph's loss. All this was bottled up in these brothers and their family units each and every day. How they would have come to regard themselves, to have done such a heinous deed. The suffering experienced by his brothers was for a reason. It had a purifying effect upon them and improved their overall character. They would now consider the consequences of their behavior, in that cruelty does not improve life, but tarnishes even your own happiness.

Gen. 42:21 And they said one to another, "We are verily guilty concerning our brother, in that we saw the anguish of his soul, when he besought us, and we would not hear; therefore is this distress come upon us." Gen. 42:22 And Reuben answered them, saying, "Spake I not unto you, saying, Do not sin against the child; and ye would not hear? therefore, behold, also his blood is required." Gen. 42:23 And they knew not that Joseph understood them; for he spake unto them by an interpreter. . . This occurred when Joseph's brothers were speaking to each other while in his presence when he was making sport of them, before he revealed his identity. These scriptures reveal a mind set of years of remorse for what they had done.

Gen. 42:37 *And Reuben spake unto his father, saying, "Slay my two sons, if I bring him not to thee: deliver him into my hand, and I will bring him to thee again."* Gen. 43:9 [Judah is speaking to his father Jacob] *"I will be surety for him; of my hand shalt thou require him: if I bring him not unto thee, and set him before thee, then let me bear the blame for ever:"* We see here a different attitude in Jacob's brothers than they formerly possessed. We see them now with a heart that cannot bear the thought of anything terrible befalling Benjamin and causing pain to their father. Remember how they formerly reveled in thoughts and plans of Joseph's demise. What an enormous change had occurred over the years as a result of the inward suffering they experienced for their actions. Joseph suffered because of them; but they also suffered terribly.

Gen. 44:22 [Judah speaking unto Joseph. Remember, it was Judah who first proposed that Joseph be sold to the Ishmeelites; who did not buy him. However his thoughts solidified when they were successful in selling him to the Midianites.] *"And we said unto my lord, The lad cannot leave his father: for if he should leave his father, his father would die. Gen. 44:31 It shall come to pass, when he seeth that the lad is not with us, that he will die: and thy servants shall bring down the gray hairs of thy servant our father with sorrow to the grave.'* Gen. 44:32 *For thy servant became surety for the lad unto my father, saying, If I bring him not unto thee, then I shall bear the blame to my father for ever.'* Gen. 44:33 *Now therefore, I pray thee, let thy servant abide instead of the lad a bondman to my lord; and let the lad go up with his brethren.* Gen. 44:34 *For how shall I go up to my father, and the lad be not with me? lest peradventure I see the evil that shall come on my father. . ."* These are the words of a changed man. Without the experience of seeing the results of his actions and feeling the ensuing pain, Judah would have developed into a different man.

Sin is Sin

Gen. 42:21 *And they said one to another, "We are verily guilty concerning our brother, in that we saw the anguish of his soul, when he besought us, and we would not hear; therefore is this dis-*

tress come upon us." Gen. 42:22 *And Reuben answered them, saying, "Spake I not unto you, saying, Do not sin against the child; and ye would not hear? therefore, behold, also his blood is required..."* These men chose to do what was wrong. Nevertheless, the sin they acknowledged was predestined to fulfill the plans of the Lord. Sin is still sin, even though it fulfills the plans of God. The same admission of sin was made by Pharaoh, even though the Lord had stated that it was Himself, Who hardened this man's heart. Ex. 7:3 *And I will harden Pharaoh's heart, and multiply my signs and my wonders in the land of Egypt.* Ex. 9:27 *And Pharaoh sent, and called for Moses and Aaron, and said unto them, I have sinned this time: the Lord is righteous, and I and my people are wicked...* We might ask ourselves, How is this possible? Simply read the scripture and accept what they say. God did not force these men to sin. Yet, it was the evil within their heart which took advantage of the situation afforded it and so manifest itself.

All of us are naked before the Lord. He understands our strengths and weaknesses. We make choices based upon what is in our heart. With any given stimulus, our behaviors will respond exactly according to what is within us. Jesus, knowing this, taught us to pray in this manner. Luke 11:4 *And forgive us our sins; for we also forgive every one that is indebted to us. And lead us not into temptation; but deliver us from evil...* Jesus did not waste words. If it were not possible to be led into temptation, He would not have advised us to pray in such a manner as to not be lead into temptation. Yes, we want to be lead, but not into temptation. Also to lead into temptation is not the same as to tempt someone. God does not tempt people. He will bring people to the place that they may be tempted and carried away, as is the case of Joseph's brothers. This may seem like a fine line of distinction, but it is an important one.

The Lord makes us righteous. People may claim righteousness based upon what they consider is their own personal worth; but this is based upon pride and self exaltation. We are warned carefully about making such boasts. 1 Cor. 10:12 *Therefore let him who thinks he stands take heed lest he fall...* Why is it so humiliatingly dangerous to make such boasts? Because if the Lord loves you, He will reveal to you how desperately wrong you are by bringing you into a situation in which you will see yourself as wretched. By doing this for you, He would have delivered you from the terrible bondage of personal pride to further purify your soul.

Joseph, emotionally, came to peace with himself because of what his brothers had done to him. The forgiveness he had for his brothers came from the understanding that the things which occurred in his life were ordained by God. The sin against him was sin even though it fulfilled the plans and purposes of God. Gen. 50:16 *So they sent [a message] to Joseph, saying,* [this was a lie concocted by Joseph's brothers because they feared retaliation] Gen. 50:17 *'Thus you shall say to Joseph, "Please forgive, I beg you, the transgression of your brothers and their sin, for they did you wrong."' And now, please forgive the transgression of the servants of the God of your father. And Joseph wept when they spoke to him.* Gen. 50:18 *Then his brothers also came and fell down before him and said, "Behold, we are your servants."* Gen. 50:19 *But Joseph said to them, "Do not be afraid, for am I in God's place?* Gen. 50:20 *"And as for you, you meant evil against me, but God meant it for good in order to bring about this present result to preserve many people alive.* Gen. 50:21 *"So therefore, do not be afraid; I will provide for you and your little ones." So he comforted them and spoke kindly to them. . .* Though Joseph came to forgive his brother, they never came to close fellowship because there was no element of trust in their relationship. Forgiveness alone is never enough for fellowship. It impossible to have a heart to heart relationship with anyone you cannot trust.

7
The Life of Samson

Judg. 13:2 *And there was a certain man of Zorah, of the family of the Danites, whose name was Manoah; and his wife was barren, and bare not.* Judg. 13:3 *And the angel of the Lord appeared unto the woman, and said unto her, "Behold now, thou art barren, and bearest not: but thou shalt conceive, and bear a son.* Judg. 13:5 *For, lo, thou shalt conceive, and bear a son; and no razor shall come on his head: for the child shall be a Nazarite unto God from the womb: and he shall begin to deliver Israel out of the hand of the Philistines..."* In the life of Samson, we see the Lord starting with an impossible situation. Manoah and his wife have no children. It makes no difference what they do socially, having no children in a primitive society causes you to be identified as someone in whom something is not right. These people would see the joy of relatives and friends with the birth of children; but this joy was withheld from them. They would even observe all the help these children provided; if they were male, they helped their father work the land; if they were female, they were great companionship and help for their mother with all the chores. What an emptiness these people experienced. Numerous prayers were offered to the Lord, but why no children? There had to be a reason for this!

As is common with the Lord, He delights in taking seemingly hopeless situations and filling them with a promise which brings faith. They were accustomed to praying and had a considerable amount of faith. We see Manoah praying and fully expecting the Lord to answer his prayer. Judg. 13:8 *Then Manoah entreated the Lord and said, "O Lord, please let the man of God whom Thou hast sent come to us again that he may teach us what to do for the boy who is to be born."* Judg. 13:9 *And God listened to the voice of Manoah; and the angel of God came again to the woman as she was sitting in the field, but her husband was not with her...* Manoah is already expecting to have the child, and that it is to be a son!

This was a simple prayer of faith which God had prepared Manoah his whole life to pray. It was a prayer according to the will of God because it was delightfully answered. Note the extent of faith in Manoah and his wife. She runs to get her husband when the angel reappears, indicating that they had prior conversation, as to what they would do when he reappeared to either one of them. Judg. 13:9 *And God listened to the voice of Manoah; and the angel of God came again to the woman as she was sitting in the field, but Manoah her husband was not with her.* Judg. 13:10 *So the woman ran quickly and told her husband, "Behold, the man who came the [other] day has appeared to me."* Judg. 13:11 *Then Manoah arose and followed his wife, and when he came to the man he said to him, "Are you the man who spoke to the woman?" And he said, "I am."* Judg. 13:12 *And Manoah said, "Now when your words come to pass, what shall be the boy's mode of life and his vocation?"* This man of faith fully expects the boy's life to be predestined. If Manoah did not believe that this future son did not have a determined future, he would not have asked such a question of this angel. Furthermore, none of this is of any importance whatsoever if Samson's life was not predestined with specific purpose. Even Samson's parents were hand picked of the Lord.

These people were being prepared for a very special child from the Lord. If they would have had other children prior to this child, the attitude at home would have been different toward Samson. He would be one of many. But Samson was the firstborn child. There is record of brothers only at his death (Judg. 16:31 *Then his brothers and all his father's household came down, took him, brought him up, and buried him.*). This is important because Samson was pampered from birth, always getting his way. Emotionally, he was conditioned to being in control. This was the mentality which the Lord wanted formed within him to fulfill his ordained destiny. If Samson would have been easygoing and accustomed to things not going his way, he would have reacted differently to all the disappointing stimuli presented to him by the Philistines. An example of his dominance toward his parents was his order, not request, to get him the Philistine woman who appealed to him. Judg. 14:2 *So* he came back and told his father and mother, *"I saw a woman in Timnah, one of the daughters of the Philistines; now therefore, get her for me as a wife..."*

Were there no suitable women in Israel for Samson? Socially, marrying someone of the same heritage and value system makes for a more enjoyable family life. A choice such as this is destined toward controversy and compromise – two attributes of which Samson was conditioned to react in complete opposition. Judg. 14:1 *Then Samson went down to Timnah and saw a woman in Timnah, one of the daughters of the Philistines.* Judg. 14:2 *So he came back and told his father and mother, "I saw a woman in Timnah, one of the daughters of the Philistines; now therefore, get her for me as a wife."* Judg. 14:3 *Then his father and his mother said to him, "Is there no woman among the daughters of your relatives, or among all our peoples that you go to take a wife from the uncircumcised Philistines?" But Samson said to his father, "Get her for me, for she looks good to me."* Judg. 14:4 *However, his father and mother did not know that it was of the Lord, for He was seeking an occasion against the Philistines. Now at that time the Philistines were ruling over Israel..*

Your Plans May Not Be His Plans

It may seem like a hard thing to swallow that the Lord would stir up controversy or be in opposition to peace or be opposed to things going your way, but this is exactly the case. Matt. 10:34 *"Think not that I am come to send peace on earth: I came not to send peace, but a sword..."* The Lord did not want peace between Israel and the Philistines. Judg. 14:4 *...for He [the Lord] was seeking an occasion against the Philistines...*

The Lord's direct involvement with peace between people is spelled out clearly in the account of the Tower of Babel. Gen. 11:4 *And they said, "Go to let us build us a city and a tower, whose top may reach unto heaven: and let us make us a name, lest we be scattered abroad upon the face of the whole earth."* Gen. 11:5 *And the Lord came down to see the city and the tower, which the children of men builded.* Gen. 11:6 *And the Lord said, "Behold, the people is one, and they have all one language; and this they begin to do: and now nothing will be restrained from them, which they have imagined to do.* Gen. 11:7 *Go to, let us go down, and there confound their language that they may not understand one another's speech."* Gen. 11:8 *So the Lord scattered them abroad from thence upon the face of all the earth: and they left off to build the city. . .* This involvement by the Lord with the alterations of the plans of all mankind has never stopped, but continues today.

It is the Lord Who is the architect of our human future. An architect is the planner and designer who controls the final outcome of what is to be built. Thus the design, foreordained, is carried out according to the architect's specifications. Anything which is attempted to be done, not according to that plan, is eliminated at the proper time, so as to not alter what is planned. Babel would carry the people of the world into a direction the Lord had not ordained. Therefore, the Lord separated these people and thus nullified their efforts.

The future they intended did not conform with what God had planned. The future is planned; to some this is good news, to others it is a point of contention. It makes no difference whether the things I write are acknowledged or rejected. Everything will continue regardless, with God having things exactly as He intends them for His own plans or purposes. We can be like King David. Ps. 16:8 *I have set the Lord always before [5048h. neged from 5046; in front of, in sight of, opposite to;] me: because he is at my right hand, I shall not be moved.* Or, we can stumble through life blind. There are those of us who are like King David, and those who are blind. At this time in history, we are mixed together.

Two Kingdoms

We all belong to God. We all do not belong to the Lord Jesus Christ because not all people are in covenant relationship with Him. There are two groups of beings, both belong to the Lord God Jehovah; one group is part of the Kingdom of Light and the other group is part of the Kingdom of Darkness. Those who belong to God through the Lord Jesus Christ are part of the Kingdom of Light.

These two kingdoms are separate, but all things belong to God.

Ps. 50:10 *"For every beast of the forest is Mine, The cattle on a thousand hills. Ps. 50:11 "I know every bird of the mountains, And everything that moves in the field is Mine..."* This scripture is stating, that literally all things are His. Some of us acknowledge this fact and some of us do not, or are oblivious to this reality. Those of us who accept this truth have not all come to contemplate the depth of what we are acknowledging. Job 1 91 *And said, "Naked came I out of my mother's womb, and naked shall I return thither: the Lord gave, and the Lord hath taken away; blessed be the name of the Lord..."* Ps. 24:1 *A Psalm of David. The earth is the Lord's, and the fullness thereof; the world, and they that dwell therein...* Our own belief structures do not alter the truth. These beliefs effect only how we react to the truth. The truth is the truth. Our personal understanding is a matter of response; but truth will remain unchanged. Jesus Christ is the truth; this is a very simple and straightforward statement, yet the world is filled with different religious denominations, each declaring a slightly different version of the truth.

Truth is like a chest of instruments and tools. They are only useful to you if you understand their purpose. If you do not comprehend what you are looking at, you are merely staring at that which is foreign. That which is foreign will be of no benefit to you.

Samson's Marriage Falls Apart

Samson's marriage to the Philistine woman was doomed before it ever started. Judg. 14:3 *Then his father and his mother said to him, "Is there no woman among the daughters of your relatives, or among all our people, that you go to take a wife from the uncircumcised Philistines?" But Samson said to his father, "Get her for me, for she looks good to me."* Judg. 14:4 *However his father and mother did not know that it was of the Lord, for He was seeking an occasion against the Philistines. Now at that time the Philistines were ruling over Israel...* We can either accept or reject what the scriptures are clearly stating. If we accept what they are saying, we only fool ourselves if we twist them or ignore the facts as presented. It states clearly that the attraction Samson had for this Philistine woman was of the Lord in that "He was seeking an occasion against the Philistines." Samson's mother and father also were ignorant of the Lord's working in this matter as the scripture states, "his father and mother did not know that it was of the Lord." Samson himself did not understand what was happening to him, as is evident from any recorded acknowledgment to this realization. God does not need people to understand what He is doing or His purposes to carry out His intentions. Samson is a perfect example.

Samson's angry reaction to the events at His marriage feast was indirectly orchestrated by God. God Himself will never do evil, but He will open the door for forces who take pleasure in destructive acts to do His will, as long as it is according to the outcome He desires. We have talked about this previously in part in the account of the demise of Ahab (1 Kin. 16:28 – 2 Kin. 10:30). Some people's understanding of God is some soft Entity Whose hands are tied so that He can do very little except observe and provide a little grace. Nothing is farther from the truth. Deut. 4:39 *Know therefore this day, and consider it in thine heart that the Lord he is God in heaven above, and upon the earth beneath: there is none else...* The Lord has no boundaries. He does exactly as He desires and no one can successfully challenge Him.

Samson's life was not his own and neither is yours. His life, like ours, came from God and it is His to do with as He sees fit. Judg. 13:25 *And the spirit of the Lord began to move him at times in the camp of Dan between Zorah and Eshtaol...* We see the same statement in the New Testament phrased in a different manner. Phil. 2:13 *For it is God which worketh in you both to will and to do of his good pleasure...* The Lord not only works within us but He also works around us, putting us in one situation or another. If we can only grasp this, we would be far more at ease. Note how relaxed the Lord Jesus was in the storm. Mark 4:38 *And he was in the hinder part of the ship, asleep on a pillow: and they awake him, and say unto him, "Master, Carest thou not that we perish?"* Jesus was at peace with everything around Him because He understood that the Father had put Him in this position. Jesus knew that the Father loved Him, therefore He rested. We also must come to have the same realization to have the same peace.

Judg. 14:5 *Then Samson went down to Timnah with his father and mother, and came as far as the vineyards of Timnah; and behold, a young lion came roaring toward him.* Judg. 14:6 *And the Spirit of the Lord came upon him mightily, so that he tore him as one tears a kid though he had nothing in his hand; but he did not tell his father or mother what he had done.* Judg. 14:7 *So he went down and talked to the woman; and she looked good to Samson.* Judg. 14:8 *When he returned later to take her, he turned aside to look at the carcass of the lion; and behold, a swarm of bees and honey were in the body of the lion.* Judg. 14:9 *So he scraped the honey into his hands and went on, eating as he went. When he came to his father and mother, he gave some to them and they ate it; but he did not tell them that he had scraped the honey out of the body of the lion...* It is obvious that quite a bit of time had passed between the first event (Judg. 14:6) of the killing of the lion and the second event (Judg. 14:8) of the bees making a hive in the carcass. It would take time for the carcass to degrade and dry out, making it a suitable habitation for the bees. Thus, this relationship between Samson and this woman had been ongoing for some time.

The Lord had brought Samson to be challenged by the lion for two reasons. Firstly, the Lord had a riddle in mind for the impending wedding feast which he intended to strongly impress upon Samson. Without this event, there would have been no riddle, and no enfolding of the events which followed as a result of it being solved deceptively. It was the Lord's intention that Samson find this woman irresistibly attractive so that He could pit Samson against the Philistines. The Lord had no intention of causing this marriage to work out for Samson's happiness because this would bring warm emotional ties between him and the Philistines. Samson's family, by marriage, would be Philistine. If he and this woman were to have any children, these children would also have Philistine family. Therefore, if the Lord established this marriage, He would have neutralized Samson as a force of separation between the Hebrews and the Philistines. The Lord's intentions were clear from the beginning. Judg. 14:4 *However, his father and mother did not know that it was of the Lord, for He was seeking an occasion against the Philistines. Now at that time the Philistines were ruling over Israel.* . . . This example makes it clear that we do not always understand the purposes of God in some of the decisions we make. Samson did not understand his attraction and neither did his parents. It was all of the Lord.

The second reason for the challenge of the lion was for our sakes. The Lord wanted to demonstrate to us that no adversary is our match when God is with us to triumph. The honey symbolizes further that out of great adversity, sweet blessings can flow. We need to keep this in mind when faced with difficulties in our own lives. Just as it took time for the carcass of the lion to decay and dry out, it may take time for us to see good come out of some of our experiences; but good will come. Prom. 8:28 *And we know that all things work together for good to them that love God, to them who are the called according to his purpose.*

Judg. 14:10 *Then his father went down to the woman; and Samson made a feast there, for the young men customarily did this.* Judg. 14:11 *And it came about when they saw him that they brought thirty companions to be with him.* . . . These were Philistine companions which the young woman's household provided to make the occasion more socially entertaining. In most situations, bad companions will corrupt good morals. Judg. 14:1 2 *Then Samson said to them, "Let me now propound a riddle to you; if you will indeed tell it to me within the seven days of the feast, and find it out, then I will give you thirty linen wraps and thirty charges of clothes."* Judg. 14:13 *"But if you are unable to tell me, then you shall give me thirty linen wraps and thirty changes of clothes." And they said to him, "Propound your riddle, that we may hear it."*

Judg. 14:14 *So he said to them, "Out of the eater came something to eat, And out of the strong came something sweet." But they could not tell the riddle in three days.* Judg. 14:15 *Then it came about on the fourth day that they said to Samson's wife, "Entice your husband, that he may tell us the riddle, lest we burn you and your father's house with fire. Have you invited us to impover-*

ish us? Is this not so?" These people no doubt were considered as friends by this Philistine woman's household. How evident it is that they were merely opportunistic acquaintances. So many people's lives are filled with these types of people; who are considered to be their friends, but are not. Judg. 14:16 *And Samson's wife wept before him and said, "You only hate me, and you do not love me; you have propounded a riddle to the sons of my people, and have not told it to me." And he said to her, "Behold, I have not told it to my father or mother; so should I tell you?"* Judg. 14:17 *However she wept before him seven days while their feast lasted. And it came about on the seventh day that he told her because she pressed him so hard. She then told the riddle to the sons of her people.*

Judg. 14:18 *So the men of the city said to him on the seventh day before the sun went down, "What is sweeter than honey? And what is stronger than a lion?" And he said to them, "If you had not plowed with my heifer You would not have found out my riddle."* It is obvious here that Samson put things together and understood that the reason she pressed him so hard was to learn the riddle for these "companions." What was not clear to him was the reason she did it. Judg. 14:19 *And the spirit of the Lord came upon him, and he went down to Ashkelon, and slew thirty men of them, and took their spoil, and gave change of garments unto them which expounded the riddle. And his anger was kindled, and he went up to his father's house...*

From Samson's perspective (if he were to find out), his wife had betrayed him because these Philistine companions had threatened to burn her father's house if she did not comply. Judg. 14:15 *Then it came about on the fourth day that they said to Samson's wife, "Entice your husband, that he may tell us the riddle, lest we burn you and your father's house with fire...* This would have been the understanding he would have. However, much higher purposes were at work. The Lord's thoughts are higher than our thoughts. His thoughts were not understood by Samson. Is. 55:8 *For my thoughts are not your thoughts, neither are your ways my ways saith the Lord.* Is. 55:9 *For as the heavens are higher than the earth, so are my ways higher than your ways, and my thoughts than your thoughts...* This conflict was ordained to happen because the Lord wanted to stir Samson up against the Philistines. Judg. 14:3 *Then his father and his mother said to him, "Is there no woman among the daughters of Soul relatives, or among all our peoples that you go to take a wife from the uncircumcised Philistines?" But Samson said to his father, "Get her for me, for she looks good to me."* Judg. 14:4 *However, his father and mother did not know that it was of the Lord, for He was seeking an occasion against the Philistines. Now at that time the Philistines were ruling over Israel...*

It should be becoming increasingly clear that the Lord rules in the affairs of men. If we truly understand this, then it is only the Lord Himself whom we should rightly fear; if He be for us, who can be against us; but if He be against us, who can deliver us from His hand?

If we were to judge Samson by our own modern standards, we would conclude that both he and the threatening Philistine companions at his marriage feast were violent, terrible human beings. Yet, Samson's emotional development was clearly ordered by God. Look at what his parents said to the angel before his birth. Judg. 13:11 *And Manoah arose, and went after his wife, and came to the man, and said unto him, Art thou the man that spakest unto the woman? And he said, I am.* [Manoah was speaking to the angel of the Lord.] Judg. 13:12 *And Manoah said, Now let thy words come to pass. How shall we order the child, and how shall we do unto him?* Judg. 13:14 *She may not eat of anything that cometh of the vine, neither let her drink wine or strong drink, nor eat any unclean thing: all that I commanded her let her observe.* Judg. 13:24 *Then the woman gave birth to a son and named him Samson; and the child grew up and the Lord blessed him.* For our vantage point, we can only marvel at this revelation.

We are admonished not to judge anything before the time, but how many of us truly understand this commandment of the Lord and heed it? Why?. Because God may have a purpose in the very thing we are judging. 1 Cor. 4:5 *Therefore judge nothing before the* time, until the Lord come, who both will bring to light the hidden things of darkness, and will make manifest the counsels of the hearts: and then shall every man have praise of God...* The apostle Paul understood deeply what I am writing. We need to learn to be a thankful people and not get upset when things do not go our way. God rules in the affairs of men; He will look out for you and me according to His own purposes. We accept this by faith, but have the scriptures as examples of the lives of people who lived before us and the Lord's dealing with them. None of us has the confidence we should have.

Samson's Wife Given to Another

Judg. 14:19 . . . *And his anger was kindled and he went up to his father's house.* Judg. 14:20 *But Samson's wife was given to his companion who had been his friend.* Judg. 15:1 *But after a while, in the time of wheat harvest it came about that Samson visited his wife with a young goat, and said, "I will go in to my wife in her room." But her father did not let him enter.* Judg. 15:2 *And her father said, "I really thought that you hated her intensely; so I gave her to your companion. Is not her younger sister more beautiful than she? Please let her be yours instead."* Judg. 15:3 *Samson then said to them, "This time I shall be blameless in regard lo the Philistines when I do them harm."*

What an incredible passage and turn of events! It is hard to imagine the emotions that would go through a young man's mind to have the woman of his dreams, whom he had just married, to be given to a person claiming to be your friend. Three people who were part of the inner circle of your life completely trample your emotions and plans for the future. One would wonder how this woman would have given consent to be given to another man if she loved Samson. Furthermore, how could a person claiming to be your friend, who had just gone to your marriage feast, ask for your wife? How could your father-in-law give his daughter to another man after he had just given her to you? Why didn't anyone come to you to discuss your intentions before such action? These were Samson's painful and conflicting emotions.

It is obvious that Samson's wife was consoled by this "friend" after the tragic turn of events. This friend obviously had strong emotions toward this woman whom Samson had just married because he chose to comfort her instead of going after Samson. This was a friendship toward Samson based upon his attraction to Samson's wife; by hanging around Samson, he could be near her. You can imagine the horror of this woman to be married to a man who had just slaughtered thirty of your countrymen. What effect would this have on her father? Some of her countrymen had previously threatened to burn her father's house if they were not told Samson's riddle; now what would happen? Opportunity abounded everywhere for her to have all kinds of thoughts. Samson might have been a charmer, but she was unwilling to suffer alienation with her people over the physical attraction she had for Samson. She wanted out of this relationship. The recent "discoveries" she had just made about him were more than she could bear. All of this was reason enough in her mind to wish for a different man. Samson had lost his appeal in her mind. Her actions prove that she never really loved him. Love endures and is not so easily defeated, even in great opposition. Samson, from youth, was a man not used to things not going his way. He was unable to see things clearly in this relationship.

After Samson had killed thirty of her countrymen, his wife's father could have hardly wanted to be associated as his father-in-law. What possible benefit would there be to him? The actions of Samson made him an outcast if he showed any support for the action of this young man. The best thing that could be done, in the eyes of this father-in-law, was to try to make everyone happy: his daughter, the new suitor, and his countrymen by giving this woman to a different man. This man feared Samson. If Samson were to return, he would have a story for him. To spare his own life, he wound offer him his younger daughter. This would add credence to his story; after all, Samson had left his home in a fit of anger. Judg. 15:2 *And her father said, "I verily thought that thou hadst utterly hated her; therefore I gave her to thy companion: is not her younger sister fairer than she? take her, I pray thee, instead of her."* This man also had reasons for his actions.

How about the man who poised himself to be a friend to Samson? We do not read of Samson having any friends at all, except this man; and this man betrayed him. With all the violence in Samson's life, you do not see Samson coming after this man to do him harm. Samson was a lonely person, with no companions. Like all other people, he needed the assurance that someone cared for him. The kindness of the friendship this man offered protected him, even though what he had offered was tainted by his desire for the same woman. This man's desire far outweighed whatever friendship he cast toward Samson. Samson's friendship provided him with reasons to be near the same woman. When the opportunity presented itself, of Samson making himself so heinous, he followed the true desires of his heart. He never went to find Samson to discuss his intentions because he feared that he would not receive the woman of his dreams. This man acted in his own best interests. He, too, had reasons for his actions.

Each one of us has reasons for our actions. The mere fact that we have our reasons does not free us from fulfilling the destiny God has ordained. We will always make choices for reasons we exalt at the time of our choosing. However, what we choose always fulfills the plans and purposes of the Lord. In the scriptures, it states clearly that Samson had great attraction for this particular woman because the Lord sought opportunity against the Philistines. Everyone had his reason, yet the bottom line is that the Lord accomplished His will.

Samson Takes Revenge for His Despair

Judg. 15:3 *Samson then said to them, "This time I shall be blameless in regard to the Philistines when I do them harm."* Judg. 15:4 *And Samson went and caught three hundred foxes, and took torches, and turned the foxes tail to tail, and put one torch in the middle between two tails.* Judg. 15:5 *When he had set fire to the torches, he released the foxes into the standing grain of the Philistines, thus burning up both the shocks and the standing grain, along with the vineyards and groves.* Judg. 15:6 *Then the Philistines said,*

"Who did this?" And they said, "Samson, the son-in-law of the Timnite, because he took his wife and gave her to his companion." So the Philistines came up and burned her and her father with fire.

We have to keep in mind that this woman was not just a girlfriend in whom Samson was interested. He was legally married to this woman. She was his wife! He had done everything according to the traditions of the land in which she lived. This was a woman with whom he had planned the rest of his life. He would make a life with this woman as his parents had done. Who was to say that his relationship with his wife might even be better than his father's with his mother; after all, he had picked her out himself, or so he thought. But this was not to be. Samson's life was not his own. Even with all his strength (which was really not his own), Samson felt helpless in the situation. There was nothing he could do to make things right between the two of them.

This helpless situation created within him a deep seated resentment toward a people whose lack of personal morals had brought him great grief and unrelenting pain. Samson would never be the same. His attitude toward the Philistines was now exactly the way the Lord intended! There would be no peace and friendship between Israel and the Philistines as long as he lived. These two would remain separate nations and Israel would remain a separated people. This is and was not by accident, but by divine design. It is determined by the counsel of God and cannot be altered by the acts or decisions of men or angels. All these people acted according to reasons set before them. To each was given to act according to the wiles of their "free will." Yet, the thoughts and plans of the Lord God Jehovah are above our thoughts. Each "free will" expressed itself exactly as needed to bring out a determined end! With God, the end justifies the means.

It seems extremely cruel for Samson to set foxes on fire in order to burn the fields of these people. This act is a testament to the amount of inner pain this man experienced. No person at peace or with kind inward thoughts would ever torture an animal to vent his frustration or purposely kill thirty people to get their garments. It was not that Samson had no conscience. He did, as is alluded in the following statement. Judg. 15:3 *Samson then said to them, "This time I shall be blameless in regard to the Philistines when I do them harm."* "This time" signifies that he felt remorse in the slaying of the thirty Philistines in order to pay his wager at the wedding feast. Thus, it is clear that his actions were very much on his mind because much time had passed between the burning of the grain fields and the events at his marriage, yet now he talks of "this time" being blameless. Before he felt his actions were unjustified, but now, surely, he is justified by his actions.

Samson, as a man, was nurtured by the purposes of God to act exactly as he did. The same Holy Spirit which came upon him and gave him his strength could also have restrained him; but the Lord did not. Samson could have been born a tranquil man, very gentile if that had been the Lord's will. Samson was born by a direct act of the Spirit of God upon a barren woman. The Lord Himself was fully responsible for Samson and his actions. Men could and would judge him; Samson would judge himself, but it is only the Lord Himself who understood the forces behind this man's inner workings. Rom. 9:20 . . . *The thing molded will not say to the molder, "Why did you make me like this," will it?* Rom. 9:21 *Or does not the potter have a right over the clay, to make from the same lump one vessel for honorable use, and another for common use?* It is only His judgment which is of eternal consequence. Samson is a perfect example of the reasons why only the Lord can judge (or guide in judgment). He alone understands all the details.

The Results of Samson's Actions

Samson's wife and father-in-law were burned alive by their Philistine countrymen. This ending never allowed him to have an emotional closure to the love he had for his wife. She became a permanent inner wound which never healed, galvanizing him against her countrymen – the Philistines. He would never get over her, as is evidenced by him never marrying again and seeking solace in prostitutes and worthless women.

Judg. 15:7 *And Samson said to them, "Since you act like this* [burning my wife and father-in-law], *I will surely take revenge on you, but after that I will quit."* Judg. 15:8 *And he struck them ruthlessly with a great slaughter; and he went down and lived in the cleft of the rock of Etam...* These events and actions set in motion a cycle of revenge and counter revenge between Samson and the Philistines. The Philistines, in burning this woman and her father, had thought to be making a gesture of judgment in the sight of all. They did not condone the actions of this woman and her father. They wanted peace between themselves and the Hebrews. Samson was completely blind to this reasoning because of his unsettled affections for his new wife. They were not communicating. Thus, we have the account of the Tower of Babel all over again: in other words, one person could not understand what the other was communicating. The Lord God Jehovah did not want there to be a forged alliance between Israel and Philistine; Samson was the chosen vessel to disrupt all peace initiatives.

The love of this woman, his wife, left a permanent wound. If he could have married again, it would have been the Philistine woman Delilah. Judg. 16:4 *After this it came about that he loved a woman in the valley of Sorek, whose name was Delilah...* However, this woman also deceived him when he trusted her. She was very cunning, manipulative, dishonest in her heart, and in her motives of affection. This was the type of women to whom he was attracted. Samson, with all his faith, suffered terribly because of the faithless women for which he had eyes. There is also symbolism in the strength of Samson overcoming all the enemies, as the Lord Jesus Christ also does in the lives of those who believe. Samson's life serves as an example to each of us of the tragedy of bad company.

8
The Life of Nebuchadnezzar

Thus far, we have examined more closely the lives of people professing godliness. I have alluded in some passages to the ungodly also doing the will of the Lord God Jehovah without their knowledge, but in this chapter, we will look at this more closely. The following are scriptures which refer to Nebuchadnezzar, king of Babylon. It is important to compare them with others to see some parallels.

Jer. 25:9 *behold, "I will send and take all the families of the north," 'declares the Lord,' and I will send to Nebuchadnezzar, king of Babylon, My servant, and will bring them against this land, and against its inhabitants, and against all these nations round about; and I will utterly destroy them, and make them a horror, and a hissing, and an everlasting desolation."* Jer. 27:6 *"And now I have given all these lands into the hand of Nebuchadnezzar, king of Babylon, My servant, and I have given him also the wild animals of the field to serve him.* Jer. 43:10 *and say to them, 'Thus says the Lord of hosts, the God of Israel, "Behold, I am going to send and get Nebuchadnezzar the king of Babylon, My servant, and I am going to set his throne right over these stones that I have hidden; and he will spread his canopy over them. . ."*

In these three verses, we see Nebuchadnezzar referred to as God's servant. We see that in Jer. 25:9 that the Lord Himself claims to be responsible for the destruction. In verse Jer. 27 6, we see the Lord declaring that it is Him Who is giving to Nebuchadnezzar not only the countries, but even the wild animals. It is God's will that they serve this man. In Jer. 43:10, the Lord states that it is He Who is setting Nebuchadnezzar's throne above all the thrones in the earth. There is not reference to the Devil giving this to Nebuchadnezzar, but the Lord. Without a doubt, the dark kingdom was very active in everything which occurred. However, It is the Lord God Jehovah who rules in the affairs of all men and all kingdoms. There is nothing which can occur without His express permission; and, no permission is given outside of the things He ordains. We have seen this clearly in the account of Job, the conversation between the Lord and Satan.

Nebuchadnezzar, throughout his campaigns of conquest, never claims to personally be a worshipper of the God of Israel. We see no accounts of him praying until the end of his life. Yet, he is referred to as God's servant. I have heard it argued that this man was not a real servant of God, but that this was just a figure of speech. The scriptures are clear that this title is no figure of speech. This same Hebrew word servant (5650h. ebed from 5647; slave, servant) is used also in the following scriptures:

Jer. 30:10 *'And fear not, O Jacob My servant,' declares the Lord, 'And do not be dismayed, O Israel; For behold, I will save you from afar, And your offspring from the land of their captivity. And Jacob shall return, and shall be quiet and at ease, And no one shall make him afraid.'* Ezek. 34:23 *"Then I will set over them one shepherd, My servant David, and he will feed them; he will feed them himself and be their shepherd."* Mal. 4:4 *"Remember the law of Moses My servant, even the statutes and ordinances which I commanded him in Horeb for all Israel."*

We see that the same word (ebed) "servant" is used to refer to Jacob, King David, and to Moses, as was used to refer to Nebuchadnezzar. There is no distinction. These men had different standing with the Lord God Jehovah. However, each served Him in His purposes in this earth. Nebuchadnezzar was part of the Kingdom of darkness; the others mentioned served the Lord volitionally as part of the Kingdom of Light. In the beginning, Darkness was separated from Light, but both are under the direct control of the Father. Nebuchadnezzar was not aware of his service to God until much later in his life when he was confronted with the revelation that he was not a self-made man. We will examine this revelation later in this chapter. At this point, it is enough to say that the revelation I am speaking about came not only for Nebuchadnezzar's sake, but also for ours that we might understand the workings and power of the Lord more completely.

People can serve the Lord in different capacities, having different relationships with Him. Just because the actions of some are in darkness does not mean that the things they do in darkness are not serving the greater purpose of God. Nebuchadnezzar is a prime example. The developments of Judah and Israel were ripe for judgment and change. The chaotic condition of the kingdoms of the world was also brought into order. Nebuchadnezzar was the chosen instrument to bring judgment and order to this system of degenerative order and chaos. Jehovah is a God of order.

How can someone serve God and not know Him? Many people serve each and everyone of us without their personal knowledge. Construction workers build and repair our world daily for their own interest in collecting a paycheck. Persons work at corporations for their own interest of earning a living. Their goals are self serving, yet they serve the owners and the rest of us by what they produce. These workers' goals may be completely self serving in the reasons they are working; in their mind, they are working for their wage. They do not need to know us in order to serve us. We are benefited by their labor. In the same way, those in darkness serve the Lord God Jehovah without their personal knowledge; they are working for a temporal reward for their endeavors. This system of reward for one's actions either reinforces their actions and goals or discourages or punishes them for their activities. In the same way, Nebuchadnezzar's course was ordained by God in the things he accomplished. Nebuchadnezzar thought he was serving himself, but on a much higher plane, he was the servant of God.

Government officials and police officers act in much the same fashion in service to God without their awareness in maintaining order in our societies. They are direct servants of the Lord in their duties. Rom. 13:1 *Let every soul be subject unto the higher powers. For there is no power but of God: the powers that be are ordained of God.* Rom. 13:2 *Whosoever therefore resisteth the power, resisteth the ordinance of God: and they that resist shall receive to themselves damnation.* Rom. 13:3 *For rulers are not a terror to good works, but to the evil. Wilt thou then not he afraid of the power? do that which is good, and thou shalt have praise of the same:* Rom. 13:4 *For he is the minister of God to thee for good. But if thou do that which is evil, be afraid; for he beareth not the sword in vain: for he is the minister of God, a revenger to execute wrath upon him that doeth evil.* Rom. 13:5 *Wherefore ye must needs be subject, not only for wrath, but also for conscience sake.*

Thus, you can see that there are many who serve God directly and indirectly without their personal cognizance; Nebuchadnezzar was one such person. This man increased in power and great, undaunted success because it was the Lord's will and purpose in the things he was doing. Jer. 27:6 *"And now I have given all these lands into the hand of Nebuchadnezzar king of Babylon, My servant, and I have given him also the wild animals of the field to serve him. . ."* This is a powerful statement because it implies that to oppose this man is to oppose the plans and purposes of God. How can this be? We fail to believe exactly what the scriptures are saying. The thoughts of the Lord God Jehovah are far above ours. Possibly we all are guilty of trying to bring Him down to our own level. As we grow in understanding, this vanity must cease if we are ever going to come into true and lasting inner peace.

The arrogance of many in positions of authority in the church seek to present the idea to their denominations that they understand everything very well. They would like their own followers to believe that they are on top of everything and that their group has the truth. They claim to have Him all figured out. I can assure you that this attitude is a lie. Even our great Lord Jesus Christ stated clearly that He did not know everything because the Father had not revealed it to Him. The whole Book of Revelation is the understanding that Father gave Jesus after His resurrection which He chose to give to the church through the apostle John. Even in this revelation, there were things our Lord chose not to reveal at this time. Rev. 10:4 *And when the seven thunders had uttered their voices, I was about to write: and I heard a voice from heaven saying unto me, "Seal up those things which the seven thunders uttered and write them not."*

When was the last time you heard a church leader recant something he has taught? Does this imply that these people have perfect knowledge or that they never grow in understanding? Or does it imply that many would rather believe and perpetuate a lie than to acknowledge the truth? What a sad state of affairs! So many different beliefs exist in so many church denominations and groups. Yet, if the Holy Spirit guides us into all truth, why does such an unyielding inflexible tenacity to lie exist? The very annals of logic point out that everyone cannot be right when their teachings disagree. There is one saving point, which is most important, that can transcend all this mess.

Jesus Christ Came to Save Sinners

The simple understanding that Jesus Christ died to save sinners is essential. We need to know that we have all sinned, that by our own personal worth we cannot save ourselves or promote ourselves into the Kingdom of Light. We must be brought to the place where we understand that we have all fallen impossibly short of the glory of God and that we must accept the blood sacrifice of the Lord Jesus Christ as payment of our sin debt. Jesus Christ came to save sinners. If you admit that you are a sinner, you can be saved; Jesus is the captain of our salvation. Father God has given us no other name in heaven or earth by which we can or must be saved. If we call upon Him to be our Lord and Savior, confessing that we have sinned, we will be added to His sheepfold. He who has the Lord Jesus, also has the Lord God Jehovah. He who does not have Jesus, still has his sin as an offense to the kingdom of God. No offensive person can be part of the Kingdom of Light over which the Lord Jesus reigns as "King of kings and Lord of lords." If you understand what I have just written, pray to make Him a part of your life and enter into His Kingdom. If you are not sure, it will not hurt you to pray as I have directed, that you may have peace and assurance. God be with you if you do.

We All Serve God

We all serve God. Some of us serve Him volitionally, while some serve Him indirectly in darkness, following the whims of their lives. I have showed you scriptures which expressly describe government leaders as "ministers of God." It is essential that we also acknowledge that everyone who is involved with the government as elected or hired does not volitionally seek to serve or please God. Most of them are simply doing their jobs. The Lord's thoughts are so much above all of this that even in this unconscious activity of "simply doing their job," they serve God in His purposes. At this point in history, that is enough. However, there is a time coming where volitional service to Him will be the only service acceptable. This is planned for the future and will be a better government than we see today.

Rev. 11:15 *And the seventh angel sounded; and there were great voices in heaven, saying, "The kingdoms of this world are become the kingdoms of our Lord and of his Christ; and he shall reign for ever and ever."* Rev. 11:17 Saying, *"We give thee thanks, to Lord God Almighty, which art, and wast, and art to come; because thou hast taken to thee thy great power, and hast reigned."* Rev. 11:18 *And the nations were angry, and thy wrath is come...* This is not a contradiction, as some believe. God rules today also, but it is not apparent to most.

Many credit the Devil for much of what happens. It is true that he is very active. However, God does not need to be seen to rule. He does not need to reveal Himself for people to fulfill His purposes. We see an active example (Jer. 27:6) of this in the life of Nebuchadnezzar in which he is referred as God's "servant." This method of ruling is far from ideal. It serves the purposes of God today in separating the wheat from the chaff, from those who wish to serve Him from those who do not, in separating those who love sin from those who hate it. For this separation to be effective, He must somewhat conceal Himself. However, He is actively found by those who seek Him!

The scriptures just cited from the Book of Revelation speak of a direct confrontational involvement of God in government. Today, the dark deeds of many in government serve God's overall purpose in providing ways for many to corrupt themselves in some measure while maintaining law and order. This provides evidence for judgment and justification for separation. People suffer when government officials corrupt themselves or pass laws which favor corrupt people; this is needed, and cannot be avoided in this world. Jesus said, John 16:33 *". . . in the world ye shall have tribulation: but be of good cheer; I have overcome the world. . ."* The future government will be filled with fiery judgment for anyone in government acting unjustly. That is why it is written, Rev. 11:17 *"thou hast taken to thee thy great power and hast reigned. Rev. 11:18 And the nations were angry, and thy wrath is come. . ."* Righteous government will have a cleansing effect on this world and will lead to a time of regeneration and restoration.

It is not that God is not reigning now, because He is. The difference is the standard He will apply to those in authority. The standard which shall be applied in that day is the Lord Jesus Christ. Anyone who does not ascribe to His attitude will not be fit to reign and will be removed. Why are the "nations angry?" Because business as usual will no longer be possible. The Lord God Jehovah through our Lord Jesus Christ will require a new standard fit for a new age. Without the new standard, there can be no new age. It is the standard which makes the age possible. Be assured, history has shown that the manner and types of governments have changed for age to age in the history of mankind. Each form of government had a time to reign and express itself. We are headed for a change in government that is more suited to all our needs and the world in which we live. It is the Lord Who will bring this to pass and only in His timing. No action by man or angel can speed up or slow down this time table. It is predestined and written in stone.

Nebuchadnezzar Exalts Himself and Fails to Honor God

Dan. 4:28 *All this came upon the king Nebuchadnezzar.* Dan. 4:29 *At the end of twelve months he walked in the palace of the kingdom of Babylon.* Dan. 4:30 *The king spake, and said, "Is not this great Babylon, that I have built for the house of the kingdom by the might of my power, and for the honour of my majesty?"* Dan. 4:31 *While the word was in the king's mouth, there fell a voice from heaven, saying, "O king Nebuchadnezzar, to thee it is spoken; The kingdom is departed from thee.* Dan. 4:32 *And they shall drive thee from men, and thy dwelling shall be with the beasts of the field: they shall make thee to eat grass as oxen, and seven times shall pass over thee, until thou know that the most High ruleth in the kingdom of men, and giveth it to whomsoever he will."*

Dan. 4:33 *The same hour was the thing fulfilled upon Nebuchadnezzar: and he was driven from them, and did eat grass as oxen, and his body was wet with the dew of heaven, till his hairs were grown like eagles' feathers, and his nails like birds' claws.* Dan. 4:34 *And at the end of the days I Nebuchadnezzar lifted up mine eyes unto heaven, and mine understanding returned unto me, and I blessed the most High, and I praised and honoured him that liveth for ever, whose dominion is an everlasting dominion, and his kingdom is from generation to generation:* Dan. 4:35 *And all the inhabitants of the earth are reputed as nothing: and he doeth according to his will in the army of heaven, and among the inhabitants of the earth: and none can stay his hand, or say unto him "What doest thou?"* Dan. 4:36 *At the same time my reason returned unto me; and for the glory of my kingdom, mine honour and brightness returned unto me; and my counselors and my lords sought unto me, and I was established in my kingdom, and excellent majesty was added unto me.*

Dan. 4:37 *Now I Nebuchadnezzar praise and extol and honour the King of heaven, all whose works are truth, and his ways judgment: and those that walk in pride he is able to abase...* My purpose is not to extol the reasons the Lord revealed Himself to Nebuchadnezzar, but to illustrate Who rules, Who has the power over all, and Who pulls the strings which manipulate what takes place on this earth and the entire universe. I encourage you to meditate on these passages in order to grasp hold of their implications, in the past, in the present, and in the future.

We see Nebuchadnezzar bragging about his vast accomplishments to those in his attendance while in his palace in Babylon (Dan. 4:30). He displays complete ignorance of the power and purposes of God at work in his life. For him, in his own mind, he is a "self made man" and gives credit and honor to no one. This is a very common attitude, even in our world today. Many people have the same attitude as King Nebuchadnezzar, but on a much smaller scale. Nebuchadnezzar saw nothing wrong with lauding his accomplishments, giving credit to no one but himself. Here is where the scriptures give light and understanding.

What is true for this great man Nebuchadnezzar should be applied as truth for every person alive. The truth of God's word does not apply to only some people, but to everyone. Neither you, nor I are exempt from the teaching in the scriptures. Therefore, let's examine what happened to this man and extrapolate the application to our own lives.

Nebuchadnezzar expresses great pride in who he is and what he has accomplished. Why is pride a sin? Pride does not acknowledge the hand of God in your life. Pride is the vanity of a lie, the lie that we made ourselves. We are all vessels of His creation. We do not create ourselves. Each of us is created for a specific purpose by our Maker. We all have different innate abilities and gifts which are endowed to us. We may apply ourselves to honing and perfecting the gifts we possess, but even this is a gift we need to acknowledge. Rom. 9:20 *Nay but, O man, who art thou that repliest against God? Shall the thing formed say to him that formed it, "Why hast thou made me thus?* Rom. 9:21 *Hath not the potter power over the clay, of the same lump to make one vessel unto honour, and another unto dishonour?"*

Some do not like to acknowledge that some vessels are made vessels of "dishonor." These vessels of dishonor are created just as the vessel of honor, out "of the same lump." They have a different purpose, just as different vessels in a household have different uses and purposes. At times, the vessels of dishonor are just as important as the vessels of honor. Vessels of honor may be completely unsuitable to fulfill the function and service of a vessel of dishonor. At this time, these vessels of dishonor are essential. This scripture does not say that God made only vessels of honor. I am not their eternal judge and will certainly make no attempt to explain this scripture or any other. It is important that we believe and accept what it says. If we accept what it says, we have understanding; if we explain it away to make it say something it doesn't, who knows how far from the truth you may find yourself.

Nebuchadnezzar was a "vessel" created for the function for which he was designed. He did not know this, but God was gracious to reveal it to him. The notion of a self-made man is a fallacy. Dan. 4:32 *And they shall drive thee from men,. . . until thou know that the most High ruleth in the kingdom of men and giveth it to whomsoever he will. . .* The notion that the Devil rules in the kingdoms of this earth is a lie. Just because what we see and have seen in the past is not Christ-like does not change this reality. Nebuchadnezzar was not Christ-like at all. Nevertheless, the Lord God Jehovah placed him in power. As proof of the acknowledging of this mandate, Nebuchadnezzar was to be a lunatic until he accepted and understood Who was the source of his power. If he would have given glory to the Devil for his accomplishments, Nebuchadnezzar would have remained a lunatic: "until thou know that the most High ruleth in the kingdom of men. . ."

What about the Devil? It is true that he is endowed with great power in the sphere of this world. However, the bounds of his power are set and controlled. Dan. 4:32 *And they shall drive thee from men,. . .* This is the function of one of the vessels of God. God Himself does no evil. God Himself did not make Nebuchadnezzar a lunatic. Nevertheless, He has at His disposal forces who take pleasure in this type of activity. It was these dark forces into which he was committed. The function of the phrase "shall drive thee" is not a singular event. It was the continuous action of dark forces directed against him, driving him mad. The only power Who could release him from this fate was God. Heb. 10:31 *It is a fearful thing to fall into the hands of the living God.*

This was a terrible ordeal for Nebuchadnezzar to experience. Look at the understanding he obtained. Dan. 4:35 *And all the inhabitants of the earth are reputed as nothing: and he doeth according to his will in the army of heaven, and among the inhabitants of the earth and none can stay his hand, or say unto him, What doest thou?. . .* Many today give credit to the Devil instead of the Lord. They fail to understand what this man came to understand by the chastisement of Divine edict. "He doeth according to his will, none can stay his hand..." Only the foolish and the rebellious try to judge God. There is no practical future in saying, What doest thou?

It is acceptable to cry or lament when we suffer because of our pain and emotion. It is acceptable to cry out for understanding. However, it is by faith that we understand that all things work together for the good of those called in Christ Jesus, our Lord. Rom. 8:28 *And we know that all things work together for good to them that love God, to them who are the called according to his purpose.* Therefore we need to rejoice and be thankful; we do this by faith when we do not have understanding.

9
The Pharaoh

Ex. 4:21 *The Lord said unto Moses, "When thou goest to return into Egypt, see that thou do all those wonders before Pharaoh, which I have put in thine hand: but I will harden his heart, that he shall not let the people go.* Ex. 4:22 *And thou shalt say unto Pharaoh, Thus saith the Lord, Israel is my son, even my firstborn:* Ex. 4:23 *And I say unto thee, Let my son go, that he may serve me: and if thou refuse to let him go... I will slay thy son, even thy firstborn."*

The pharaoh of whom we are to write is specifically the one in power at the writing of the passages just quoted. In Exodus, this pharaoh's name does not appear directly and I do not have specific insight to know it. So humbling and abasing is the account we are about to examine, that it is possible that the omission of his name is the final judgment to his great pride.

It is interesting to note that it was an earlier pharaoh's daughter who drew Moses out of the river and gave him his name (Ex. 2:10). The name Moses is Egyptian. Dr. Scofield points out (in the King James Study Bible which contains his notes) that the name Moses is found in portions of other Egyptian names such as: Ramose (Ramose), and Thutmoses. According to Dr. Scofield, the name Moses was familiar in the Egyptian court as a component of the compound names of several pharaohs.

The definition in the Hebrew dictionary states the meaning of his name as follows: 4872h. Mosheh from 4871; a great Israel, Israelite leader, prophet and lawgiver;... However, this is not the original definition, but the explanation the name Moses came to mean. The original meaning is stated in the scripture: Ex. 2:10 *And the child grew, and she brought him unto Pharaoh's daughter, and he became her son. And she called his name Moses: and she said, "Because I drew him out of the water..."* Thus, Moses' name originally meant "to be drawn out of the water." It was what God did with this man which gave new meaning to is name.

Back to God's Original Declaration

Ex. 4:21 *And the Lord said unto Moses, "I will harden his heart, that he shall not let the people go."* Ex. 4:92 *And thou shalt say unto Pharaoh, 'Thus saith the Lord, Israel is my son, even my firstborn:'* Ex. 4:23 *And I say unto thee, "Let my son go, that he may serve me: and if thou refuse to let him go, behold, I will slay thy son, even thy firstborn. . ."* This was what the Lord God Jehovah spoke to Moses when he was in the wilderness, after he had been absent from Egypt for forty years. It is a statement of intent. If God declares openly that He is going to harden a man's heart, this man is doomed. He does not have a choice in the literal sense over the future decisions he will make. True, he, in his own mind, will have reasons for the things he chooses, but other choices are not available to him because of the hardness in his heart. For this man, there are no other choices. This man will make choices based upon his own blind, exalted, arrogant, boastful, prideful, self-conceited, and inflated ego.

The attitude of the Pharaoh was this: Who is the Lord God of Israel that I need to kowtow to Him; is not the gods of Egypt superior in every way? Look at these disgusting people. They are in my hand as tools of my kingdom, over which I rule as a god. Am I not the Pharaoh? All their lives combined do not compare to my own importance and magnificence. They exist to serve me in my purposes, as I determine. Did not the Pharaoh before me demonstrate how contemptible are these Hebrews when he ordered the deaths of all the male babies (Ex. 1:16)? If they were worth a second thought, the pharaoh before me would have been ordered by the gods to stop this. As the pharaoh before me did as he willed, so shall I. God could have humbled the haughty man in his development, far before he got to this stage of self deception; but He chose the contrary! What a painful situation to the people in his kingdom to have such a man rule. Like men of recent history, such as Hitler, Stalin, and others, the purpose of their cruel existence may be a mystery. This man's reason for existence was for the understanding of the generations to follow.

This prideful man was created by God for a specific purpose. Ex. 9:16 *And in very deed for this cause have I raised thee up to show in thee my power; and that my name may be declared throughout all the earth...* Things would never be the same in this world. Through this man, God was able to clearly declare that there is but one true God and that everything they worshipped was a lie. Notice that the scripture declares, "And in very deed for this cause have I raised thee up..." It was not the Devil who raised up this man, but the Lord God Almighty. He was raised up for God's own purposes. This man, called Pharaoh, did not know the Lord, but that did not change the facts. God works and men do not perceive His presence. The apostle Paul understood well the workings of God when he stated: Heb. 10:31 *It is a fearful thing to fall into the hands of the living God...* You can argue if you want. The scriptures are clear. God has two plans; one is for those who know and love Him; the other is for those who live in darkness. But above all, one thing is clear; all people serve Him in the purposes He has set forth in this world. As I have said before, even those who volitionally oppose Him are serving Him in His purposes! It is impossible to successfully oppose God.

Who is the Lord?

Ex. 5:1 *And afterward Moses and Aaron went in, and told Pharaoh, "Thus saith the Lord God of Israel, Let my people go, that they may hold a feast unto me in the wilderness."* Ex. 5:2 *And Pharaoh said, "Who is the Lord, that I should obey his voice to let Israel go? I know not the Lord, neither will I let Israel go..."* The heart of this pharaoh is laid bare. He has no knowledge of Who he is confronting. In his mind, he is great in his own right. He has no concept that it is this same God (there is none other) Who has raised him up and placed him in power. He is in utter darkness, though God had made him ruler of Egypt. We cannot judge this man, for it is written, "for this cause have I raised thee up..." This does not change the substance of pride and arrogance. Did not God have the power to humble this man? Yes, of course, but He did not. Just as there are people today who are puffed up beyond measure and are not brought low. This does not mean that their condition will never be brought to judgment. This man's heart condition shone as an unchallenged beacon of presumption; but, that was all going to change.

We have a perfect example from the scriptures. Prov. 11:2 *When pride cometh, then cometh shame: but with the lowly is wisdom.* Prov. 16:18 *Pride goeth before destruction, and an haughty spirit before a fall.* I can't help but wonder if King Solomon meditated on the fate of this pharaoh along with others like him when he uttered these proverbs. Think about Goliath, with his own thoughts of superiority. 1 Sam. 17:10 *And the Philistine said, "I defy the armies of Israel this day; give me a man, that we may fight together."* 1 Sam. 17:42 *And when the Philistine looked about and saw David, he disdained him: for he was but a youth, and ruddy, and of a fair countenance.* 1 Sam. 17:43 *And the Philistine said unto David, "Am I a dog, that thou comest to me with staves?" And the Philistine cursed David by his gods.* 1 Sam. 17:45 *Then said David to the Philistine, "Thou comest to me with a sword, and with a spear, and with a shield: but I come to thee in the name of the Lord of hosts, the God of the armies of Israel whom thou hast defied."*

God has a way of bringing judgment against the thing we exalt the most. Undo pride can bring a person low, if the very thing they are prideful about cannot be exalted or is a source of embarrassment. This is exactly what happened to the pharaoh. All his power and authority was shown to be of no consequence. His powers of reason were reduced to abject foolishness to his own people and the entire world. All his gods about which his life revolved were shown to be nothing but fantasy. Every time this man asserted himself forcefully, the wealth of his entire nation was further plundered or his people suffered miserably. Under his prideful rule, Egypt was reduced to ruin. Why? There are two reasons. First, Egypt and the rest of the world were shown that there is only one true God. You may worship what you will, but He, the Lord God Jehovah alone is to be feared and revered. Secondly, this man was chosen to exemplify the futility of exalting one's self above your maker. The end of this course is only misery and defeat.

What more can I say about this? Ex. 9:16 *And in very deed for this cause have I raised thee up to show in thee my power; and that my name may be declared throughout all the earth. . .* It would be a grave error in logic or understanding to come to the conclusion that his example is an isolated instance. Although we have the Exodus account as a wonderful example and lesson to all who cherish and want to know the truth, it is but a macrocosm for the sake of gaining the attention of the whole world.

At all times throughout history, God has been exerting His power developing the earth and this world as He has seen fit, for the purposes only He fully understands. This is what faith is all about. We understand what we can. However, we cannot fully understand life or everything which goes on around us. We enter into special relationships with God only through faith in accepting the Lord Jesus Christ. Why? Because God has told us that Jesus is the way. John 6:2 *Then said they unto him, "What shall we do, that we might work the works of God?"* John 6:29 *Jesus answered and said unto them "This is the work of God, that ye believe on him whom he hath sent. . ."*

The Correct Attitude
(Diverging From Pharaoh)

What is the correct attitude? Those in darkness will think what they will think; that is what darkness is all about. But to those whom God has chosen to reveal Himself, correct attitude is part of everything He reveals. We all need to have a deep desire that we are in agreement with His plans. This appreciation is something into which we grow because there is a certain amount of pain in the working out of things. I am not saying that everything is painful. Far be it from that. What I am communicating is that in the experiences of everyday life, situations will arise that hurt. When the pain comes, it is only natural to want the pain to cease as quickly as possible. However, there are many situations which will not immediately go away. If it is God's will that we be able to eliminate the suffering immediately, then we will be successful in our faith and our efforts will be rewarded. Each experience has a life expectancy. Consider Job and what he went through. If he could have made the whole thing go away, he would have. But we would not have the Book of Job today. He also would not have received the benefit of his suffering by the things he learned.

Jesus suffered the crucifixion. What a terrible experience. Yet, God glorified His suffering. I think of the tremendous satisfaction He has for all eternity as a result of that horrendously terrifying, cruel, and painful circumstance. Only a fool would tell himself that people need not suffer in this world. If the only begotten Son of God, Jesus, needed to suffer, you and I are going to have pain in our own lives. The opposite side of the coin is also true. We will also have great joy and wonderful experiences, but everything as He has ordained. In everything, both we and the world in which we live are changed by the experiences and what transpires. We also are part of the creative process of the universe which has been ongoing since the beginning.

Matt. 6:10 *Thy kingdom come. Thy will be done in earth, as it is in heaven.* Matt. 26:42 *He went away again the second time, and prayed, saying, O my Father, if this cup may not pass away from me, except I drink it, thy will be done. . ."* An affirmative attitude toward the will of God is helpful with our lives. With such an attitude, we move through life with a solid inner peace that we are in His care and understand that He has a plan for our lives. With this knowledge comes peace. Those who do not understand this basic concept can never really have true peace because they are always fighting everything which comes along.

The Power of Blessing and of Cursing

Remember the prophet Balaam? When he learned that it was God's will to bless the children of Israel and not curse them, what marvelous prophecies flowed from his lips. Num. 22:12 *And God said unto Balaam, "Thou shalt not go with them; thou shalt not curse the people: for they are blessed."* Num. 22:35 *And the angel of the Lord said unto Balaam, "Go with the men: but only the word that I shall speak unto thee, that thou shalt speak." So Balaam went with the princes of Balak.* Num. 22:38 *And Balaam said unto Balak, "Lo, I am come unto thee: have I now any power at all to say any thing? the word that God putteth in my mouth, that shall I speak."* Num. 24:1 *And when Balaam saw that it pleased the Lord to bless Israel, he went not, as at other times, to seek for enchantments, but he set his face toward the wilderness.*

When God releases power "in the air" to bless someone, or a group, or a project, or anything, only blessings can flow. Everything about that person is charged for blessing. The amount of blessings which will flow is proportional to the amount of power God has released for that purpose. It is a waste of time for the Devil himself or any of his minions to attempt to try to break this flow, because they cannot be successful unless it is God's will. This knowledge had to be revealed and it has continued to be revealed through history. Many though, even with the numerous examples in the scriptures, are not able to rest and accept this one truth: God rules!

The Lord does not limit Himself as to what He is capable of doing. The wrong choice from a human or angelic point of view can be the right choice from God's point of purpose. The scriptures are filled with numerous examples of methods He has employed to accomplish His own will. At times, He may decide to reveal Himself directly, making His intentions clear, as is the case of Abimelech: Gen. 20:3 *But God came to Abimelech in a dream by night, and said to him, Behold, thou art but a dead man, for the woman which thou hast taken; for she is a man's wife.* Gen. 20:4 *But Abimelech had not come near her: and he said, "Lord, wilt thou slay also a righteous nation?"* Gen. 20:5 *Said he not unto me, "She is my sister?" and she, even she herself said, "He is my brother: in the integrity of my heart and innocence of my hands have I done this."* Gen. 20:6 *And God said unto him in a dream, "Yea, I know that thou didst this in the integrity of thy heart; for I also withheld thee from sinning against me: therefore suffered I thee not to touch her.* Gen. 20:7 *Now therefore restore the man his wife; for he is a prophet, and he shall pray for thee, and thou shalt live: and if thou restore her not, know thou that thou shalt surely die, thou, and all that are thine."* Gen. 20:8 *So Abimelech arose early in the morning and called all his servants and told all these things in their hearing; and the men were greatly frightened.*

The only limitations the Lord God Jehovah puts upon Himself are His own plans. God is the source of all power in the universe. Subsequently, all power which exists had to originate from Him. What He has determined to be is unalterable. Any attempt to alter this power (when it is God, Himself) is complete futility. The life forces of man and angels are in His hand. A fallen angel will only traumatize his own existence if he persists in opposition. He will not be successful in changing what God has planned, but will just heap upon himself misery. Let me cite some examples: Gen. 6:2 *That the sons of God saw the daughters of men that they were fair; and they took them wives of all which they chose.* Jude 1:6 *And the angels which kept not their first estate, but left their own habitation, he hath reserved in everlasting chains under darkness unto the judgment of the great day...* This is quite an example to other angels contemplating this or any other self-willed activity. There are other examples, but I will cite only one other scripture which shows that the spirits in darkness fear God's intervention. They, even though they are haters of God, are careful to respect the limits He sets, because He will deal with them in short order. Matt. 8:29 *And, behold, they cried out, saying, "What have we to do with thee, Jesus, thou Son of God? art thou come hither to torment us before the time?"* Matt. 8:31 *So the Devils besought him, saying, "If thou cast us out, suffer us to go away into the herd of swine..."* I understand that this concept may be hard for some to accept or comprehend, but too much false teaching has been promoted to make men fear the Devil instead of their Creator.

Back to the Pharaoh

Every experience has a "life expectancy" determined by God. It cannot be shortened or lengthened. When Egypt was ordained to have seven years of plenty, seven years was what they had. When Egypt had seven years of famine, all the prayers of all the people in Egypt and Canaan did not shorten that drought (Gen. 41:15-54).

(Remember, Jacob also suffered from the lack of rain. It is inconceivable that this man of prayer refrained from praying for rain.) That which can be changed, will be changed. That which cannot be changed, will not be changed. The past, the present, and the future are set in stone, and cannot be altered.

Why couldn't the pharaoh simply change his mind when he saw all the destruction, and let the Israelites go? Because God would not let him successfully change his mind. Prov. 21:1 *The king's heart is in the hand of the Lord, as the rivers of water: he turneth it whithersoever he will. . .* God would not let this man go until He was finished with what He had planned to reveal to the world. This man was chosen to play a key role in this revelation. The Lord did not ask this man for permission to do these things.

Look at the pharaoh's reaction midway through the judgments upon Egypt. Ex. 9:27 *And Pharaoh sent, and called for Moses and Aaron, and said unto them, "I have sinned this time: the Lord is righteous, and I and my people are wicked* [in the case of hail].*"* Ex. 13:16 *Then Pharaoh called for Moses and Aaron in haste; and he said, "I have sinned* [in the case of locust] *against the Lord your God, and against you. . ."* In both cases, the Lord hardens this man's heart so that he acts foolishly in defiant behavior.

After the Lord gets His people out of the clutches of Egypt, He demonstrates that He is not through having sport with them yet. Whatever wickedness is hidden within a heart, God is able to bring it out and manifest it to all. The Egyptians had not fully confessed that He, the Lord Jehovah is God, and there is none other. These Egyptians still held out hope in their hearts that they would be victorious in their cruelty to re-enslave the Hebrew people. It was this desire, to bring them back into bondage, and their lack of acceptance of God's rule, which opened the door for further judgment. Ex. 14:5 *And it was told the king of Egypt that the people fled: and the heart of Pharaoh and of his servants was turned against the people, and they said, Why have we done this, that we have let Israel go from serving us?*

Imagine this for a while. After all that these people suffered, they are still blind at heart. I am saying this from a human point of view. It was the Lord Who hardened these hearts, therefore their reasoning was faulty. It was not just the pharaoh, whose heart was hardened, but most of the Egyptian people; not all the Egyptian people, but enough to make an example of them. There were those whose eyes and hearts were open and receptive to the truth. Not much is mentioned about these people as to their experiences with the judgments which God brought upon Egypt, but it does state that they left Egypt with Israel; God made special provisions for them. He accepted them fully as His own. Lev. 24:22 *Ye shall have one manner of law, as well for the stranger, as for one of your own country: for I am the Lord your God.* Deut. 10:19 *Love ye therefore the strangely for ye were strangers in the land of Egypt.* Num. 9:14 *And if a stranger shall sojourn among you, and will keep the Passover unto the Lord; according to the ordinance of the Passover, and according to the manner thereof, so shall he do: ye shall have one ordinance, both for the stranger, and for him that was born in the land...*

The word stranger means: 1616h. ger (stranger [25]) from 1481a; gur; a sojourner;... The same word is also translated as alien, foreigner, immigrant, sojourner, and stranger. Therefore we see that in the midst of much judgment, there are many people whom the Lord spares because they have a different heart. Almost anything is possible with people of the right heart and attitude. The Lord cared to save the Egyptians.

The Red Sea Experience

I have included the following scriptures to refresh your memory. You may skip over them to the next paragraph if you are very familiar with their content.

Ex. 14:10 *And when Pharaoh drew nigh, the children of Israel lifted up their eyes, and, behold, the Egyptians marched after them; and they were sore afraid: and the children of Israel cried out unto the Lord.* Ex. 14:13 *And Moses said unto the people, "Fear ye not, stand still, and see the salvation of the Lord, which he will show to you to day: for the Egyptians whom ye have seen to day, ye shall see them again no more for ever.* Ex. 14:14 *The Lord shall fight for you, and ye shall hold your peace.* Ex.14:16 *But lift thou up thy rod, and stretch out thine hand over the sea, and divide it: and the children of Israel shall go on dry ground through the midst of the sea.* Ex.14:17 *And I, behold, I will harden the hearts of the Egyptians, and they shall follow them: and I will get me honour upon Pharaoh, and upon all his host, upon his chariots, and upon his horsemen.* Ex. 14:18 *And the Egyptians shall know that I am the Lord, when I have gotten me honour upon Pharaoh, upon his chariots, and upon his horsemen.* Ex. 14:19 *And the angel of God, which went before the camp of Israel, removed and went behind them; and the pillar of the cloud went from before their face, and stood behind them:"* Ex. 14:20 *And it came between the camp of the Egyptians and the camp of Israel; and it was a cloud and darkness to them but it gave light by night to these: so that the one came not near the other all the night.* Ex. 14:21 *And Moses stretched out his hand over the sea; and the Lord caused the sea to go back by a strong east wind all that night, and made the sea dry land, and the waters were divided.* Ex. 14:22 *And the sons of Israel went through the midst of the sea on the dry land, and the waters were like a wall to them on their right hand and on their left.* Ex. 14:23 *And the Egyptians pursued, and went in after them to the midst of the sea, even all Pharaoh's horses, his chariots, and his horsemen.* Ex. 14:27 *And Moses stretched forth his hand over the sea, and the sea returned to his strength when the morning appeared; and the Egyptians fled against it; and the Lord overthrew the Egyptians in the midst of the sea.* Ex. 14:28 *And the waters returned, and covered the chariots, and the horsemen and all the host of Pharaoh that came into the sea after them; there remained not so much as one of them.*

The spirit that drove these Egyptians had to be extremely strong. You will notice that God separated the two camps by a pillar of light on one side toward the Hebrews and the same pillar was a wall of darkness to the Egyptians. Any man in his right mind would have been terrified, but not these Egyptians; they were confident!

Next we see the Red Sea parted so that the water was a wall on one side and on the other side, forming a corridor of dry land for passage. Such a marvelous spectacle would have awed a rationally thinking man into worship and submission. Not so with the Egyptians. Their hearts were seething with hatred and revenge. Upon them came a blindness that was so complete that they were unable to appreciate or grasp anything around them except the thoughts of satisfaction from bloody revenge.

Did the Devil have a part in all this? We know that God is love. Yet, He has a host of spirits which will work with Him in an instant to fall upon men such as this. Thus, while the Devil and his forces consumed the Egyptians working with God to fulfill His judgment, the children of Israel had complete protection. God had set the boundaries, and they were firmly maintained. Few people appreciate or understand the fullness of the meaning that "God rules."

10
The Lord Jesus Christ

1 Pet. 1:20 *Who* [the Lord Jesus Christ] *verily was foreordained before the foundation of the world, but was manifest in these last times for you,...* The word foreordained means the following: 4267g. progino_sko_ from 4253 and 1097; to know beforehand. This same word is translated in other scriptures as foreknew, foreknown, knowing beforehand, and know previously. It is important that we get this idea clearly. Therefore, it is worth the time to think about this for understanding.

First of all, it states "before the foundation" of the world. Adam is the foundation of the world. This truth is a separate teaching which I will not elaborate upon here. The point is "before." This means that the Lord Jesus was foreordained (foreknew) before Adam. The apostle John states, John 1:1 *In the beginning was the Word, and the Word was with God, and the Word was God...* It is important to understand that the Lord Jesus Christ is not just some last minute reaction to problems which occurred on this earth. This "foreknowledge" is total and complete. You and I cannot fully comprehend knowing the end from the beginning; however, this is exactly the place which God inhabits. The manifestation of the Lord Jesus Christ to us was not an unplanned reaction to something which came up by God. He is able to prevent problems before they occur by eliminating the circumstances. God had already planned His revelation of Himself through the Lord Jesus Christ before He created Adam (1 Pet. 1:20).

We see further confirmation of the thoughts of God at the time He expelled Adam and Eve from the Garden of Eden. Gen. 3:15 *And I will put enmity between thee* [the serpent] *and the woman, and between thy seed and her seed; it shall bruise thy head, and thou shalt bruise his heel...* In this scripture, we see God revealing much of His plans for the future. It is not difficult to understand that this scripture does not correspond to natural serpents. Natural serpents do not talk, nor do they possess the mental faculties to tempt people to commit acts against God. This serpent is Satan. Jesus said, John 8:44 *Ye are of your father the Devil, and the lusts of your father ye will do. He was a murderer from the beginning, and abode not in the truth, because there is no truth in him. When he speaketh a lie, he speaketh of his own: for he is a liar, and the father of it.* Thus, the seeds of the serpent are all people contrary to the Lord Jesus Christ.

The woman in this scripture is not Eve. "And I will put enmity between thee and the woman. . ." It does not mean that serpents have it out for all women, nor does it mean that all women will have it out for snakes. The woman is the symbolic representation of the church. Rev. 21:9 *And there came unto me one of the seven angels which had the seven vials full of the seven last plagues, and talked with me, saying, Come hither, I will show thee the bride, the Lamb's wife. . .* The seed of the woman in this scripture refers to those who come forth as a result of the church and the Lord Jesus Christ. The animosity between those born of the Spirit and those born of the flesh is obvious in every social gathering. This is a daily fulfillment of the mid portion of this scripture: "and enmity between thy seed and her seed. . ."

Lastly, the last portion of this scripture states, "it shall bruise thy head, and thou shall bruise his heel. . ." The seed in the latter portion of this scripture takes on the masculine gender, "his." This is because this seed is speaking of the many membered body of Christ – Jesus being the head, and we being the many membered portion making up that body. Rom. 16:20 *And the God of peace shall bruise Satan under your feet shortly. The grace of our Lord Jesus Christ be with you. Amen.*

You can see that very early in the account in Genesis, God chose to reveal what He had planned, foreordained, predestined to occur. Look around you, see and understand that all this was spoken before all the events which occurred making it a reality. All this became reality not because it was a prediction, but because God had determined the future.

Gen. 1:26 *And God said, Let us make man in our image, after our likeness: and let them have dominion. . . .* It took the birth of the Lord Jesus Christ for this scripture to begin to display the meaning the Lord God Jehovah intended. Jesus is the "first born of many brethren." He is the image of the invisible Father. Jesus Christ is the pattern Son. He is the Alpha and the Omega. We all must be born again in Christ to enter into the power of this aspect of God's creation. The following scripture is not a "stopgap" measure to save man who, unbeknownst to God, fell. It is the continuation of a plan He had from the very beginning. John 1:14 *And the Word was made flesh, and dwelt among us,. . .* God's plan existed before the foundation of the world.

Abel's Revelation

Gen. 4:2 *And she [Eve] again bare his brother Abel. And Abel was a keeper of sheep, but Cain was a tiller of the ground.* Gen. 4:3 *And in process of time it came to pass, that Cain brought of the fruit of the ground an offering unto the Lord.* Gen. 4:4 *And Abel, he also brought of the firstlings of his flock and of the fat thereof. And the Lord had respect unto Abel and to his offering:* Gen. 4:5 *But unto Cain and to his offering he had not respect. And Cain was very wroth, and his countenance fell.*

Abel's offering was accepted because it corresponded to the plan of God. Sin was in the world. Sin, in one fashion or another, is the act of taking something which does not belong to you. It may be respect, false credit, a physical object, lack of honor, lack of support, on and on, so that what is appropriated, results in a lie, a theft or a murder. Thus, there is a debt in God's scheme of accounting in His laws which govern His creation.

The one who sins is a debtor. It is hard for us to comprehend the serious consequences of every sin. We see it all the time and it is committed all around us. For many, sin is a way of life. They never give much thought to the consequence of what they are doing. However, sin separates a person from God and is an act of spiritual suicide. It may seem that it is other people who suffer from someone's deeds, but those who sin irrevocably cut themselves off from God. Everyone who sins and is without the heart to repent is without hope. Repentance, necessary though it is, is not enough. In the accounting of God, the debt remains. Sin has a cost which must be repaid. Since all sin causes death, life must be given to pay the debt. Abel's offering is a revelation of God's thinking. God's Spirit had dealt with Abel's heart to make such an offering of "the firstlings of his flock and of the fat thereof. . ." By this, He was communicating that He would send His son, Jesus Christ, to be the payment for sin to all those who have faith in this offering. We see in the account of Cain and Abel, that Cain did not have regard for this offering. Rather than admit the truth, he killed his brother. Cain demonstrates the first example of the enmity God promised between the seed of the Devil and the Godly seed.

This offering of Abel was just the symbolic representation of the true thinking of God. That is why He had respect for it. The sacrifice was representative of the Lord Jesus Christ. This symbolic representation of the firstling of the flock is rich in revelation of Jehovah's future plans, and is a theme He repeated over and over again.

Rev. 13:8 *And all that dwell upon the earth shall worship him, whose names are not written in the book of life of the Lamb slain from the foundation of the world.* We see here a reference to the Lord Jesus Christ depicted as a "Lamb." This symbolism of Him is used throughout the scriptures. Rev. 13:8 is a reference to Abel's sacrificial offering. Jesus Christ is the "firstling of the flock and the fat thereof." He is the only sacrifice for which the Father has respect and acceptance. Cain's sacrifice was totally unacceptable.

All mankind falls into two categories: those who follow in Abel's footsteps and those who follow Cain. To those who follow Cain, the word still comes: Gen. 4:7 *"If you do weld will not your countenance be lifted up? And if you do not do well, sin is crouching at the door; and its desire is for you, but you must master it."* "Doing well" refers to emulating Abel's sacrifice and worship. God was not interested in the natural fruit of the earth. He was interested in that which is born by faith and not of our own self efforts – Jesus Christ.

This same theme is repeated over and over again in the scriptures. We see the pattern in Abraham. Abraham had two sons, Isaac and Ishmael. Isaac was born of faith by the supernatural workings of the Spirit of God. Ishmael was born by the efforts of the flesh. We saw the efforts of Moses when he was about forty years old. He killed an Egyptian oppressing his countrymen and hid the body in the sand. Moses ended up having to flee for his life as a result of his efforts. His efforts correspond to the offering of Cain, just as the birth of Ishmael.

Some Important Differences Between the Elect and the Non-Elect

Both our Cain and our Abel experiences are designed to teach us about our Father's will. There is a difference between those who are called to be God's elect from those who will, like Cain, choose to remain in darkness. Rom. 8:28 *And we know that all things work together for good to them that love God, to them who are the called according to his purpose.* Abraham and Moses went on to understand and put behind them the works of the flesh. Cain refused to submit to the revealed will of God for his life. I personally believe that both the failed attempt in the flesh and the success experienced from the function of faith are valuable to Christians. However, those who walk in darkness persist in refusing to alter their thinking. The works of the flesh become a way of life.

The things we suffer teach us valuable lessons that serve in the creative process. Consider Moses' act of killing the Egyptian. This resulted in him fleeing from Egypt to be prepared by God for a role he was to fulfill forty years later. The scriptures say of the Lord Jesus Christ, Heb. 5:8 *Though he were a Son, yet learned he obedience by the things which he suffered;. . .* Thus, we can conclude that even our stumbles are ordained of the Father because it is all part of the creative process and is designed for a specific ending. This is a very controversial subject over which many people struggle. Even in the apostle Paul's day, people accuse him of saying, "Let us do evil, that good may come." Why? Because of a lack of understanding.

The writings of the apostle Paul: Rom. 3:8 *And not rather, Let us do evil, that good may come? whose damnation is just...* If we affirm that all things work together for the good of God's elect and we say that "even the wrong we do will invariably work out for the best," then we can be accused as the apostle Paul. Nevertheless, Paul understood what I am endeavoring to communicate. A terrible wrong which anyone of us may commit; the pain and shame it brings will have many ramifications. One of those ramifications, if godly sorrow is present, will result in tremendous purification and spiritual growth.

Consider the following scripture: Dan. 11:35 *And some of them of understanding shall fall, to try them, and to purge, and to make them white, even to the time of the end: because it is yet for a time appointed...* Let's read the same scripture in a different translation. Dan. 11:35 *"And some of those who have insight will fall, in order to refine, purge, and make them pure, until the end time; because [it is] still [to come] at the appointed time...* Thus, one translation states that the fall is to make them white; the other translation phrases it in order to refine, purge, and make them pure. Both translations state the same thing. This "fall" is not without purpose or merit. It serves a function and provides a benefit to those who experienced it, even though the definition of "fall" implies that these people are doing something wrong.

It may seem like a paradox, but God will bring you to a "fall" if it is needed. This is not the same as saying that God will tempt you. God hates sin. But the Father will put up with sin for a season if the end result warrants it. Remember the parable about the wheat and the tares. The roots of the tares (weeds) can be intertwined with your own roots. You are of greater value than the cost of the sin. The Lord knows how to get you to reject the weeds and choke them out. Jesus, knowing that an unrepentant dark desire may be eventually dealt with by the Father, advised us to pray in this manner: Matt. 6:13 *And lead us not into temptation, but deliver us from evil:...* We are to avoid sin. Nevertheless, the Father will answer only those prayers which are according to His will. He may choose to lead us into situations in which hidden sin is brought into the open so that it can be brought to judgment. For those who love Him, this judgment, although painful, will lead to greater purification and worship.

Sadly, some will love their inner sin so completely that judgment will not successfully separate them from their desires. These people, although loved, are unsuitable for the Kingdom of the Lord Jesus Christ. They have no commonalty of thinking or tastes to have eternal fellowship with those chosen for that kingdom. These people would find themselves alone and exposed in a sea of light. The Lord in His mercy has chosen to separate them, to be with those of like thinking. This separation is necessary for everyone's sake.

Ordained to be Crucified: Two Positions

Jesus Christ was ordained to be crucified. This plan of the Father was not a last minute decision but was in His plans from the beginning. As the end is known from the beginning by the Lord God Jehovah, the crucifixion of His only begotten Son was not a decision in response to anything which we had done. God does not act as a reactionary to our actions, so that we act first and He responds. God is the author and finisher of our faith. He first loved us. Many people envision a God that is somewhat akin to a firefighter, who is constantly putting out fires which either man or the Devil start. These well-meaning, albeit short sighted people, see the Father as always struggling to regain control of a situation which is going awry. This understanding comes from the deception that man and angels are ever in control. This misunderstanding is not new. Even Nebuchadnezzar thought that he had built Babylon by his own power and that he owed his success to himself. The Lord brought him to understand that the earth is the Lord's and He gives it to whomever He chooses.

God created Adam knowing full well that he would fall. This is because he had an inherent weakness. This weakness was not an accident. He could have been created without this character defect. If the Lord would have made him without this weakness, man would be much different emotionally. Man would be a different being.

The Lord does not make mistakes! He could have made a man who would not fall; but instead, He made Adam. There was no question in God's mind that this man might fall. Adam was created with the capacity to fall and God knew that he would. Did Adam live in world filled with temptation beckoning him on every side? No. Adam made a conscious decision to reject God's word because he placed little or no value upon it. The Lord could have given him understanding and a mind to value, reverence, and fear His word. But He did not. God created Adam as needed so that we could develop into the beings we were destined to become. God's creation of Adam and all that was to follow was and is part of His continual creationary work. There was no mistake – no surprise sin. God does not run around trying to fix situations that never should have occurred. He is the Creator. With God, there are no surprises. Nothing is unaccounted for. Therefore, you and I should enter into rest. He has everything under control.

We have two positions. The most common position is that the plan to crucify the Lord Jesus Christ came into being as a result of Original Sin of Adam and Eve. The second position is that the Lord Jesus Christ was crucified in plan from the beginning of time. The plan to crucify Him was not a new thought as a result of unexpected sin on behalf of Adam and Eve. This second position is my position and, although controversial is according to the scriptures. Acts 2:23 *this [Man], delivered up by the predetermined plan and foreknowledge of God, you nailed to a cross by the hands of godless men and put [Him] to death.*

When did Jehovah have a predetermined plan? He had a predetermined plan from the very beginning. His plan was complete and lacked nothing from the earliest thoughts of the creation of the universe. Is. 46:9 *Remember the former things of old: for I am God, and there is none else; I am God, and there is none like me,* Is. 46:10 *Declaring the end from the beginning and from ancient times the things that are not yet done, saving My counsel shall stand, and I will do all my pleasures. . .*

The Lord God Almighty is not a God of reaction to the things man does. I am not saying that He does not act as in every situation. What I am saying is that God's actions toward us are either in the form of judgment or blessing. Both of these acts serve to further create us and everything around us. From the creature's point of view, it appears that they have control. This is one way our creator can motivate us to continue down a certain path or abandon our ways. However, often relatively innocent people (from man's perspective), doing everything apparently right, sometime suffer terribly. Is this suffering always judgment? From God's perspective, it may not always be judgment. Look at the life of King David. David suffered terribly as a result of King Saul's jealousy. Yet, everything David suffered made him into a man of faith. He, through his suffering, got to know God intimately. In David's experience, the terrible things which occurred in his life in the end proved to be blessings. This is not to say that he did not have any directly revealed judgments. He did. In God's thinking, it is the end result that is most important. We must always bear this in mind. He is the Master Architect. We and everything in the universe are the architecture! Yes, we do interact with Him, and He is moved with our infirmities. However, this weakness of God is stronger than man (1 Cor. 1:25).

The Lord Jesus Christ, from the beginning of time, knew He was to be crucified. All the scriptures reiterate over and over again the theme of the sacrifice of the innocent suffering death to secure the blessings of the Father for the needy and the guilty. Ps. 40:7 *Then said I, Lo, I come: in the volume of the book it is written of me,...* This same scripture is quoted in the writings of the apostle Paul. Heb. 10:7 *Then said I, Lo, I come to do thy will, O God...*

Everything About Lord Jesus Christ is Told in The Scriptures

Psalms 40:7 states that in the "volume of the book" is written about Christ Jesus. This is a powerful statement from the scriptures themselves, because it was written before Jesus was born as incarnate man. Everything about Him was told as fact from the vantage point of the beginning!

You might ask yourself, "If everything about Him was predicted, Why didn't the Devil disrupt some of those predictions?" If the Bible were mere predictions of the future, then some of them could be disrupted so that they did not come true. Mere predictions do not imply force of implementation. However, the bible does not contain predictions, but statements of fact. These "facts" are plans which have existed from the creation of the universe. They are the privilege of the Creator over what He is creating. These predetermined plans cannot be altered or disannulled because there is power contained within the words greater than any obstacle or opposition. Obstacles or opposition always work for God, because it is impossible to successfully oppose Him.

Revelations

As the Father gives us revelations of His intentions and thoughts, He also grants revelations to the angels. When revelation comes to us, it is for the purpose of our cooperation and understanding so we can flow with what He is doing or about to do. He grants this same revelation to the angels. Even the only begotten Son, the Lord Jesus Christ, did not know all things, but relied upon revelations from the Father. Mark 13:32 *"But of that day or hour no one knows, not even the angels in heaven, nor the Son, but the Father alone."* Rev. 1:1 *The Revelation of Jesus Christ, which God gave unto him, to show unto his servants things which must shortly come to pass; and he sent and signified it by his angel unto his servant John:*

Thus, revelation of God's plans (plans are not predictions) is given to man and angels; even the Lord Jesus Christ received revelation. Let's look at another scripture. Gen. 1:26 *And God said, "Let us make man in our image, after our likeness: and let them have dominion over the fish of the sea, and over the fowl of the air, and over the cattle, and over all the earth, and over every creeping thing that creepeth upon the earth. . ."* The word "God" in the original text means: 430h. elohim plural of 433; God, god;. . . The traditional understanding of this verse is a so-called conversation between the God Head Trinity (Father, Son, and Holy Spirit). However, this is not correct. This scripture is a statement of direct revelation from the Father to His angelic sons of His intentions toward mankind. It is a call for unity. It announces His intentions clearly to the angels with a request for them to labor with Him toward that end. God wanted His intentions clear that there be no misunderstanding. Shortly after this revelation came the fall of Lucifer and angels who banded with him. These angels sought special ranks and position over what God had planned for mankind.

To desire a particular place in the kingdom God had revealed was one thing. To plot, scheme, and seize positions not prepared for you is another. Actions such as this can only be considered renegade and self-willed. This was the position of the wayward angels, with Lucifer, their chief visionary.

When the mother of the sons of Zebidee requested of Jesus a favor: that her two sons might sit, one on His right side and the other on His left. Jesus told her that these positions were for those whom it was prepared by the Father. Matt. 20:23 *to sit on my right hand, and on my left, is not mine to give, but it shall be given to them for whom it is prepared of my Father...* Jesus is of a different Spirit than the spirit of the attitude found in Lucifer and his cohorts.

What I wish to say in this is that with all the revelation these angels had received, they did not understand that the crucifixion of Jesus Christ was the Father's plan from the beginning of time – and not their own. This revelation was to come later. These angels thought by getting rid of Jesus, they would be able to assume the positions they coveted. Jesus communicated their thinking in a parable. The key statement from this parable is as follows: Mark 12:7 *But those husbandmen said among themselves, This is the heir; come, let us kill him. and the inheritance shall be ours.* By opposing God's plan they actually served to fulfill it!

It was not that the Father was refraining from communicating his plans about Jesus. He did. However, Lucifer who became Satan and his cohorts were isolated from fellowship. They were no longer in the light. They could no longer distinguish truth from fantasy. The writings of one confused man seemed no different from the fantasies of another. When Isaiah wrote his book by the Holy Spirit, it was not until the resurrection of the Lord Jesus Christ that they comprehended that the book he wrote was the Word of God. They certainly did not understand the symbolism contained in the books of Moses. If they understood what they were doing, they would not have crucified the Lord of Glory.

Let's look at some of Isaiah's writings to examine how clear were the declared intentions of God: Is. 53:1 *Who hath believed our report? and to whom is the arm of the Lord revealed?* Is. 53:2 *For he [the Lord Jesus Christ] shall grow up before him as a tender plant, and as a root out of a dry ground: he hath no form nor comeliness; and when we shall see him, there is no beauty that we should desire him.* Is. 53:3 *He is despised and rejected of men; a man of sorrows, and acquainted with grief: and we hid as it were our faces from him; he was despised, and we esteemed him not.* Is. 53:4 *Surely he hath borne our griefs, and carried our sorrows: yet we did esteem him stricken, smitten of God, and afflicted.* Is. 53:5 *But he was wounded for our transgressions, he was bruised for our iniquities: the chastisement of our peace was upon him; and with his stripes we are healed.* Is. 53:6 *All we like sheep have gone astray; we have turned every one to his own way; and the Lord hath laid on him the iniquity of us all.* Is. 53:7 *He was oppressed, and he was afflicted, yet he opened not his mouth: he is brought as a lamb to the slaughter, and as a sheep before her shearers is dumb, so he openeth not his mouth.* Is. 53:8 *He was taken from prison and from judgment: and who shall declare his generation? for he was cut off out of the land of the living: for the transgression of my people was he stricken.* Is. 53:9 *And he made his grave with the wicked, and with the rich in his death; because he had done no violence neither was any deceit in his mouth.* Is. 53:10 *Yet it pleased the Lord to bruise him; he hath put him to grief: when thou shalt make his soul an offering for sin, he shall see his seed, he shall prolong his days, and the pleasure of the Lord shall prosper in his hand.* Is. 53:11 *He shall see of the travail of his soul, and shall be satisfied: by his knowledge shall my righteous servant justify many; for he shall bear their iniquities.* Is. 53:12 *Therefore will I divide him a portion with the great, and he shall divide the spoil with the strong; because he hath poured out his soul unto death: and he was numbered with the transgressors; and he bare the sin of many, and made intercession for the transgressors. . .*

There we have it! A powerful passage of the plans of the Father. These plans are clearly laid out in detail about the birth, life, death, and resurrection of the Lord Jesus Christ. This passage declares that it "pleased the Lord to bruise him" and to "make his soul an offering for sin." There is a difference between making predictions and making plans. The Father's predestination of the Lord Jesus Christ is clearly declared in the scriptures.

Many people have a lot of difficulty with the idea of predestination. One of the first things these well meaning people object to is the idea that God had anything to do with tragedy, illness, wicked leaders or other perceived evil. Yet, we have just read that it "pleased the Lord to bruise" the Lord Jesus Christ. It pleased the Father to make innocent Jesus a sacrifice for sin. Jesus suffered real pain by the hands of wicked and cruel hearted people. Jesus' death was not instantaneous and merciful, but slow and by torture. He was despised. He was lonely. He suffered from rejection. He experienced deep grief. Search the gospels and epistles. You will find no record of Jesus laughing or smiling. This is not to say that He walked around with a long face. The scriptures clearly state that He was "a man of sorrows, and acquainted with grief: and we hid as it were our faces from him;. . ." In spite of His inner feelings, Jesus did rejoice and considered it all joy to do the Father's will. It was the Father Who placed Jesus in this situation; a situation which He knew from the beginning of time would cause Him to suffer grievously. If Jesus was given up to suffer by the hand of wicked people, do you think that there is any person in this world that is more loved of the Father than Him?

Look at what Jesus said of calamities and evil that were scheduled to occur: Matt. 24:6 *And ye shall hear of wars and rumors of wars: see that ye be not troubled: for all these things must come to pass, but the end is not yet. Matt. 24:7 For nation shall rise against nation, and kingdom against kingdom: and there shall be famines, and pestilences, and earthquakes, in diverse places.* Matt. 24:8 *All these are the beginning of sorrows.* Matt. 24:9 *Then shall they deliver you up to be afflicted, and shall kill you: and ye shall be hated of all nations for my name's sake. . .* In the words of Jesus, "these things must come to pass." Everyone should understand that the Lord does not use words loosely. This word "must" is a key word in this passage of scripture. It means that these events were set to occur and could not be changed.

We have talked a little about prayer. Prayer is important and is part of our laboring with the Father. However, no amount of prayer will alter what the Father has planned. A beast when it is injured may lash out aggressively at anyone trying to help it because it does not comprehend the efforts of the one trying to help. As much as it is difficult to understand, evil has its purpose and place in the world. This does not mean that we embrace evil, but we need to understand that if it did not have a function in this age, God would have eliminated it.

Look at what Jesus said about evil: Matt. 5:39 *But I say unto you, That ye resist not evil: but whosoever shall smite thee on thy right cheek, turn to him the other also. . .* This statement seems to go against the grain. But we need to understand what our Lord is telling us. Evil has work to accomplish. It has brought each and every believer to the realization of their need of a savior. Evil provides a contrast so that light can be distinguished from darkness. It also has works to manifest and fruit to be tasted which teach us all about the necessity to be loyal and affirmative observers of God's Word. If evil was eliminated in this world now, it would negate the plan of salvation. For our own edification, I have listed the ways the word "evil" in this scripture is translated elsewhere in the bible: bad , crime, envious, envy, evil one, evil things, malignant, more evil, more wicked, vicious, what is evil, wicked, worthless. The Father does have a plan to eliminate evil. That plan is the Lord Jesus Christ. 1 John 3:8 *He that committeth sin is of the Devil; for the Devil sinneth from the beginning. For this purpose the Son of God was manifested, that he might destroy the works of the Devil. . .*

The works of evil must be destroyed from within each and

every one of us. Destroying evil on the outside cannot eliminate evil from this world, because it comes from within and manifests without. Thus, it is impossible to eliminate evil on the outside without first eliminating its root within the heart of man. If you destroy the root, the plant will die. How simple and pure a plan. And yet, there is so much resistance to the truth from the would be dragon slayers. Instead of pointing at evil all around, each one of us must instead deal with the issues within us. Jesus said this, Luke 6:41 *And why beholdest thou the mote that is in thy brother's eyes but perceivest not the beam that is in thine own eye?* Luke 6:42 *Either how canst thou say to thy brother, Brother, let me pull out the mote that is in thine eye, when thou thyself beholdest not the beam that is in thine own eye? Thou hypocrite, cast out first the beam out of thine own eye, and then shalt thou see clearly to pull out the mote that is in thy brother's eye...* This "beam" corresponds to the evil I am writing about.

Thus, everything in this present world is designed to teach us about ourselves. Those destined to understand their need, accept Jesus Christ; He is the only solution and salvation provided to us by the Father. Those who reject Jesus Christ are destined to become an example to all throughout the ages yet to come.

Lamb Slain from the Foundation of the World

We have already read about Abel's offering, which was the first of its kind which pleased the Father because the revelation of the Lord Jesus Christ was manifest within it. And we saw that the scriptures support the understanding that the future crucifixion of the Lord Jesus was set to occur even before the foundation. 1 Pet. 1:20 *Who [the Lord Jesus Christ] verily was foreordained before the Foundation of the world, but was manifest in these last times for you,...*

We read in the Book of Revelation the following scripture: Rev. 13:8 *And all that dwell upon the earth shall worship him, whose names are not written in the book of life of the Lamb slain from the foundation of the world...* What the apostle Peter is saying and what this scripture is saying is basically the same with one difference. What was foreordained for the Lord Jesus to suffer was known only to the Father and to our preincarnate Christ. Abel's offering and those which followed were the enfolding of the revelation of a future ordained event – the crucifixion of the Lord Jesus Christ. Over and over again, the Father repeated this central theme, "the innocent dying in the place of the guilty," as the acceptable sacrifice. No example of predestination is more fully demonstrated than the Father's plan to offer His only begotten Son Jesus as the perfect sacrifice to suffer the penalty of death as a substitute for we who are guilty.

Was God's plan a secret? No. However, as is common, we fail miserably at understanding what He is communicating. We read earlier of a passage form Isaiah (verses 53: 1 – 12), in which the sacrifice of the Lord Jesus is spelled out in great detail. With everything God does, there is a danger of seeing without understanding. Luke 8:10 *And he said, Unto you it is given to know the mysteries of the kingdom of God: but to others in parables; that seeing they might not see, and hearing they might not understand. . .* Our heart must be right in the eyes of our Lord. It is He Who makes the decision to give us all understanding; otherwise we, too, can see without truly seeing and hear without truly hearing. Jesus said, "Blessed are the pure in heart, for they shall see God." Some people think that this means sometime in the future. But Jesus meant that we can see God now, today, at this moment.

Abraham's Symbolic Sacrifice of Issac

I am purposely skipping over Noah's sacrifice of the "clean animals" after the flood because I wish not to diverge into discussing the meaning of clean animals. Therefore, the next truly notable figure we see is Abraham. Abraham marks the beginning of an expansion of the Lord's purposes with regard to justification by faith. God began to communicate clearly of the type of relationship which He sought and what was pleasing to Him. This relationship is based upon pure faith. Even in the realm of the relations between people, faith is an essential ingredient for trust. In our relations, we go to great lengths to create faith in the forms of escarole accounts, performance bonds, legal documents with penalty clauses, and so forth. Faith is the essential agreement to build relationships and societies. There can be no positive working relationship between anyone without having faith in them that they will do what they say. This is true between God and man. Mutual coexistence is not faith.

The Lord Jesus Christ is the Father's "performance bond" that He will do exactly what He has promised. Those who lived before the birth of Jesus knew only that certain acts were acceptable. They acted in obedience to what the Father had revealed to them as evidence of the faith. These acts were open revelation about Christ Jesus.

In the following scriptures, the obedience of the patriarch Abraham displays clear revelations of the predestined sacrifice of Christ. Gen. 22:2 *And he [the Lord God Jehovah] said, Take now thy son, thine only son Isaac, whom thou lovest, and get thee into the land of Moriah; and offer him there for a burnt offering upon one of the mountains which I will tell thee of.* Gen. 22:7 *And Isaac spake unto Abraham his father, and said, My father: and he said, Here am I, my son. And he said, Behold the fire and the wood: but where is the lamb for a burnt offering?* Gen. 22:8 *And Abraham said, My son, God Will provide himself a lamb for a burnt offering: so they went both of them together.* Gen. 22:9 *And they came to the place which God had told him of; and Abraham built an altar there, and laid the wood in order, and bound Isaac his son, and laid him on the altar upon the wood.* Gen. 22:10 *And Abraham stretched forth his hand, and took the knife to slay his son.* Gen. 22:11 *And the angel of the Lord called unto him out of heaven, and said, Abraham, Abraham: and he said, Here am I.* Gen. 22:12 *And he said, Lay not thine hand upon the lad, neither do thou anything unto him: for now I know that thou fearest God, seeing thou hast not withheld thy son, thine only son from me.* Gen. 22:13 *And Abraham lifted up his eyes, and looked, and behold behind him a ram caught in a thicket by his horns: and Abraham went and took the ram, and offered him up for a burnt offering in the stead of his son.*

This account in Genesis, which occurred about 2,000 years

prior to the birth of the Lord Jesus Christ, is so clear that it requires almost no comment. The Father foretold His intention to sacrifice His beloved only begotten Son, as the sacrifice He Himself would provide in our place. Think about this. Again, this passage is not a prediction of events which followed; it is an informative statement of things planned. We will look at another area in which the Lord Jesus Christ was symbolically sacrificed repeatedly for about 1,400 years before examining some other interesting facts.

The Sacrifice of Jesus Established in the Law

Deut. 21:23 *His body shall not remain all night upon the tree, but thou shalt in any wise bury him that day; for he that is hanged [on a tree] is accursed of God; that thy land be not defiled, which the Lord thy God giveth thee for an inheritance. . .* The apostle Paul, referring to the same scripture, makes a point of this truth to the early church. Gal. 3:13 *Christ hath redeemed us from the curse of the law, being made a curse for us: for it is written, Cursed is every one that hangeth on a tree. . .*

What was the sole purpose of this statement being placed in the law? Why was this statement in the midst of the law of Moses? This statement is a demonstration of the provision and forethought of God. This statement is written for our sake. The Father set in order the framework to lay upon Jesus the sins of all who look upon Jesus in faith. Faith is what it takes to appropriate the sacrifice of Christ and begin a new life. Although Jesus died in the place of us all, His sacrifice cannot be applied to anyone who rejects the promise of the Father.

Let me show you what I'm talking about from the scriptures. Num. 21:8 *And the Lord said unto Moses, Make thee a fiery serpent, and set it upon a pole: and it shall come to pass, that every one that is bitten when he looketh upon it, shall live.* Num. 21:9 *And Moses made a serpent of brass, and put it upon a pole, and it came to pass, that if a serpent had bitten any man, when he beheld the serpent of brass, he lived. Those who looked upon it lived: those who refused, died. . .* This brass serpent set upon a pole is a symbolic picture of the Lord Jesus Christ – God's plan from the very beginning. Faith appropriates the power of God unto salvation. Only those who looked upon the serpent lived. This is because these people put faith in the plan of salvation provided to them by Jehovah. The Lord had painted a clear picture of things to come. As it was true then, it is true today. Although the saving grace contained in the crucifixion of the Lord Jesus Christ is provided to all mankind, it is only those who look to Him for salvation who will receive this power into their lives. Those who refuse to look upon the Lord Jesus Christ in faith as the "fiery serpent" in the wilderness will die in their sins.

John 1:12 *But as many as received him, to them save he power to become the sons of God, even to them that believe on his name:*. . . The plan of God has never changed. Some say that the plan has changed. But it hasn't. God spoke His thoughts over and over again in symbolism and by the prophets. All the promises and symbolism Jehovah put forth was a call to respond by faith. All this revolved around relationship.

The Lord freely justified those who believed Him. He did so because of their faith – faith in what God told them. Complete understanding was never an issue. Trust is. It is the type of faith to which He responds without failure. King David, when he had experienced a lifetime of harrowing situations, came to the place where he stated with satisfaction and joy, Ps. 37:25 *I have been young, and now am old; yet have I not seen the righteous forsaken, nor his seed begging bread.*

Yet the entire Old Testament is layer upon layer of preparation for the revelation of the only begotten man (Son) He had planned to come forth in His own image, the Lord Jesus Christ. This He stated clearly in Genesis: Gen. 1:26 *And God said, Let us make man in our image, after our likeness.* . . We today are also part of that revelation as part of the body of Christ. The Lord Jesus is the head of that body. The Father has only one begotten Son. Either you are part of Him or you will never be conformed into His very image. All this the Father had planned from the very beginning.

Jesus Sacrificed in the Law

To talk about everything written about the sacrifice of Christ in the Law, I would need to write an entire book and would not be able to fully discuss everything that is implied. Therefore, sufficient here will be to state that all the animals sacrificed in the rituals contained in the Law pertain to Christ Jesus. First, the animal chosen had to be perfect; that is without defect or blemish:

Ex. 12:5 *Your lamb shall be without blemish, a male of the first year: ye shall take it out from the sheep, or from the goats:*... Ex. 29:1 *Take one young bullock and two rams without blemish,*... Lev. 1:3 *a burnt sacrifice of the herd, let him offer a male without blemish:*... Lev. 1:10 *a male without blemish*... Lev. 3:1 *a sacrifice of peace offering, a male or female, without blemish before the Lord*... Lev. 4:3 *If the priest that is annointed do sin, then let him bring for his sin, a young bullock without blemish unto the Lord for a sin offering*... Lev. 4:23 *a kid of the goats, a male without blemish:*... *Lev. 4:28 a kid of the goats, a female without blemish,*... Lev. 4:32 *a lamb for a sin offering, he shall bring it a female without blemish*...

Each one of the above offerings refers to the ultimate sacrifice of the Lord Jesus Christ and has a particular meaning. It would be interesting to discuss the differences and the facets of the revelations contained in the various animals. For our purposes, it is sufficient that we see Christ Jesus. Each type of sacrifice contains a revelation of Jesus Christ and our relationship to the Father. Each sacrifice speaks of the provisions He has made for us. Actually, it was the Father in Jesus reconciling the world unto Himself. Remember Abraham's statement to Isaac (Gen. 22:8): ...*God will Provide himself a lamb for a burnt offering.* The plan and salvation of the Father was laid out in these sacrifices. They all refer to the future sacrifice of Jesus. It goes without saying that each one of us may also be called upon to follow in His footsteps. It may be necessary to suffer at times according to the will of the Father.

In every case, the sacrifice of necessity had to be "without blemish." God would not accept just any sacrifice; it had to be perfect. The exchange for sin had to be a trade-up. God would not be robbed by receiving that which was not worth much in exchange for His graces. God's graces are of inestimable value. Anyone trying to pawn off on God something flawed was, in essence, trying to cheat Him by receiving that which was not flawed in exchange. If God was to be gracious, then He would be gracious, but no one would take from Him by subtlety. Therefore, every sacrifice had to be "without blemish."

However, symbolism itself is not enough to please God forever. He is interested in the real thing; the substance behind the symbolism. Isaiah prophesied this very thought. Is. 63:5 *And I looked, and there was none to help; and I wondered that there was none to uphold: therefore mine own arm brought salvation unto me; and my fury, it upheld me.* John the Baptist, filled with the revelation of God because of the Holy Spirit which dwelt within him, understood God's thoughts. Therefore, he prophesied when he saw Jesus. John 1:29 *The next day John seeth Jesus coming unto him, and saith, Behold the Lamb of God, which taketh away the sin of the world. . .*

The gist of the entire law made one thing clear. Without the shedding of blood, there was no remission of sin (Heb. 9:22). If you reject the blood sacrifice or do not have a blood sacrifice, you have no forgiveness of your sins. Without the blood sacrifice, your relationship with the Father is not based upon forgiveness. Religion without the blood sacrifice may make you feel good, but it is devoid of salvation. Jesus Christ is our blood sacrifice to everyone who looks to Him in faith. This is exactly what God revealed through Moses in the account of the brass serpent on the pole. The Lord Jesus Christ is that brass serpent.

Resurrection

Jesus referred to His resurrection while fulfilling His earthly ministry. It may not seem extraordinary to predict one's death, but it is another matter to state openly that you would not remain there. One of His first references to this resurrection was telling His disciples that as the prophet Jonah was in the belly of the fish three days and three nights, He also would remain the same amount of time in the grave (Luke 11:29, Matt. 12:40). Two things are evident here. First, that this is a planned event. The second, is that this had been planned long before Jesus stated it openly. This is the reason Jonah spent this precise time in the fish and the symbolism that he had to sacrifice himself in the sea (symbolic of the world) to save the lives of those in the ship which bore him.

But this was not the only reference Jesus made toward His death and resurrection. He also spoke of destroying the temple and rebuilding it in three days (John 2:18-21). It is evident that the people listening to Him heard His words, but did not understand what He was telling them. At the mock trial before sentencing Him to crucifixion, He was accused of stating that He would destroy the temple and rebuild it in three days (Matt. 26:61). In this, the Father was speaking clearly through His Son Jesus, but no one understood what He was telling them. Even at the crucifixion, those passing by shook their heads and repeated this same saying, challenging Him to save himself. Again, this demonstrates so clearly that people can listen intently, remember what was spoken, but not understand a word of anything they heard. This pattern of hearing without understanding or seeing, without grasping the significance, was demonstrated repeatedly throughout the Old Testament in the lives of the prophets and the entire body of the scriptures; it is also true today.

In the face of all this, we are asked not to judge anything prematurely. The Lord knows those who are His. So many denominations, and those claiming not to be denominations, tell their followers that only their group will be saved. They claim that they alone know the truth and all the rest of the believers are to be lost because they do not believe exactly the same way. This lie in the midst of the truth they bear does not come from the Lord Jesus Christ; it is from the fallen angel presiding over the group. It is in an effort by this angel to preserve a membership in order to have a group to present to the Lord as a token to regaining His favor at Judgment Day. These fallen angels know full well that the Lord has committed their judgment to us (1 Cor. 6:3). Not all religious groups have the central theme of salvation through our Lord Jesus

Christ. In these instances, it can only be concluded that the spirit behind this religion, denomination, sect or order has no desire to attain favor with the Lord Jesus. All those who reject Jesus in their worship of the father are doomed to exclusion (1 Cor. 16:22, 1 John 2:23), whether they be man or angel.

There is something else about foreknowledge in Jesus' statements that I wish to communicate. John 2:19 *Jesus answered and said unto them, "Destroy this temple, and in three days I will raise it up."* John 2:18 *Then answered the Jews and said unto him, "What sign showest thou unto us, seeing that thou doest these things?"* John 2:19 *Jesus answered and said unto them, "Destroy this temple, and in three days I will raise it up."* John 2:20 *Then said the Jews, "Forty and six years was this temple in building, and wilt thou rear it up in three days?"* John 2:21 *But he spake of the temple of his body.* The thought and concept of the Body of Christ, with Jesus as the Head of that body, was being communicated to all. The problem is no one understood a word He was saying until years later. This fact is clearly demonstrated by the witness brought against Him at His trial. Look at what they quoted Him as saying: Mark 14:58 *We heard him say, "I will destroy this temple that is made with hands, and within three days I will build another made without hands."*

Jesus was also speaking about His body, those believers born again as a result of His resurrection. This body of believers, justified and purified by His blood sacrifice, would become the sanctified "temple of God." This also was the sign of which He spoke of to those who questioned Him (John 2:18). By this, they shall know that you are My disciples, "by your love for each other." Everywhere we look today we see the sign of which Jesus spoke. The church which was raised up and built without hands is filling the whole earth. Contained within the church is the dwelling place of God by His Spirit. Thus, the church is the body of Christ and is the "temple of God" on this earth.

This sign spoken by the Lord Jesus Christ was not a prediction of the future, but a statement of the plans of the Father. God does not predict the future; He creates it! This is a simple statement.

Yet, how many there are who struggle with this reality. Jacob's ladder is such a visual picture of the understanding of those obtaining salvation (Gen. 28:12). The ladder reaches from earth to heaven, indicating levels as rungs starting from ground zero to the full height. To get a clear picture of this ladder, I want you to visualize the earth as a dark place and heaven as being very bright and full of light. The ladder extends from darkness into progressively brighter and brighter light until, at the top rung, is fullness of light. Those on the earth are walking around in darkness. But those on the ladder ascending it are coming into more and more light as they climb upwards.

We have a vivid, symbolic representation of the benefits of increasing understanding and growth in the Lord Jesus Christ. Those at the bottom of the ladder have little understanding; there is still quite a bit of darkness. Those at the higher rungs of the same ladder see things that are not seen by them on the lower rungs or see things hard to visualize because the light of their understanding is dim. Jesus, in His earthly ministry, wanted to talk of heavenly things, but knew that they were beyond those to whom He was ministering (John 3:12). And so it is true today!

The apostle Paul put it slightly differently, but was stating the same thought. If a person has little knowledge, spiritually speaking, he is a babe in understanding. These people, as natural babies and young children, need milk and food easily digestible. Otherwise, their immature digestive system will reject or simply not digest what is fed to them (1 Cor. 3:2, Heb. 5:12-13, 1 Pet. 2:2).

Upon This Rock I Will Build My Church

When Jesus questioned His disciples about who they thought He was, Simon answered Him correctly (Matt. 16:13-19): *"Thou art the Christ, the Son of the living God."* This correct statement earned him a new name, "Peter," which means little rock. This name began to symbolize the larger truth, the "Rock" or foundation for the future church. When Jesus stated: "upon this rock, I will build My church," He was not stating that He would make Peter the first Pope, as some have construed. This confession of revelation which Peter had stated is the basis for everything Jesus wanted to accomplish. Without the revelation that Jesus is the Christ, the Son of God, there can be no beginning in the Kingdom of God. What was true then, is true today. Jesus is the cornerstone of our faith; this is seen clearly to most.

What is not seen clearly, and is a mystery to many, is the next thing Jesus told them, "the gates of hell shall not prevail against My church." Jesus is not stating a prophesy of a prediction of the future. He is telling His disciples about a planned event – the church. God could have told Noah, "The waters of the flood will not prevail against the ark I commissioned you to build;" it would mean the same thing. God ordained the flood. God ordained the ark. Both are ordained by Jehovah. Both are under His control. Both exist because they fulfill His purposes. The flood swept away an evil unbelieving generation; the ark preserved His faithful chosen. Today, hell, in the same way, sweeps away an evil unbelieving generation and the church is the ordained ark of salvation to those fleeing the waters of destruction.

Do you see that this is the same? You do not need to worry. If you put your trust in God through the Lord Jesus Christ, you will be saved. Yes, you should fear. But who or what do you fear? Jesus said that we should fear Him Who after He has killed, also has the power to cast into hell (Luke 12:5). God alone has that power. God controls both sides of the coin. If you please Him, who can be against you? It may be hard to comprehend, but even the Devil would bless you if the Father so ordered. There exists no angel, man or power that can hold back the hand of Jehovah from accomplishing exactly what He pleases. God has the power to watch over you and keep you safe, if that is His plan for your life. The Father wishes to be all things to you. Why don't you let Him into your life? Anyone who turns his life over to God through the Lord Jesus Christ will not regret it.

I am the Alpha and the Omega

This says it all: Rev. 1:8 *"I am the Alpha and the Omega," says the Lord God, "who is and who was and who is to come, the*

Almighty." We see the angel of God declaring as a spokesman to the apostle John that He is the beginning and the end. He is stating that He is the start and He is the finish. What He is communicating is that the power is with Him to create exactly what He planned from the beginning; and that the end will be exactly as He set it out to be. There is no chance implied here! There is no prediction of the future. We see a clear statement of fact from the vantage point of the Creator. Note that He states, "I am." He does not state "I was," nor does He state "I will be." This is very significant.

If I were to state to you that the past, the present, and the future all exist, you may be intrigued, but may dismiss the concept because it is difficult to grasp. Yet, from the Father's position, all things were complete from the beginning. Nothing will be one iota different than what He created. Look at what the apostle Paul writes: Heb. 4:3 *For we which have believed do enter into rest, as he said, As I have sworn in my wrath, if they shall enter into my rest: although the works were finished from the foundation of the world. . .* If you check out the other translations, you will see the same thought being communicated. Notice that it states that the works "were finished." It could have read "were started" or "were began," but it distinctly states that the "works were finished."

Why can we "enter into [His] rest"? Because all is already finished! The real problem is that we do not grasp the concept and, therefore, work so hard to make things happen. Does this mean that we do nothing? Not at all. Then what is our position if the future, like the past, is already set?

Entering into God's rest is a matter of understanding. It does not mean that we do nothing. Jesus worked the works of the Father. He said that He did nothing of Himself. Let's look at the scripture to which I am referring. John 5:19 *Then answered Jesus and said unto them, "Verily, verily, I say unto you, The Son can do nothing of himself, but what he seeth the Father do: for what things soever he doeth, these also doeth the Son likewise. . ."* If Jesus could do nothing of Himself, neither can you. With us, the Father is looking for our cooperation. He seeks for us to join in with Him, as does the Lord Jesus. If you can see that the works are already finished "from the foundation of the world," then while you work, you will have peace, and rest in the understanding that God rules always and at all times. Calamities may arise, but even calamities are not without purpose.

Jesus said that when we pray, we need to understand that we posses that for which we pray, and in due time, it will be manifest (Mark 11:24). We can possess only what the Father has planned and ordained; remember what Jesus said in John 5:19. See how Jesus prayed when He raised Lazarus from the grave: John 11:42 *"And I knew that Thou hearest Me always; but because of the people standing around I said it, that they may believe that Thou didst send Me."* John 11:41 *And so they removed the stone. And Jesus raised His eyes, and said, "Father, I thank Thee that Thou heardest Me..."* Jesus prayed out loud for the sake of the observing people. He already knew that it was the Father's will for Lazarus to be raised from the dead. This is clearly seen in that He used the past tense of "hearest" in the scripture saying, "Thou heardest." Jesus had sought the Father beforehand and knew His will. Therefore, knowing Jehovah's will, Jesus had perfect faith to pray in this manner before the people and had full assurance of receiving Lazarus from the grave.

Jesus' Suffering and Ours is According to the Will of the Father

It is not true that Jesus never struggled with everything around Him. There were many things that He had a mind to do or change which were not the Father's will to do or change. We, like our wonderful Lord, are surrounded daily with the same obstacles and temptations. Jesus is the Father's pattern. The Father brought the Lord Jesus through all the obstacles. Today, with the help of our Lord, the Father, by His Spirit, will bring us through all difficulties, as He also did Jesus. The Father had determined in the very beginning that you and I make it through all difficulties. This does not mean that you will not suffer. It is probably not possible to live in this world without suffering. Suffering is part of the creative process to make you into what He has determined from the beginning. The "omega" in the process is the image of God (Gen. 1:20), to be as our master, the Lord Jesus Christ (Luke 6:40).

Look at what it says of our Lord Jesus: Heb. 5:7 *Who in the days of his flesh, when he had offered up prayers and supplications with strong crying and tears unto him that was able to save him from death, and was heard in that he feared;* Heb. 5:8 *Though he were a Son, yet learned he obedience by the things which he suffered;* Heb. 5:9 *And being made perfect, he became the author of eternal salvation unto all them that obey him;. . .*

I want us to stop here and take a close look at these scriptures. Too often the Lord Jesus is portrayed as not having much difficulty with the fleshly side of Him. This picture is simply not true. Jesus was a man of strong passions and desires. The passions and desires of His flesh were so strong that they were of great concern to Him. He understood early on that He of His own power was not able to overcome the baser side of Him inherited from His mother Mary. What I am stating may be a shock to some because they do not see our Lord identifying with us in all things. Yet the proof of what I am stating is contained in the fact that "He offered up prayers and supplication to Him with strong crying and tears. . ." No one prays with that kind of passion for casual needs! Jesus knew that He would be swept away by His fleshly desires without help, swept away to the point of failure. Righteous living and abstinence from sin is a gift to mankind by Jehovah. It is not attainable by one's own efforts. It was not attainable to the Lord Jesus without grace and power from the Father. The scripture states He "was heard [the prayers were answered] in that He feared. . ." .

What things Jesus suffered to learn obedience is a matter of speculation. (Heb. 5:8 *Though he were a Son, yet learned he obedience by the things which he suffered.*) These specific "things" are not important. The point being made is that we must all learn two things. First, the ability to overcome is not within our own strength. Look at what the apostle Paul writes: 1 Cor. 10:12 *Therefore let him who thinks he stands take heed lest he fall. . .* The fall from grace of which the apostle is writing is assured if your attitude and understanding needs adjustment and enlightenment. The fall that this person experiences comes because of self-righteous thinking. It should not be viewed as punishment, but a creative act of Jehovah in order to teach the proud individual an important truth. By grace, you have been saved through faith (Eph. 2:8), and not of ourselves; it is a gift of God. If we do not understand this simple truth, our fall is ordained. Forces will be brought into our lives until we gain understanding. When we gain this understanding through the creative work of the Father, humility is a matter of our hearts and has become more than just a doctrine.

We can see in our Lord Jesus the understanding that the ability to stand and the gift of righteousness is from the Father. From a human point of view, most people would agree that the Lord Jesus Christ had a right to call Himself good. We hear people all the time say things like, this or that person is good. Yet note what Jesus says when someone calls Him good. Matt. 19:16 *And, behold, one came and said unto him, "Good Master, what good thing shall I do, that I may have eternal life?"* Matt. 19:17 *And he said unto him, "Why callest thou me good? there is none good but one, that is, God: but if thou wilt enter into life, keep the commandments. . ."* (see also Mark 70:18, Luke 18:19.) Jesus understood that it was the power of the Father which kept Him from falling (why else do you think He prayed with strong crying and tears to be delivered from temptation?); you and I need to understand the same thing. Righteousness is a gift from Jehovah. Jesus did not forget this for one moment; neither should we.

The second point is hinged upon the first point. We have need of obedience to inherit the blessings of the Father. A bunch of self-willed barbarians will not inherit the kingdom God has placed under Jesus. The Father has a kingdom for the rebellious and those who have no heart for His Word called the Kingdom of Darkness. Although our Father rules over both kingdoms (He is God to all), all of us must be translated out of the Kingdom of Darkness into the Kingdom of the Lord Jesus Christ (the Kingdom of Light) by a creative act of God (Col. 1:13).

Some people struggle with the idea that the Father rules over both the Kingdom of Darkness and the Kingdom of Light. It is easy to comprehend the Father ruling in the kingdom of His Son Jesus, but most people see the kingdom of darkness as nothing but a collection of rebels. It is true that the latter kingdom is a collection of rebellious spirits. However, to suggest that there is no order in this kingdom is without foundation. Jesus acknowledged this order when He was accused of casting out devils by the Beelzebub, the prince of devils (Matt. 12:24). Jesus said that no kingdom divided against itself could stand. He went on to explain that if Satan's kingdom were divided, it would not stand. Matt. 12:26 *"And if Satan cast out Satan, he is divided against himself; how shall then his kingdom stand?"* There is an authority and power structure in the kingdom of darkness to maintain hierarchy.

The apostle Paul, knowing the authority in the Kingdom of Darkness, proposed turning a rebellious Christian over to Satan for him to learn to choose the ways of the Kingdom of the Lord Jesus Christ (1 Cor. 5:5). How could this man be turned over? There is an authority structure to receive him! Furthermore, as far as Jehovah ruling over both kingdoms, read the following scriptures: Deut. 10:14 *Behold, the heaven and the heaven of heavens is the Lord's thy God, the earth also, with all that therein is. . .* The word "all" is stated clearly. You may not grasp the significance of this scripture, but it is fact. Another translation phrases it this way: Deut. 10:14 *"Behold, to the Lord your God belong heaven and the highest heavens, the earth and all that is in it. . ."* This is why Jehovah can translate (transfer) someone from the "power of darkness" into the Kingdom of His Son, because He has authority and power over both!

Salvation, for every man who ever lived, is by grace. Without the Father's favor, failure is an inevitability. Therefore, understanding that it is all by grace, where does obedience enter into the picture? There are two types of suffering: suffering according to the will of God because you are doing His will and suffering according to the will of God because you are committing wrongful acts. If you suffer according to the will of God, doing His will, there is contained within the suffering inner peace and provisions to sustain you. If you are suffering because of wrongful acts, the experience contains within it added dimensions of mental turmoil and loss, all designed to change your attitude and eliminate your pleasure and satisfaction in wrongful deeds. Thus, both sufferings are from the Father; however, the rewards are different. Willfully doing God's will brings us to experience riches and fullness of life. Matt. 19:17 *And he said unto him, Why Callest thou me good? there is none good but one, that is, God: but if thou wilt enter into life, keep the commandments...* Life emanates from the Father through Jesus Christ to us as a result of obtaining His favor. Jesus obtained the Father's favor by obedience unto crucifixion; therefore, God has highly exalted Him (Phil. 2:8-9).

Jesus, the Name the Father is Exalting

Jesus said that He could do nothing except the things he saw the Father was doing (John 5:19). The same is true for us. Today, the Father is exalting the name Jesus. If we exalt this name, we are flowing with the Father. Remember the account of Balaam (Num. 22:5 – 24:25). When he discovered that it was God's will to bless Israel, the prophesies flowed from his lips. There can be no power against anything the Father has planned. If power of opposition exists, there is a reason for it which agrees with the Father. All power emanates from God.

Why is the Ark of the Covenant and the articles of the Old Covenant, sacrifice and worship, missing? Why does not present day Israel have any legitimate stand in their Old Covenant faith? There can be no basis for Old Covenant worship unless everything is done according to tenant's of the Law governing worship. Let me explain further. The following is a list of scriptures for which a person will be cut off from relationship with God:

Ex. 12:15 *Seven days shall ye eat unleavened bread; even the first day ye shall put away leaven out of your houses: for whosoever eateth leavened bread from the first day until the seventh day, that soul shall be cut off from Israel.* Ex. 12:19 *Seven days shall there be no leaven found in your houses: for whosoever eateth that which is leavened, even that soul shall be cut off from the congre-*

gation of Israel, whether he be a stranger, or born in the land. Ex. 31:14 *Ye shall keep the Sabbath therefore; for it is holy unto you: every one that defileth it shall surely be put to death: for whosoever doeth army work therein, that soul shall be cut off from among his people.* Lev. 7:21 *Moreover the soul that shall touch any unclean thing, as the uncleanness of man, or any unclean beast, or any abominable unclean thing, and eat of the flesh of the sacrifice of peace offerings, which pertain unto the Lord, even that soul shall be cut off from his people.* Lev. 7:27 *Whatsoever soul it be that eateth any manner of blood, even that soul shall be cut off from his people.* Lev. 20:6 *And the soul that turneth after such as have familiar spirits! and after wizards, to go a whoring after them, I will even set my face against that soul, and will cut him off from among his people.* (This is palm readers psychics, tarot cards, and the like.) Lev. 20:18 *"If a man who lies with a menstruous woman and uncovers her nakedness, he has laid bare her flow, and she has exposed the flow of her blood; thus both of them shall be cut off from among their people.* Lev. 23:28 *And ye shall do no work in that same day: for it is a day of atonement, to make an atonement for you before the Lord your God.* Lev. 23:29 *For whatsoever soul it be that shall not be afflicted in that same day, he shall be cut off from among his people.* Num. 9:13 *But the man that is clean, and is not in a journey, and forbeareth to keep the passover, even the same soul shall be cut off from among his people: because he brought not the offering of the Lord in his appointed season, that man shall bear his sin.* Num. 15:29 *Ye shall have one law for him that sinneth through ignorance, both for him that is born among the children of Israel, and for the stranger that sojourneth among them.* (Those who sin in ignorance are still held responsible. The Law holds them accountable, but to a lesser degree than someone sinning defiantly. Though the sin may be considered less serious in our eyes, it still separates the person from God until it is accounted for in the manner prescribed in the Law.) Num. 15:30 *But the soul that doeth ought presumptuously, whether he be born in the land, or a stranger, the same reproacheth the Lord; and that soul shall be cut off from among his people.* Num. 15:31 *Because he hath despised the word of the Lord, and hath broken his commandment, that soul shall utterly be cut off, his iniquity shall be upon him.* Num. 19:20 *But the man that shall be unclean, and shall not purify himself, that soul shall be cut off from among the congregation, because he has defiled the sanctuary of the Lord: the water of separation hath not been sprinkled upon him; he is unclean.* Num. 19:21 *And it shall be a perpetual statute unto them, that he that sprinkleth the water of separation shall wash his clothes; and he that toucheth the water of separation shall be unclean until even.*

Any person "cut off" cannot have a relationship with Jehovah according to the Jewish faith. Once they are "cut off," they must satisfy the exact requirements of the "law" and the "covenant" in which they trust, or remain "cut off." I do not know of a single person (outside of the Lord Jesus Christ) who is innocent of violating this "law." Of these people who are "cut off," I do not know of any who have satisfied the requirements of the "law" to be reinstated. In today's world, it is not possible to practice Judaism "lawfully" by design of the Father. It is no accident that the articles of worship needed to fulfill the "law" in the natural have been removed from mankind. God has chosen to glorify His Son Jesus. There is no other name given under heaven by which we all must be saved. The Lord Jesus Christ fulfilled the requirements of the "law" for every person who looks to Him in faith. Thus, the Father is exalting the Lord Jesus Christ. He has removed from the Jews their articles of worship. God had made it impossible for the Jews to bypass Jesus.

Let's look at a few more scriptures: Deut. 16:16 *Three times in a year shall all thy males appear before the Lord thy God in the place which he shall choose; in the feast of unleavened bread, and in the feast of weeks, and in the feast of tabernacles: and they shall not appear before the Lord empty:. . .* Lev. 23:27 *Also on the tenth day of this seventh month there shall be a day of atonement: it shall be an holy convocation unto you; and ye shall afflict your souls, and offer an offering made by fire unto the Lord. . .*

If people are to celebrate Judaism, claiming to have a relationship with Jehovah according to the region based upon Mosaic tradition, they must in all points satisfy the requirements set forth by the "law" in which they base their stand. If these people violate the "law" in one point, then they are excluded from further worship until they satisfy the requirements set forth in the "law" for reinstatement. Today, anyone claiming to have a relationship with the Father based upon Mosaic traditions is based upon a lie. According to the very "law" in which they are basing their stand, they are "cut off."

Furthermore, the "law" states that anyone not keeping the law is under a curse (Duet 30:1-8). The rituals of purification and celebrating the Day of Atonement are not possible today outside of the Lord Jesus Christ. It is God's doing that articles of worship formed under the supervision of Moses have been removed permanently from the Jew's possession. To the confused, the removal of these sacred objects was the Devil's doing; to those enlightened, God the Father did this so that all people must look to His Son Jesus. Jesus is the fulfillment of these objects, therefore God hid them from human attention to direct all eyes toward Jesus.

Everything I am telling you here is a display of predestination. Jesus, before the foundation of the world, was to replace all natural things. His name is exalted and will continue to be exalted. The exaltation of the Lord Jesus Christ is not a result of the collection of many accidental occurrences. It is the plan of God.

Rev. 22:13 *"I am the Alpha and the Omega, the first and the last, the beginning and the end."* In this scripture, the Lord Jesus Christ is speaking about Himself and those in Him. Jesus is the beginning of the creation of God and He is the end. Jesus is also everything in between. That is to say that all things, everywhere, at all times through history, served a predetermined end. Jesus could have stated that He is every letter of the alphabet; this fact is implied by stating that "I am the Alpha and the Omega." Settle it in your heart; it is impossible for anyone of us to understand all things. Even the things which are horrible in our own eyes serve some purpose. Jesus is the end of the creation of God. The entire power of the Father is resident within Him! His image is the beginning; His image is the present pattern for our creation; and His image is the future of all within Him.

Why are things the way they are today if Jesus has all the power of the Father? Because it is not God's plan to do away with evil at this time in history. Accept the fact that even evil has a purpose in this present age, according to the plan of God. All power in heaven and earth is in the Lord Jesus Christ (Matt. 28:18). Jesus presently has this power. If He wanted (He has all power), He could bring this era to an end today! If it is not ending this moment, it would logically have to follow that He does not want it to end as of yet. Stop worrying so much and put your faith in the Lord Jesus Christ.

11
Prayer: Its Nature, Purpose, and Place in Our Lives

I've been asked, "If everything is predestined, why should I pray?" This is a good question, but it reflects a fundamental misunderstanding of our place in this age and our relationship with our Father. Many look at prayer similar to someone picking up a phone and ordering something to eat, or picking something out of a catalog and making a request. A lot of scriptures are quoted by those who promote this understanding. They say, "If you can believe in it, you can have it." This again is error. Let me assure you of one thing that must be the foundation of all things you desire in prayer; God will not give you anything apart from His will (1 John 5:14), and neither should you desire it. If the desire in your spirit is born of Him, then He also will supply you with the necessary faith to understand that you have the thing you request (Mark 11:24). This may sound strange, but I wish to reflect a fundamental reality of prayer.

Jehovah's Will is Immutable

If God were like man, changing His mind and His purpose, His word would be worthless to us. No promise ever made by Him would be reliable; none of us, man or angel, would have any security. Those who know Him have come to understand that this is not the case. We have strong security from the knowledge that once He has said something, we can rest with full assurance and peace of mind that He will not go back on His word. The most fundamental doctrine of our faith is that God does not change! How secure we are in this fact. Let's look at a couple of scriptures: Mal. 3:6 *For I am the Lord, I change not; therefore ye sons of Jacob are not consumed.* James 1:17 *Every good gift and every perfect gift is from above, and cometh down from the Father of lights, with whom is no variableness, neither shadow of turning.*

We need to approach prayer with this understanding. Prayer is entering into the will of God. Its very nature is to seek those things which are according to the plans and purposes of the Father. When we pray, we seek to be consciously one with God. Prayer is communion with God. If you pray without seeking His communion, then you are most probably praying amiss.

Our first concern is to seek the Father's mind. We know the mind of God by His Spirit which He has given to us who believe. If you have not God's Spirit, then you are not part of the Kingdom of the Lord Jesus Christ. If you do not belong to God through the Lord Jesus Christ, then you are part of the Kingdom of Darkness. If you are part of the Kingdom of Darkness, you have a different perspective toward God and prayer. You cannot know God without having His Spirit. Without God's Spirit, you are in darkness. If you are in darkness, you have no assurance that God hears your prayers because you do not have His mind. We have the mind of Christ if we are in communion with Him through the Lord Jesus Christ. The mind of Christ is to seek and know the Father's will, which is His pleasure to reveal to us by His Spirit. This may seem like a lot of double talk. However, this is the basis for asking according to the Will of God. God will not answer any prayer that is not according to His Will for your life or anyone else's.

Therefore, we see two principles arise from our discussion:

PRINCIPLE ONE: God is immutable. He cannot and will not change His mind.

PRINCIPLE TWO: Ask only according to God's will. Using the name of our Lord Jesus in prayer does not make the Father change His mind.

Agreement with God as a Way of Life

Seventeen or eighteen years ago, I had a vision as I knelt to pray. In an instance, I saw all the people of the world and could see their faces. A living darkness covered and clung to them, consuming their lives. The situation in the world was very grim. Problems around the globe were so many and so severe that government leaders' hearts were failing them and they could not come up with solutions. The situation around the world had reached a state where things were seemingly hopeless. In the midst of this sea of darkness, I saw individual sons of God. These were people who had been transformed through the work of the Holy Spirit in Christ Jesus.

These sons of God glowed like burning embers in a sea of darkness. The stage of world events was set for a needed change. Things could not go on as they were because the problems were too great. These "sons" went into abandoned church buildings (I believe is symbolic) and began to preach the very simple message, "Turn your life over to God." (There is only one way to do that; it is through the Lord Jesus Christ.)

Almost unanimously, people who heard this simple message complied. These people were then transformed into burning embers, just as the one who brought the simple message. They began to glow in the darkness. Every person obedient to this simple message was given supernatural solutions to his problems. The darkness literally rolled off them.

I also saw those who refused the message. The darkness clung to these people, almost like worms, consuming them unto destruction. There was no reprise and no escape from the darkness except to obey the simple message.

At the beginning of the vision, the "sons of God" appeared like stars shining in the night sky. The sea of darkness was interrupted by the light of the individual stars. As the message they carried was received, these sparks of light grew as a spark of fire spreads in a field of dry grass. This happened all over the world, so that what started as small embers of fire grew at a regular rate from small fires to progressively larger fires everywhere. This occurred in each place one of the "sons of God" was exposing the message. The fires grew at their borders until the boundaries of one fire reached the boundaries of adjacent fires – each fire progressing toward each other circumferentially until all the darkness was dispelled. When all the borders of the fires had spread fully and met with all the adjacent fires, there was no more darkness left in the earth. The earth was filled with Light.

I have shared this vision with you because it illustrates the point I wish to make. Agreement with Jehovah is a way of life. Agreement is not a wavering, inconsistent expression of conduct in order to get something. It is a way of life as a member of the Kingdom of the Lord Jesus Christ. We of the Kingdom of Light have a specific mentality. We are destined to be of the same mind as the Lord Jesus Christ. We need to think the way He thinks. This, for us, is a way of life.

Therefore, "If you ask anything according to His will, He hears us" (1 John 5:14). What is the purpose in God hearing you? What is the purpose in your request? Another word for God's will is "desire." Therefore, let's rephrase the statement: "If you ask anything according to His 'desire', He hears us." The word 'desire' is not as strong a statement as 'will,' therefore it is the most correct English in the translation. Nevertheless, the word 'desire' is used in one place in the scriptures in place of 'will.'

God's will is immutable and so is His desire. The Father always gets exactly what He desires. The desire and the will of the Father is the same. God will only do what He desires. What God desires from an eternal vantage point is always good. We now begin to see things more clearly. We could rephrase this same scripture, keeping in the same Spirit of communication to say: God will not honor any request which is contrary to His plans. The next principle, therefore, is:

PRINCIPLE THREE: Learn what is God's will and desire, as much as you are able, in everything. You will discover that anything you attempt beyond His will, is a waste of effort.

Enter into life, by living your life in agreement with God. Settle it in your heart beforehand, that in all things, it is your pleasure to do and live God's will as much as He reveals it to you. Accept the experiences of life as His perfect fingers, forming and molding you for a higher function. When He is finished with you, you will be unique and perfect for the purpose He has for you.

Selective Sight

Let's start with a question. When you look, what do you see? What we see is very important because we have a relation with our environment. Jesus said that if our eye was evil, our body would be full of darkness. Matt. 6:23 *But if thine eye be evil, thy whole body shall be full of darkness. If therefore the light that is in thee be darkness, how great is that darkness...* Two people can see the same thing and understand what they see differently. Some people only see the Devil at work all around, everywhere in the world. These people suffer greatly because the light they think they have is darkness. They, because of their lack of understanding, cannot comprehend why "a good God would allow such things to occur." Everywhere they glance, their eye does not have the ability to see the glory of Jehovah. These unfortunate people see a great struggle between good and evil, but incorrectly perceive God struggling to maintain order. I assure you that God does not struggle with anything. Jesus said "these things must first take place (Luke 21:9, 18);... do not let your hearts be troubled." (John 14:27)

The understanding heart sees things differently. If you see that God is in control and that He rules at all times, then you rest in the assurance that He has all things under control. Jesus said that even the hairs on your head are numbered and that a sparrow cannot fall to the ground without the Father's authority being involved (Matt. 10:29-30). Jesus is telling us to relax; the Father is in control. Therefore, we need to have singleness of sight. It is a mind filled with darkness that has an "evil eye." If you understand, your eyes see God everywhere. That is why Jesus is cautioning us to keep things in perspective. Matt. 6:22 *The light of the body is the eye: if therefore thine eye be single [clear], thy whole body shall be full of light.*

Look what King David said by the Holy Spirit: Ps. 16:8 *I have set the Lord always before me: because he is at my right hand, I shall not be moved...* Everywhere David looked, he saw Jehovah; he was not moved because of that. David saw, too, that not even a sparrow fell to the ground without God's authority. Today we have many people trapped in the deception that they see the Devil at work everywhere. This misconception is a form of misguided worship. These people credit the Devil for the work of God. Let me illustrate. Depending on your understanding, you could say that our Lord Jesus Christ was crucified by the Devil or by God. The scriptures clearly state that it is the Father Who sacrificed His Son. Jesus said He had the power to lay His life down and the power to take it back up again. Just because the Devil has a part in the works of God does not mean that he should be credited with the place of God. We are admonished to fear only Jehovah. If God says you can be touched, you will be touched. If God says that you are not to be touched, then no one can touch you. Settle it in your mind; God rules everywhere, at all times!

Saying all this, we come to the place where it becomes obvious that we need to have selective sight. Selective sight is the "single eye." We see all things from a Christian perspective, that is from the mind of Christ. Because of our relationship with our Lord Jesus, we walk in His footsteps. We see things the way He sees things. If we are having difficulties, which we all do, He leads us so that we can learn from our mistakes. We all make mistakes, fear and hate them; but, we all need them. We learn from the things we suffer. If we are very stubborn, we learn very slowly and end up suffering a little more. If we are teachable and love the Light, God can receive us as sons through Jesus Christ. The Father has a purpose for everything we experience. God is our maker; we do not make ourselves.

The ability to see or be blind is a gift from our Creator, our Father. We need to "selectively see" throughout our lives in service to God. We are blind and deaf to everything except what He wants us to see and hear. Note what is written in Isaiah. Is. 42:19 *Who is blind, but my servant? or deaf, as my messenger that I sent? who is blind as he that is perfect, and blind as the Lord's servant?* In another translation, it is stated this way: Is. 42:19 *Who is blind but My servant, Or so deaf as My messenger whom I send? Who is so blind as he that is at peace with Me, Or so blind as the servant of the Lord?* Therefore, being that we are blind and deaf to everything except to what God wants us to see and hear, our prayers need to be directed accurately.

Many times throughout our lives, our Lord Jesus will reveal something to us which requires prayer. We are workers together with Him fulfilling the will of the Father. The work we do in prayer is not so much what we see with our eyes, but what we know in our spirit. Our natural eyes will deceive us when it comes to doing the work of God. God communicates with our spirit. This is how it all started. In Genesis we read over and over again, "Evening and morning, and the next day" (Gen. 1:5, 1:8, 1:13, 1:19, 1:23, 1:31, and Ex. 27:21). Why? Because God starts with darkness and brings forth His work into the light. The pattern is set.

We know it is our spirit which is in communion with the spirit of the Father. We pray accordingly, as our spirit guides us. As we grow spiritually, we understand not to pray contrary to our inner conviction because it is a fruitless venture. Learn to discipline yourself not to pray amiss (James 4:3).

Why Do We Pray?

If everything is predestined and can only be done according to Jehovah's will, why pray at all? This is a good question, but comes from incomplete understanding. When we pray, we enter into the creative works of our Father. We also only do the things we already see Him doing, just as our Lord Jesus. Jesus communicated this thought to us in His gospels: John 5:19 *Jesus therefore answered and was saying to them, "Truly, truly, I say to you, the Son can do nothing of Himself, unless it is something He sees the Father doing; for whatever the Father does, these things the Son also does in like manner. . .* We are fellow workers with Him, working according to what is pleasing to the Father. We also enter into the work of the Lord Jesus Christ by the fruit we bring forth in our lives. John 5:17 *But He answered them, "My Father is working until now, and I Myself am working."* Prayer is entering into the creative work of God, therefore it is not to be taken lightly.

If we are one with the Father, then we are one with His power. Jesus prayed that we would be "one" with Him and His Father (John 17:20-23). If we are one with the Father, then the power which emanates from Him is part of our oneness. This power I am speaking about is the same power by which the Father created all things visible and invisible; we are told that all things were made through the "Word" of Jehovah and that this Word became flesh in our Lord Jesus Christ. Through our faith in our Lord Jesus Christ and the miraculous work of God's spirit, we are one flesh with Jesus. The life and power which emanates from us is no longer our own, but is an extension of the life of Christ Jesus.

By our position in faith, we admit submission to God's authority. It is from this position of submission to His authority where we find His power in our prayers. We understand that all power originally emanated from the Father. He will not oppose His own purposes. Therefore, you can have anything you request which does not alter His purposes.

Prayer is more than just making requests. Our prayer is not mere words uttered in passing. Prayer is entering into the creative work of God. When we pray, it is an extension of our lives and our work. It is Jehovah's purpose that we become fellow workers, sons doing the work of the Father. Look what He said in the beginning of the revelation of His plans for us in Jesus Christ: Gen. 1:26 *And God said, Let us make man in our image, after our likeness: and let them have dominion over the fish of the sea, and over the fowl of the air, and over the cattle, and over all the earth, and over every creeping thing that creepeth upon the earth. . .*

Jesus Christ is the image of God. Everything outside of the Lord Jesus Christ is not in the image of God. Genesis 1:26 is the great commission to work with the Father to accomplish His directive, "make man in our own image." The sons of God, the angels, are already in the image of God. Therefore, it was spoken to them, "Let us make man in our own image." When we pray for anyone or anything, the release of the Father's power is tied to the great commission.

The Devil took that great commission and converted it to what he thought was his own purposes – to make man in his own image. That is why Jesus said to the Pharisees, (John 8:44) *Ye are of your father the Devil, and the lusts of your father ye will do. He was a murderer from the beginning, and abode not in the truth, because there is no truth in him. When he speaketh a lie, he speaketh of his own: for he is a liar, and the father of it. . .*

Thus the purpose of prayer is to fulfill the purposes of the Father. John 5:20 *"For the Father loves the Sons and shows Him all things that He Himself is doing; and greater works than these will He show Him, that you may marvel. . ."* God's purposes must be fulfilled for your prayer to be answered. If those purposes are to heal your diseases, to rescue you from trouble, give you money or anything else according to His will, then your petition is answered. The future is immutable because Jehovah's Will is immutable.

PRINCIPLE FOUR: The purpose of prayer is to enter into the work of God, to fulfill His purpose (will).

The Comfort of Understanding

The gift of understanding is a precious one. Every thinking, reasoning person alive will face crises in their lives. Very little needs to be said of the purpose of prayer in times of sorrow, grief, and bewilderment. As I have stated before, it is impossible to alter the will of God by any request or effort. He will always answer any prayer according to His will. If we are sorrowful, He will comfort us. If we are upset, He will lead us to more reasonable thoughts. If we are deceived, He can teach us. If we are lonely, He can provide us companionship. If we are hateful, He can soften our heart. If we are jealous, He can free us from our envy. In everything which brings us pain, the Lord God Jehovah will bring us help if we have a mind and sincerity to receive it.

All people and all things belong to God. There is no creature that does not belong to the Father. This is not to say that all have the same relationship with the Father. There is a place where each relationship is special. We see two basic relationships between us and our Creator, both by birth; one relationship is as a descendant of Adam, the other is through the Lord Jesus Christ. The difference in these two relationships is also the difference in prayer.

All people born in Adam, the root of mankind, are in the Kingdom of Darkness. Let's look at a few scriptures. Is. 9:2 *The people that walked in darkness have seen a great light: they that dwell in the land of the shadow of death, upon them hath the light shined...* 1 Cor. 15:21 *For since by man (this man is referring to Adam) came death, . . .* 1 Cor. 1 5:2 2 *For as in Adam all die,. . .* Thus, the relationship of all people born through Adam is not one of life. If you are in Adam your life has a temporal purpose. You are considered a temporal being. This is why eternal life is promised to the followers of the Lord Jesus Christ. Eternal life is not an option outside of the Lord Jesus. Beyond their Adamic existence, these people's lives will have no further purpose. They, for all intents and purposes, are dead. Their existence is a mute point with respect to future events in the universe. This existence is a dead end; it is death. These people follow in the footsteps of their father, Adam. They compose a part of the Kingdom of Darkness, a kingdom of nothingness, a kingdom isolated and cut off from everything else. I will discuss this in great detail in the chapter, Heaven and Hell.

In the Lord Jesus Christ, our relationship is based upon a birth which expands and has purpose beyond our present earthly bodies and duties. When we pray, we are exercised in the development of this relationship. Prayer, for us, is more of an open line of communication. Our Father and our Lord Jesus comforts us in that we have been given a hearing ear by the Holy Spirit which dwells in us. If a person does not have the Holy Spirit, then he is not part of the special relationship that is possible only through the Lord Jesus. We, in the Kingdom of Light, are comforted because we hear.

PRINCIPLE FIVE: Prayer is an open line of communication.

If you are in the Kingdom of Darkness, you do not have the benefit of God's indwelling Spirit. When you pray, it is a true leap of faith. You belong to the Father, but you do not belong to the Lord Jesus Christ. Jehovah communicates to you when you cry out to Him because He cares for you without partiality. There are those who claim that God does not hear anyone outside of those in covenant relationship with Him. This is not completely true. Jesus said: Matt. 5:45 *for he maketh his sun to rise on the evil and on the good, and sendeth rain on the just and on the unjust...*

We see some other examples in the scriptures of God communicating with those outside of covenant relationship. Gen. 20:3 *But God came to Abimelech in a dream of the night, and said to him, "Behold, you are a dead man because of the woman whom you have taken, for she is married."* (This king had taken Abraham's wife, Sarah, into his harem.) We see God communicating His Will quite clearly. God also communicated the reason his country was having difficulties with pregnancies. Gen. 20:17 *And Abraham prayed to God; and God healed Abimelech and his wife and his maids, so that they bore children. . .* We can, therefore, see that God withholds blessings when He is demanding a change. God communicated with this man to make His will clear. This communication had the potential of expanding in this man's life. This man could go further to come into covenant relationship or remain as he was. God blessed him to communicate with him.

This man also was heard of God when he confessed some ignorance of the situation (Gen. 20:4-6). God further communicated with him. Gen. 20:7 *"Now therefore, restore the man's wife, for he is a prophet, and he will pray for you, and you will live. But if you do not restore her, know that you shall surely die, you and all who are yours."* God's purposes are maintained in all His communications with the unsaved. He signifies that the place Abraham has is special. God elevates Abraham to bless this man by his prayer for him. Abimelek of the Kingdom of Darkness cannot circumvent Abraham or fail to recognize his special place. Abimelek is comforted in submission to the will of God.

PRINCIPLE SIX: Effective prayer is submission to the will of God. It contains within it the attitude of submission.

There are other examples similar and varied from the one just sighted. The Kingdom of Darkness is as it means, without light. If there is no light, you cannot see. If you cannot see, you cannot understand clearly. John 1:5 *And the light shineth in darkness; and the darkness comprehended it not. . .* In absolute darkness, you are unable to see anything. If someone speaks to you, giving you an explanation of things around you, it is necessary for you to take him by his word because you do not see. It is Jehovah Who gives the seeing eye. You do not develop a seeing eye on your own just as a totally blind person cannot develop sight. Sight is something with which you are born. Yes, it is possible to develop blindness. But the one who has had sight and develops blindness has some understanding of the world of light from the things he has seen. Those born in darkness have never seen; for them, to see is a gift.

If you are born in darkness and are given eyes to see, what you see is light. You never really see objects, but the light which it reflects. The light illuminates everything that is in the darkness. Thus, light is the only thing you can see in the darkness; the "things" you see are revealed by the light. God cannot fully comfort those in darkness because they cannot see; therefore they cannot understand. God does at times hear and comfort those in darkness, but it is only when their hearts are right or when it is according to His own purposes. The purpose of God is to bring forth Jesus Christ in this earth. Everything outside of Jesus Christ is darkness. If you have a heart to enter into the Lord Jesus Christ, then you can enter into the comfort of God. The Lord Jesus Christ is the comfort of God; He is also the understanding of God to us. Acts 13:48 *And when the Gentiles heard this, they were glad, and glorified the word of the Lord: and as many as were ordained to eternal life believed.*

There are those who wish that God would hear everyone's prayer indiscriminately. Let me assure you that this will never be the case in this present age. The comfort of God is the assurance of the Lord Jesus Christ. Everything is connected to the Father's plan to glorify the name of Jesus. Included in that plan is to comfort those who put their trust in that name. 2 John 1:9 *Whosoever transgresseth, and abideth not in the doctrine of Christ, hath not God. He that abideth in the doctrine of Christ, he hath both the Father and the Son. . . .* Thus rejection of the Lord Jesus Christ and His teachings separates you from the comfort of God. Comfort will only come from Jehovah through the Lord Jesus to those of a repentant, remorseful heart. God will not defeat His own purposes by circumventing that which He is establishing through Jesus. Any apparent exception is only for the purpose of opening the door to lead someone down the path to meet Christ.

The following scriptures all contain a common thread of understanding as the curtains of the Tabernacle in the Wilderness contained the "golden wire" passing through the various fabrics (Ex. 39:3). This golden wire is a common truth. It is the nature of the Lord Jesus Christ. Ps. 34:18 *The Lord is nigh unto them that are of a broken heart; and saveth such as be of a contrite spirit...* Ps. 51:17 *The sacrifices of God are a broken spirit: a broken and a contrite heart, O God, thou wilt not despise...* Is. 57:15 *For thus saith the high and lofty One that inhabiteth eternity, whose name is Holy; "I dwell in the high and holy place, with him also that is of a contrite and humble spirit, to revive the spirit of the humble, and to revive the heart of the contrite ones."*

In each instance, God informs us of the attitude of heart to which He has an open ear. Jesus gave us an example of two people praying and made it clear as to whom the Father would respect. Luke 18:10 *Two men went up into the temple to pray; the one a Pharisee, and the other a publican.* Luke 18:11 *The Pharisee stood and prayed thus with himself, God, I thank thee, that I am not as other men are, extortioners, unjust, adulterers, or even as this publican.* Luke 18:12 *I fast twice in the week, I give tithes of all that I possess.* Luke 18:13 *And the publican, standing afar off, would not lift up so much as his eyes unto heaven, but smote upon his breast, saying, God be merciful to me a sinner.* Luke 18:14 *I tell you, this man went down to his house justified rather than the other: for every one that exalteth himself shall be abased; and he that humbleth himself shall be exalted...*

Our righteousness is a gift, as is a proper heart's attitude. The sooner we give glory to God and acknowledge this truth, the sooner we will experience greater grace and rest in our walk in this world. King David prayed, "Create in me a clean heart, O God; and renew a right spirit within me" (Ps. 51:10).

Miraculous Prayer

There is a special form of prayer which has mystified us from the beginning of the Father revealing Himself to us. All answered prayer is a manifestation to us of God's involvement and our oneness with Him. This sense of oneness is important to our development as sons or daughters of God. We, as we develop into the image of the Lord Jesus Christ, must also develop a confidence of us being an integral part of His Kingdom. We are ambassadors acting upon His behalf in the world around us (2 Cor. 5.20). Prayer is a manifestation of our ambassadorial power. This is why Abimelek was told to have Abraham pray for him and his countrymen (Gen. 20:7). Abraham was one of God's ambassadors in the world of his time. The power manifest in miraculous prayer is a very visible display of our ambassadorship in the Kingdom of God and is also a visible testament to God's active concern for our needs.

The following example is the pattern for miracles throughout the scriptures. In this passage of scriptures, we will see that Jehovah provides the circumstances for a miracle. In other words, God sets the stage for a miracle to occur. Furthermore, if God does not set the stage for a miracle, no miracle is possible. Miraculous manifestation is only possible when it has been planned ahead of time. Let's look at the following scriptures:

John 9:1 *And as Jesus passed by, he saw a man which was blind from his birth.* John 9:2 *And his disciples asked him, saying, Master, who did sin, this man, or his parents, that he was born blind?* John 9:3 *Jesus answered, Neither hath this man sinned, nor his parents: but that the works of God should be made manifest in him.* John 9:4 *I must work the works of him that sent me, while it is day: the night cometh, when no man can work.* John 9:6 *When he had thus spoken, he spat on the ground, and made clay of the spittle, and he anointed the eyes of the blind man with the clay,* John 9:7 *And said unto him, Go, wash in the pool of Siloam. He went his way therefore, and washed, and came seeing.*

There was a purpose for this man's blindness "that the works of God should be made manifest." Jesus knew before He prayed that the Father had one exact purpose in Him "seeing" this blind man. Jesus knew that this man was preordained to receive a miraculous healing. Jesus acknowledged that "He could do nothing of Himself" (John 5:19). Thus, this man's healing was not the will of the Son, but the Father. Jesus said that He came "not to do His own will" (John 4:34, John 5:30, John 6:38). This man's blindness had a specific "life expectancy" determined by God. Neither this man nor his parents sinned that this situation existed but, "that the works of God should be made manifest." Our attitude in prayer should be exactly as that of Lord Jesus. We pray to enter into the manifestation of the works of God. If we have this mind, which was also in Christ Jesus, we will eliminate much error in prayer.

Remember the life of Joseph and the dreams of the pharaoh involving the drought that was to come upon the whole land. Remember also the drought which came upon the land of Israel in the days of Elisha. Both droughts were ordained by God. Jehovah had a purpose in Egypt and a purpose in Israel. No amount of praying would make these droughts end sooner than ordained. These droughts had a "life expectancy" to fulfill the purposes of God in this earth. Each drought had a different purpose. To imagine that Jacob, living in the land of Canaan, did not pray for rain before he sent his sons to Egypt to buy grain is inconceivable. This man was very spiritual, but had lost faith concerning his son Joseph. His prayer for rain was one of bewilderment. No rain would come even though his name was Jacob, a man highly revered by God.

When Elijah prayed so that it would not rain, his prayer was exactly according to the will of God. It was not his own idea. The faithful in Israel could have prayed endlessly, and many people did, but no rain would come because it was contrary to the plans of Jehovah. When Elijah saw that the purposes of the Father had been fulfilled, he knew that he could pray for rain and that his prayer would be answered miraculously. James 5:17 *Elias [Elijah] was a man subject to like passions as we are, and he prayed earnestly that it might not rain: and it rained not on the earth by the space of three years and six months.* James 5:18 *And he prayed again, and the heaven gave rain, and the earth brought forth her fruit. . .* In each case, the stage was set by God; He orchestrated the events. Miracles just don't happen as a result of us exercising our own will and mixing in some faith we conjure up by our personal initiative. True miracles are always by the will of God. For a miracle to occur, God supplies a very special faith at the time it is needed. If that special faith is not supplied, the miracle will not occur because you will it. Yes, there are some false signs and wonders, but this ordained deception is not the order of our discussion. We must come to an understanding of the rulership of our Father and submit, fully understanding, that we are here only to do His will and not our own. This understanding is the source of agreement which makes it possible for God to move through you unhindered and prevents you from going astray. For a miracle to occur, we must have His mind before we pray. Spiritual communication is the key word here between our Father and us because of our Lord Jesus Christ.

We read in scriptures that Jesus learned obedience by the things He suffered. Heb. 5:8 *Though he were a Son, yet learned he obedience by the things which he suffered;* Heb. 5:9 *And being made perfect, he became the author of eternal salvation unto all them that obey him;...* Many people do not understand that Jesus learned perfect obedience, just like you and I. Look at the following to illustrate my point. Matt. 13:58 *And he did not many mighty works there because of their unbelief...* It was not that Jesus did not want to bless these people by a glorious manifestation of the power of the Father. He did. What was lacking was the gift of faith imparted by Jehovah. Jesus could not do the works on His own. Jesus, you, I or anyone cannot do the mighty works of the Father without Him fully setting the stage; it is impossible. What will occur is our own personal suffering in which it is hopeful that we learn obedience. In the eyes of our Father, our obedience is our perfection. Wherever there is an obedient son or daughter, miracles will follow.

I would like to tell you of one modern day miracle of which I have personal knowledge. One of my patients had severe cancer of the bladder. He had one surgery to remove an advanced tumor. At the time of the surgery, it was discovered that there were many other small cancerous growths also within the bladder. Conditions were not suitable at that time to do anymore surgery. His surgical wounds were closed and he was under observation with periodic exams until conditions progressed that would allow him to have a second surgery. Scoping of his bladder revealed that the lining was covered with numerous cancerous tumors. He was scheduled for surgery.

While he lie on the gurney awaiting the planned surgery, there was a substantial delay. An intravenous line was running and he saw one bag of solution empty, followed by another. After lying there for about 90 minutes, the man broke emotionally. In his despair, he wondered if he was so far gone, it wasn't worth the effort to try to save him. He began to weep. In this state, crushed emotionally and in great anxiety, he prayed, "Lord, please help me." This man's heart and spirit made the connection. The sincerity was there. The exact words are not as important as the heart's intent. It is with our heart through our spirit that we enter into worship.

As soon as he had prayed, he noticed angels standing around his surgical cart in rows. The first row stood at the four corners and had shields. He said that there was something different written on each shield. He tried to speak to the angel at the head of the cart, asking, "Is that your name written on the shield?", but he would not answer him. There was a second row of angels with swords drawn. Not once did any of these angels speak to him. He looked very intently at every detail. He said that he noticed that he could somewhat see through and beyond them. A deep peace and inward quietness replaced his raging anxiety.

The hospital staff brought him into the surgical suite. He woke up a short time later. His treating doctor told him with amazement that he had a spontaneous remission; that he could find no trace of cancer. This man continued to have periodic scoping of his bladder for several years to evaluate reappearance of any new cancerous growths, but none developed. The specialist told him that there was no need to see him anymore. This miracle occurred a little more than eight years ago. This man's devotion to God, his life, and the manner in which he practices his profession were profoundly affected by the faith which was given to him.

Many miracles are born on the stage of adversity. God sets the stage for miracles to occur. Look at the adversity of the Children of Israel when they fled Egypt and the pharaoh. They found themselves with their backs to the sea and pharaoh's army in hot pursuit to chop them to pieces. Who had led them to this impossible place in which they had no retreat? Jehovah did, through His obedient servant Moses. They did not get into this seemingly impossible situation on their own; they were lead. Most of them, probably almost all, cried out in despair with fear and anxiety. They had followed and now, because of it, were trapped in their situation.

This is how God sets the stage for miracles. To these people, it seemed to be a dark day indeed. However, to God, He had everyone exactly where He wanted them. The Egyptians were in a rage, the powers of darkness driving them. The Hebrews were in terror, their hearts trembling.

Ex. 14:10 *And when Pharaoh drew nigh, the children of Israel lifted up their eyes, and, behold, the Egyptians marched after them; and they were sore afraid: and the children of Israel cried out unto the Lord.* Ex. 14:11 *And they said unto Moses, "Because there were no graves in Egypt, hast thou taken us away to die in the wilderness? wherefore hast thou dealt thus with us, to carry us forth out of Egypt?"* Ex. 14:12 *"Is not this the word that we did tell thee in Egypt, saying, Let us alone, that we may serve the Egyptians? For it had been better for us to serve the Egyptians, than that we should die in the wilderness."* Ex. 14:13 *And Moses said unto the people, "Fear ye not, stand stills and see the salvation of the Lord, which he will show to you to day: for the Egyptians whom ye have seen today, ye shall see them again no more forever.* Ex. 14:14 *The Lord shall fight for you, and ye shall hold your peace."* Ex. 14:15 *And the Lord said unto Moses, Wherefore criest thou unto me? speak unto the children of Israel, that they go forward:* Ex. 14:16 *But lift thou up thy rod, and stretch out thine hand over the sea, and divide it: and the children of Israel shall go on dry ground through the midst of the sea.* Ex. 14 17 *And I, behold, I will harden the hearts of the Egyptians and they shall follow them: and I will get me honour upon Pharaoh, and upon all his host, upon his chariots, and upon his horsemen.* Ex. 14:18 *And the Egyptians shall know that I am the Lord, when I have gotten me honour upon Pharaoh, upon his chariots, and upon his horsemen."*

God is in control in every instance of this miracle which He orchestrated. Prior to this, it had not been recorded that God had ever delivered any other person in such a manner. This miracle was for His purposes, not for ours or theirs. Yes, He saved them. But this salvation was for His own name's sake. He had no need to lead them into a trap. God has no lack of planning or tactical wisdom. Thus, it was not that He was saving them for their sakes. He had placed them there with the intention of delivering them that "the Egyptians shall know that I am the Lord, when I have gotten me honour upon Pharaoh, upon his chariots, and upon his horsemen."

The name Jehovah was destined to stand out as "God." Today, because of everything that He has done in the past, it is understood that when we write the capital "G" in the word god, it only refers to Jehovah. For many people, the title "God" is His name. When they pray, they consider no other possibility; their heart is openly communicating with their Maker. For these people, the Creator's proper name is "God." It is not that they refuse to use His proper name; "God," in their minds, is His proper name. For these people, there is only one true God. Therefore, they do not regard it as an issue. In their minds and hearts, the very word God is only in reference to Him. Thus, in the minds of many, His official name is God, because they realize that there is only one true God.

Except for a few isolated primitive peoples, cut off from all social contacts, most of us accept His official name simply as "God." To most of us in the civilized world, there is only one God; every spiritual being is considered as inferior and in a lower position; we know them as a "want-to-be's." I, personally, have no problem with the use of the Father's title for His name. The title, when understood correctly, says it all. I, though, prefer using a formal name for God. I am of no particular religious denomination, but see no reason to only use a title. The scriptures are not nearly as clear when we only use the title "Lord" or "God." Look at the following scripture as an example: Ps. 100:1 *A Psalm of David. The Lord said unto my Lord, Sit thou at my right hand, until I make thine enemies thy footstool...*

In the future, I sincerely doubt that anyone will ever use the word "God" in reference to anyone but the Almighty. This knowledge is increasing and expanding through the ministry of our Lord Jesus Christ. In the Lord Jesus Christ, the Father has invested all power and authority to fully complete the task of revelation of His name in this earth. The true revelation of the Father is only given in connection with personal relationship with the Lord Jesus Christ. He who does not have Jesus, does not have the Father. It is impossible to have one without the other. If you have Jesus, you have the Father. If you claim to have Jehovah, but you do not have Jesus, you are still in the Kingdom of Darkness. John 5:24 *Verily, verily, I say unto you, He that heareth my word, and believeth on him that sent me, hath everlasting life, and shall not come into condemnation; but is passed from death unto life...* The greatest miracle of all occurs daily, in the translation of a person from the Kingdom of Darkness into the Kingdom of Light.

We could talk about many other miracles recorded in the scriptures, as well as others occurring daily in our present world. There is a common gold wire that passes through all miracles. God is the salvation in every situation through the faith He supplies.

Misguided Prayer

There is an area of misguided prayer that we have not discussed. It may seem ridiculous, but some people attempt to use faith to affect the outcome of sporting events. Please do not allow yourself to sink to that level. The Father is all for glorifying the name of the Lord Jesus Christ in this earth, but not an athletic team, unless there is a specific purpose. It is proper to ask that a participant in a sport, who openly confesses Jesus, be blessed to perform at his best. This is always proper, unless the participant needs to discover the benefits of humility.

In any athletic event, it is likely that contenders on opposite sides have like faith. Does God take sides to dash the hopes of one so that the other can rejoice? Does not God love all equally? Would it not be better that all contestants walk away with the inner knowledge that each had played his best? Look what James says of such prayer: James 4:4 *You ask and do not receive, because you ask with wrong motives so that you may spend it on your pleasures.*

Other Avenues of Prayer

We could go on and on about specifics. I do not wish to get extremely detailed and exhaustive. There is prayer for restitution, binding and loosing, and involving every avenue of life. Enough is said about all prayer and discovery in prayer that we must maintain an attitude of submission to His will and purposes. Everything else is a waste of time and personal resources.

12
Heaven and Hell

If life is predestined, what about Heaven and Hell? Can we say that a person is destined to go to hell? This is an important issue and needs to be understood clearly. The scriptures state plainly that it is the desire of God that all be saved and come to the knowledge of the truth. 1 Tim. 2:3 *For this is good and acceptable in the sight of God our Savior;* 1 Tim 2:4 *Who will have all men to be saved, and to Come unto the knowledge of the truth. . .* These scriptures are from the King James Version. "Who will have all men saved" may be misunderstood as the forceful, immutable will of God. Good and acceptable is different from determinate will. This scripture is stating the Father's desire, not will. This fact is born out more clearly in the New American Version: 1 Tim. 2 3 *This is good and acceptable in the sight of God our Savior,* 1 Tim. 2:4 *who desires all men to be saved and to come to the knowledge of the truth.*

We need to grasp the attitude of our Father in everything we are going to explore. Having revealed the power and reality of predestination, I am aware of the controversy aroused upon thinking about one's personal destiny. We need to explore this controversy, not from an emotion, but from a rational point of view. To whet our appetites further, consider Judas, the man who betrayed our Lord Jesus Christ. But before we look specifically at Judas, we need to remind ourselves of a scriptural text we examined earlier. God is the potter, we are the clay. The statement is easy enough to mouth. However, many who mouth this reality never stop to contemplate its full implications. We read in Isaiah: Is. 64:8 *But now, O Lord, thou art our father; we are the clay, and thou our potter; and we all are the work of thy hand. . .*

"We are all the work of thy hand." Please show me, for the sake of argument, someone who is not the work of His hand. There is no person of whom you can say, this person made himself. Yes, you can work at something to be a success. But it is God Who makes it possible. A farmer works hard to prepare the soil; he then plants his crop. The farmer may even water and weed his planting, tilling and fertilizing it. Nevertheless, the survival of that crop is dependent upon conditions far beyond his control. The farmer has no control over forces beyond him. If the weather is too hot, too dry, too cold or too wet, the crop will not survive. Social and governmental forces may disrupt his field, robbing him of a worthy increase. Biologic forces and other forces of nature may also consume his labor.

God controls the forces beyond us that dictate our success. It makes no difference whether we be a man or an angel, there exist forces beyond our control. It is God Who determines the success of our ventures; this has always been true and will always be true in the future. Thus, Jehovah determines the direction we develop by controlling our success in the ventures we undertake.

Look at what the apostle Paul wrote: Rom. 9:21 *Hath not the potter power over the clay, of the same lump to make one vessel unto honour, and another unto dishonor. . .* God is the "potter." We are the "clay." He does have the power over us to form us as He sees fit. He does make one vessel for an honorable use. He also makes vessels for dishonor and terrible deeds. The Children of Israel were commanded by God to slaughter every man, woman, and child, even the animals, in the city of Jericho at the time of the taking of the promised land. Was this a wonderful deed or terrible? Terrible. But it was Jehovah's will.

The apostle Paul points out in his dissertation that the scriptures declare that God raised up the very defiant Pharaoh in the days of Moses that he could judge Egypt Rom 9:17 *For the scripture saith unto Pharaoh, "Even for this same purpose have I raised thee up, that I might show my power in thee, and that my name might be declared throughout all the earth."* The scriptures do not give this credit to the Devil, but to God. Men need to start fearing Jehovah and not the Devil! The function of people in the world and their inevitable destiny after this eternal existence, is a different matter. The predestined actions and deeds of an individual are separate from judgment. We will look more at this as we examine what the scriptures reveal.

Judas

We return to our discussion of Judas, a man raised up to betray our Lord Jesus Christ. This man was handpicked to reject the Lord of Glory for a handful of silver. The plan to use Judas existed from the foundation of the world and was declared in Zechariah. Zech. 11:12 *And I said unto them, if ye think good, give me my price; and if not, forbear. So they weighed for my price thirty pieces of silver.* Zech. 11:13 *And the Lord said unto me, "Cast it unto the potter: a goodly price that I was prised at of them." And I took the thirty pieces of silver; and cast them to the potter in the house of the Lord...*

We see our Lord at the last supper with full understanding of the Father's will. Jesus has complete knowledge of the plan to crucify Him. This, Jesus submits to willingly, because it is our Father's will. John 13:1 *Now before the feast of the passover, when Jesus knew that his hour was come that he should depart out of this world unto the Father, having loved his own which were in the world, he loved them unto the end.*

John 13:2 *And supper being ended the Devil having now put into the heart of Judas Iscariot, Simon's son, to betray him;...* Mark 14:18 *And as they sat and did eat, Jesus said, "Verily I say unto you, One of you which eateth with me shall betray me."* Mark 14:19 *And they began to be sorrowfull, and to say unto him one by one, "Is it I?" and another said, "Is it I?"* Mark 14:20 *And he answered and said unto them, "It is one of the twelve, that dippeth with me in the dish."*

John 13:20 *"Verily, verily, I say unto you, He that receiveth whomsoever I send receiveth me; and he that receiveth me receiveth him that sent me."* John 13:21 *When Jesus had thus said, he was troubled in spirit, and testified and said, "Verily, verily, I say unto you, that one of you shall betray me."* John 13:25 *He then lying on Jesus' breast saith unto him, "Lord, who is it?"* John 13:26 *Jesus answered, "He it is, to whom I shall give a sop, when I have dipped it." And when he had dipped the sop, he gave it to Judas Iscariot, the son of Simon.* John 13:27 *And after the sop Satan entered into him. Then said Jesus unto him, "That thou doest, do quickly."* John 13:28 *Now no man at the table knew for what intent he spake this unto him.* John 13:30 *He then having received the sop went immediately out: and it was night.* John 13:31 *Therefore, when he was gone out, Jesus said, "Now is the Son of man glorified and God is glorified in him."* Matt 26:24 *The Son of man goeth as it is written of him: but woe unto that man by whom the Son of man is betrayed! it had been good for that man if he had not been born."*

Satan could enter Judas because he was chosen to commit this deed. Judas' heart was prepared to be hard for this hour. Even though it is revealed to Judas that our Lord knew what he had planned, it did not dissuade him. Judas was never ordained to be part of the Kingdom of Light. In the midst of the sins, wonders, and miracles he could only think of the worldly advantages of being close to Jesus, advantages which brought him personal wealth (John 12:6). Judas was in the ministry for the money. The thought of Jesus being King and him being in a high political office was what drove Judas. Love of the Lord Jesus Christ was not a motivation in this man's life. The love of this present world so blinded Judas that he was unable to grasp or hear much of what Jesus was saying.

Judas loved darkness, and the ways of darkness. Nothing Judas saw was able to turn his heart to personally accept the life Jesus was presenting. The love, respect, and hands-on revelation before him did not gain his desire to enter into the truth. The Father gave to this man as much opportunity to turn to the light as He gives to any person. Yet, Judas loved the darkness of this present age more than anything he had seen or heard. Was he without opportunity to believe? Was he treated badly by Jesus? No, he was entrusted with the money bag even though Jesus knew that he was a thief. Judas was given every opportunity to repent.

Why didn't he repent? The Holy Spirit must be present to personally convict of sin. Judas lacked inner conviction of a need to change. If any of the words of Jesus would have appealed to this man, the Holy Spirit would have had a grasp upon him to bring him to godly repentance. The appeal of Jesus to Judas was strictly a worldly one. This man was a true lover of darkness.

John 3:19 *And this is the condemnation, that light is come into the world, and men loved darkness rather than light, because their deeds were evil.* John 3:20 *For every one that doeth evil hateth the light, neither cometh to the light; lest his deeds should be reproved.* John 3:21 *But he that doeth truth cometh to the light, that his deeds may be made manifest, that they are wrought in God.* Judas never was part of the Kingdom of Light.

Judas' life was not without purpose, as every one of us has a purpose in life. Judas' purpose was fulfilled in betraying the Lord Jesus. At one instance, he had an opportunity to repent, but rejected the concept of forgiveness. After he had successfully betrayed Jesus, Judas attempted to return the money. At that time, he experienced true godly sorrow for his actions. When he discovered that his deeds were irreversible, he plunged himself into despair instead of the doctrine of the Jesus. Judas did not have the word of reconciliation in his heart because he had not been listening while Jesus was teaching. His heart was so filled with treachery and manipulation that his ears were dull of hearing. Judas did not comprehend the Word of God.

Look what the apostle John writes: John 1:5 *And the light shineth in darkness; and the darkness comprehended it not.* Even when Judas' heart was filled with sorrow, convicted to the point of repentance, his heart was so dark that he could not comprehend the concept of embracing forgiveness. Instead, he again chose the darkness to solve his pain and destroyed his life in suicide. God is greater than our hearts. If we see clearly the greatness of God in Jesus Christ, we understand that we can be forgiven. The darkness in Judas' heart killed him. Judas' life was filled with darkness – a darkness he loved and embraced. His future would be filled with the darkness he loved. Jesus remorsefully says of him, "It had been good for that man if he had not been born."

You Must Be Born Again

There is a lot of argument among various religious circles about going to heaven when you die. Some people even joke about Saint

Peter at the pearly gate making decisions as to who will enter and who will be turned away. When asked, other people will tell you that they hope they make it to heaven. Some will tell you that they have lived a good life and that they expect to go to heaven because they, in their opinion, are basically good. Even some Christians worry about getting to heaven. All such thinking reflects a basic lack of understanding. These ideas about getting to heaven are erroneous.

The concept of heaven and hell is the division of two spiritual kingdoms. Heaven and hell are not as much two places, but the separation of two creations. These creations are the Kingdom of Light and the Kingdom of Darkness. All of spiritual creation falls into one of these two kingdoms; as two sides of the same coin, one side faces the light, the other turns away from the light. The light exposes all things and all details; in the darkness, nothing is clear.

In darkness, people ask themselves the "meaning" of life because they cannot see. If they could see, they would not be asking such a rudimentary question. This very question is a sign of spiritual darkness within them. They cannot see, therefore, they ask. For those born in darkness, light is only a concept; they do not comprehend it (John 1:5).

If you are born in a particular country, you are considered a citizen of that country. Unless you make an effort to change the reality into which you were born, you will remain a citizen of that country all your days. This is the natural order of things. Having considered this basic premise, I want to look at the words of our Lord Jesus, "You must be born again."

John 3:7 *"Do not marvel that I said to you, 'You must be born again.'* John 3:5 *Jesus answered, "Truly, truly, I say to you, unless one is born of water and the Spirit, he cannot enter into the kingdom of God."* John 3:6 *"That which is born of the flesh is flesh, and that which is born of the Spirit is spirit."*

This statement of Jesus is the key to everything about which we are talking. It is a statement of fact. "That which is born of flesh is flesh." "That which is born of Spirit is spirit." Jesus did not say, "You should be born again." He said, "must." Why must you? Because it is a matter of creation.

As I mentioned earlier, we see two basic relationships between us and our Creator; both are by birth. All people born in Adam, the root of mankind, are in the Kingdom of Darkness. 1 Cor. 15:21 *For since by man came death,...* 1 Cor. 15:22 *For as in Adam all die,...* Thus, the relationship of all people born through Adam is not one of life. If you are in Adam, your life has a temporal purpose. Beyond this existence, your life will have no further purpose. You, for all intents and purposes, are dead. This existence is a dead end; it is death. These people compose the Kingdom of Darkness, a kingdom of nothingness, a kingdom isolated and cut off from everything else.

Let me see if I can make this clearer. Whatever kingdom you are born into, you shall remain forever. If you are in Adam, you are in the Kingdom of Darkness. Except in the circumstance we shall examine later in this chapter, if you are born a descendent of Adam, you shall remain in the Kingdom of Darkness forever. It takes a miraculous act of creation by God through the Lord Jesus Christ to translate you from the Kingdom of Darkness into the Kingdom of the Lord Jesus Christ, which is the Kingdom of Light. You become "born again." You become a new creation. You are "born" into the Kingdom of Light. You become a citizen by birth. Whatever kingdom into which you are born, you shall remain forever. Physical death is merely a staging ground to enter into the next phase of your existence in the kingdom of which you are born. If you are part of darkness when you die, you will continue in darkness. If you are part of Jesus (the Kingdom of Light) when you physically die, you will continue in that kingdom. Eccl. 11:3 *If the clouds be full of rain, they empty themselves upon the earth: and if the tree fall toward the south, or toward the north, in the place where the tree falleth, there it shall be.*

The direction the tree falls illustrates what I have been writing. The tree remains in the place it falls. The place you fall in physical death is where you remain. If you die in Christ, there you shall remain. The decision of whether you end up in heaven or hell is determined by your position at physical death. Death is the next step in your development into the kingdom in which you are a member. If you die outside of Christ, then you will develop further outside of Christ. If you die in Christ, then you will develop further in Him. Hell is the extension of the Kingdom of Darkness. Heaven is the extension of the Kingdom of the Lord Jesus Christ. The translation from one kingdom to the other is a miracle. It is not based upon one's own efforts. No person can transform himself. Thus, those in Christ are a new creation (2 Cor. 5:17).

What about the question of morality? If a person is not a Christian, is there any reward for wholesome living? I will examine this issue later in this chapter.

When Life is Death

Let me expand on this concept of life a bit further. If we examine the concept of life, we refer to a system that continues to express itself in a function. We may know someone suffering in a coma. This person has biologic life, but we all admit that this is not a "life." We may even talk about a person trapped in a terrible scenario of circumstances, causing a cruel situation and say also of this person that they have "no life." I am using our powers of reason to look beyond mere existence. From our vantage point, "mere existence" is not the essence of life. "Living" is more than merely existing. History is full of examples of people who endured idealizations of suicide because they felt their life was not worth living. Thus, from a human perspective, life is more than existence.

There is another aspect of life which we need to examine. In order for life to continue, it requires an outside source. We all have different standards for that which we call really living. Nevertheless, life, in order to continue, requires an outside source. Since we are not talking about mere existence, we will continue to talk about "life" worth living from the individual perspective. Each of us needs to have interaction with our environment. If our interaction is satisfactory, then the quality of our life is satisfying.

What each of us considers satisfying depends upon what is in our heart. Some people's satisfaction is dependent upon causing suffering and harm to others. These people feel they have a life when they can do exactly as they desire. "Life," although satisfying to them, causes suffering in the lives of others. These people weave themselves into the fabric of society throughout the world. Their continuance is part of what makes the world what it is today and has been throughout history. These people are not a source of life to others, but death. Others must continue to sacrifice their "lives" to maintain the satisfaction of these individuals. In their own eyes, they are "living," but in the experience of those paying the price, they are a source of suffering and death, like a poison. From a spiritual perspective, this "life" is death. For the world to become a paradise, these people and their appetites must be sequestered from any further interaction. This is exactly God's plan, a plan predestined from the foundation of the world.

Let's look at the words of the Lord Jesus: Matt. 8:22 *But Jesus said unto him, "Follow me; and let the dead bury their dead. . ."* Notice that the Lord did not say, "Let the unbelievers bury their dead." Jesus' words were carefully chosen to illustrate the reality of two worlds, two creations, two kingdoms. Those in spiritual darkness are dead in the eyes of our Lord. These need not wonder "if they are going to heaven when they die." Those who are spiritually dead in the flesh will remain in the kingdom of darkness when they physically die. They are part of old creation and will remain so unless recreated by a miraculous act of God through the Lord Jesus Christ. There is no other name than Jesus under heaven by which we must be saved (Acts 4:12). From our perspective, this is an absolute!

John 3:14 *We know that we have passed from death unto life, because we love the brethren. He that loveth not his brother abideth in death. . .* Any person professing to be a Christian will have love for other Christians; it makes no difference if they have denominational doctrine differences. There is a reality of oneness that goes far beyond some apparent differences in understanding. The life of Christ within us bears witness with the life which is in other brethren. We are all part of the same body. The body does not reject its parts when they become injured or diseased, but fights to restore and heal it. Why? Because there is an integral love within the body for each of its members. If a person has hatred or distaste for other Christians, while they themselves claim to be Christian, then there is reason to doubt that they have ever experienced the "new birth." In that case, it is probable that they are but religious members of the old creation and remain in death. Gal. 6:15 *For neither is circumcision anything, nor uncircumcision, but a new creation. . .* The "new creation" is everything. If you are not part of the "new creation," you are dead while you live.

Of His Own Will Begot He Us (James 1:8)

Where does our destiny fit in the scheme of destiny and predestination? We need to understand that predestination has its limits. These limits are defined by the nature of the creation itself. When the Lord Jesus Christ agonized in the garden over the humiliating, barbarous death He faced on the cross, He tells us that He has a choice. Matt. 26:52 *Then said Jesus unto him, "Put up again thy sword into his place: for all they that take the sword shall perish with the sword."* Matt. 26:53 *"Thinkest thou that I cannot now pray to my Father, and he shall presently give me more than twelve legions of angels?"* Matt. 26:54 *"But how then shall the scriptures be fulfilled, that thus it must be?"* Jesus is telling us that He has a choice. If He abandons the cross, then He abandons us. We have no salvation without Jesus. Nevertheless, it is a freedom He has.

We see Jesus reiterating His freedom of choice in the following scriptures: John 10:17 *"For this reason the Father loves Me, because I lay down My life that I may take it again."* John 10:18 *"No one has taken it away from Me, but I lay it down on My own initiative. I have authority to lay it down, and I have authority to take it up again. This commandment I received from My Father."* However, in the midst of all this is the concept of predestination clearly stated in the scriptures in the past tense! The victory and fulfillment of all things was stated many times in the Old Testament. We see one example of this in the following scripture: Is. 63:5 *And I looked, and there was none to help; and I wondered that there was none to uphold: therefore mine own arm brought salvation unto me; and my fury, it upheld me. . .* This statement from the Father, although spoken hundreds of years before the fact, is declared in the past tense. He did not say, "will bring salvation" or "might bring salvation." It says "brought salvation to me."

Jesus was predestined to fulfill the plan of God. The heart of the Son was known to the Father before the foundation of the world. The Father knew Jesus better than He knew Himself! Jesus agonized over the prospects of failure, but the Father knew the Son. He would not fail. He would not choose to be contrary to Jehovah's will. Heb. 5:7 *Who in the days of his flesh, when he had offered up prayers and supplications with strong crying and tears unto him that was able to save him from death, and was heard in that he feared;. . .* Jesus chose and delighted to do the will of the Father. You have similar choices within the scheme of predestination. Yet, it is your heart's desire which will be made manifest. This desire is deeper than the words we mouth. Our heart's desire is from the core of our being. Desires of this nature are the elements of our very essence: what we love, and what we hate, our personal tastes, the philosophies of life we embrace and reject. It is these desires that God investigates and brings to the surface for examination and manifestation. Therefore, it is written: John 3:19 *"And this is the judgment, that the light is come into the world, and men loved the darkness rather than the light; for their deeds were evil.* John 3:20 *"For everyone who does evil hates the light, and does not come to the light, lest his deeds should be exposed.* John 3:21 *But he who practices the truth comes to the light, that his deeds may be manifested as having been wrought in God."*

The choices cited in these scriptures are on the basis of the essence of the heart's desire. It is the reason why all people will not be saved and come to the knowledge of the truth. We are each a matter of creation. Our hearts choose on the basis of what we are. The Father works with our hearts to bring out what is within. Our lives are so designed that we can examine our tastes. On the basis of our experiences, we discover our heart's desires. Our appetites are satisfied, increased or decreased by our experiences. I am making no judgment as to whether these experiences are good or evil;

only that we have them, to discover what is in our hearts. Call it judgment, if you wish, or discovery. God will bring you to your heart's desire. This coming to know one's self is part of our development and progression in creation.

Each of us is part of a very special element of nature. We have the ability to develop in the image of God. Because of this special endowment created within us, we also can develop into someone quite different than our Creator. It is this spark of God in each of us that is our rescue or our fall.

If God made you different, you would not be you. You could be similar or very close to what you are right now, but you would not be the same person. The thoughts you think and the actions you take would all be different. Your motivations and tastes would also be altered. This all has to do with what people like to refer to as their "free will." You are what you are because of creative forces beyond your control. The genetic information in your mother's egg was not determined by you. In your father's sperm, there were thousands of different possibilities; each sperm carries information for a different genetic being. It was God Who determined the genetic code making you unique. Just prior to conception, there were other possibilities for you; but you are what you are because of the unique combination chosen by God.

Now comes the question about what this has to do with Heaven and Hell. As we have examined predestination in the previous chapters, we could see and come to the conclusion that God manipulates all things on earth along the path He determines. He raises a king and puts him down. He humbles and exalts people for specific purposes. He controls the weather. He traps people in circumstances beyond their control in order to fulfill His purposes. However, along this path, God reveals Himself to all the people in the conditions He orders. This revelation of Himself in the midst of circumstances is to bring people to knowledge of "the Lord God Almighty, which is" (Rev. 4:8).

When this knowledge comes, do you worship and submit or hide and turn away from the truth? This grand exposure is given to each and every one of us. Our reaction is our choice. Jehovah may manipulate all things to create the world, but He lets us choose or reject Him. We cannot say that we love Him and accept Him if we reject the truth. If we reject the truth, we are in rebellion and are turned away from Him. Look what the scriptures say about this: John 14:6 *Jesus saith unto him, "I am the way, the truth, and the life: no may cometh unto the Father, but by me..."*

Your true self is discovered by you. You were made with the potential to be like God Himself. This special endowment by your maker gives you the authority to develop into a different kind of "god" or being – one who is quite different than your maker. When everything is boiled away, this final choice is your own. Predestination may have trapped you in events and circumstances, but you make the choice on the basis of loving or hating the light. You cannot dwell in the light if you hate it! Those who hate the light have difficulty accepting even this much of the truth.

Thieves on the Cross

Consider the two thieves crucified with Jesus (Matt. 27:38). Let's look at those passages. Luke 23:39 *And one of the malefactors which were hanged railed on him, saying, "If thou be Christ save thyself and us also."* Luke 23:40 *But the other answering rebuked him, saying, "Dost not thou fear God, seeing thou art in the same condemnation?"* Luke 23:41 *"And we indeed justly; for we receive the due reward of our deeds: but this man hath done nothing amiss."* Luke 23:42 *And he said unto Jesus, "Lord, remember me when thou comest into thy kingdom."* Luke 23:43 *And Jesus said unto him, "Verily I say unto thee, Today shalt thou be with me in paradise."*

This passage further illustrates what I am saying. Both of these men fulfilled their lives. Both men had lived troublesome lives, causing much suffering to the society in which they lived. Both had run their course revealing something about the nature of sin to every life they touched. Although they had lived this life and were now condemned to death for their actions, they ultimately would end up spiritually in the same place as the judge who condemned them. These people were part of the Kingdom of Darkness as sons of Adam. The judge was also a son of Adam. All would continue in the kingdom in which they were born. But one man had a glimmer of the love of the truth in his heart. A lifetime of corruption had not snuffed it out. When he came into the presence of the Prince of Peace, his innermost being responded in affection.

The affection the one thief had for Jesus and the understanding of what He was, opened the door for his translation from the Kingdom of Darkness into the Kingdom of the Lord Jesus Christ. Had there been no attraction to the light of God, this man would have remained in darkness. All those who have a love for the light will come to the light when their heart is prepared to appreciate it. One's entire life may be one scenario after another of a demonstration of compulsive behavior, like Pavlov's dog. However, the love or hatred of the light is the core of our being. God will bring our hearts to make a choice.

What about the other thief? He had the opportunity to change his stance. He hung on the cross next to Jesus for hours, during which time he could have poured out his heart. He was and is like so many people in this world. He, like many of us, suffered and hung on a cross of affliction, thrust upon him as a result of the judgments of life. This man, like many people today who reject Christ, become a true spokesmen of the kingdom of which he was a part and which he represented. Instead of seeking comfort in our Lord, he gnashed his teeth at Him. People like him claim to need no crutches in life. After all, they reason, it is God's fault they are in this present circumstance. These people fail to understand that the suffering of this world, if submitted to the Lord Jesus Christ, would transform them into magnificent beings in the image of God. Their submission to the cross of Christ would transform their suffering into icons of glory. Instead of cursing, they could literally boast of them in the light of the mercy of God through the Lord Jesus Christ.

Nebuchadnezzar

Earlier in this book, we looked at the life of Nebuchadnezzar. We saw how Jehovah gave him the kingdom's of the world to rule over and crush any opposition. He was an absolute dictator, ruling with the authority to kill or reward at his personal discretion. This man's power, though he was a member of the Kingdom of Darkness, was vested in the hands of God.

We will begin with a dream of Nebuchadnezzar and the interpretation by one of his magistrates, Daniel: Dan. 4:10 *Thus were the visions of mine head in my bed; I saw, and behold, a tree in the midst of the earth, and the height thereof was great.* Dan. 4:11 *The tree grew, and was strong, and the height thereof reached unto heaven, and the sight thereof to the end of all the earth:* Dan. 4:12 *The leaves thereof were fair, and the fruit thereof much, and in it was meat for all: the beasts of the field had shadow under it, and the fowls of the heaven dwelt in the boughs thereof, and all flesh was fed of it.* Dan. 4:13 *I saw in the visions of my head upon my bed, and, behold, a watcher and an holy one came down from heaven;* Dan. 4:14 . . . *Hew down the tree* . . . Dan. 4:15 *Nevertheless leave the stump of his roots in the earth, even with a band of iron and brass, in the tender grass of the field; and let it be wet with the dew of heaven, and let his portion be with the beasts in the grass of the earth:* Dan. 4:16 *Let his heart be changed from man's, and let a beast's heart be given unto him: and let seven times pass over him.* Dan. 4:17 *This matter is by the decree of the watchers, and the demand by the word of the holy ones: to the intent that the living may know that the most High ruleth in the kingdom of men, and giveth it to whomsoever he will, and setteth up over it the basest of men.* Dan. 4:18 *This dream I king Nebuchadnezzar have seen. Now thou, O Belteshazzar, declare the interpretation thereof, forasmuch as all the wise men of my kingdom are not able to make known unto me the interpretation: but thou art able; for the spirit of the holy gods is in thee.* Dan. 4:19 *Then Daniel, whose name was Belteshazzar, was astonished for one hour, and his thoughts troubled him. The king spake, and said, Belteshazzar, let not the dream, or the interpretation thereof, trouble thee. Belteshazzar answered and said, "My lord, the dream be to them that hate thee, and the interpretation thereof to thine enemies."* Dan. 4:24 *"This is the interpretation, O king, and this is the decree of the most*

High, which is come upon my lord the king:" Dan. 4:25 *"That they shall drive thee from men, and thy dwelling shall be with the beasts of the field, and they shall make thee to eat grass as oxen, and they shall wet thee with the dew of heaven, and seven times shall pass over thee, till thou know that the most High ruleth in the kingdom of men, and giveth it to whomsoever he will."*

I have cited this long passage as a matter of history. When we examine the fulfillment of Nebuchadnezzar's dream, we see his reaction to the revelation of God in his life and God's judgment. Does he curse, become bitter, and inevitably turn away from the light? No, quite the opposite. This man rejoices and gets excited about this great revelation. He turns with purpose directly into the light. Though he was the greatest earthly emperor and in spiritual darkness, he turns from his old way with purpose into the revelation God has given him. This man, by his actions, demonstrates that he has made a choice. It is obvious that he loves the light and intends to make it a part of his life.

Look what Nebuchadnezzar says at the end of his judgment: Dan. 4:34 *"And at the end of the days I Nebuchadnezzar lifted up mine eyes unto heaven, and mine understanding returned unto me, and I blessed the most High, and I praised and honoured him that liveth for ever, whose dominion is an everlasting dominion, and his kingdom is from generation to generation:"* Dan. 4:35 *"And all the inhabitants of the earth are reputed as nothing: and he doeth according to his will in the army of heaven, and among the inhabitants of the earth: and none can stay his hand, or say unto him, What doest thou?"* Dan. 4:36 *"At the same time my reason returned unto me; and for the glory of my kingdom, mine honour and brightness returned unto me; and my counselors and my lords sought unto me; and I was established in my kingdom, and excellent majesty was added unto me."* Dan. 4:37 *"Now I Nebuchadnezzar praise and extol and honour the King of heaven, all whose works are truth, and his ways judgment: and those that walk in pride he is able to abase."*

This is the man of whom God chose to conquer the then known world. His entire life was driven by destiny, as is witness by this scripture: Dan. 4:32 *And they shall drive thee from men [speaking of the fulfillment of his dream], and thy dwelling shall be with the beasts of the field: they shall make thee to eat grass as oxen, and seven times shall pass over thee, until thou know that the most High ruleth in the kingdom of men, and giveth it to whomsoever he will. . .* After he had run his course, it is obvious that when presented with the truth, he turned to it and not away. With such a heart, he made a clear choice away from darkness and into light. Even though he lived at a time when God made specific revelation of Himself to the house of Israel, we find a man translated from darkness into the Kingdom of Light. God presented him a choice. He made it. God will honor it.

Jabez's Prayer

This life is a proving ground to bring out what is actually in our hearts. It is not so much to show God what is there, because He already knows us. God does not judge as man judges. His judgment is just. The Father's plan is to give to everyone according to what we have chosen. God is good and will reward each person with the final situation that best suits their inner cravings. I am not saying that there are no restrictions. There are those who would depose God in their desires. What I am saying is this, in final judgment He will not give you what you hate. If you love iniquity, He will not give you righteousness. If you hate the truth, He will not force it upon you; in that case, you will never comprehend the light. You may observe it, but you will not understand it.

The unresolvable issue about God's judgment from the perspective of those in darkness is that they cannot understand it because it is a manifestation of light. Each person and fallen angel will receive exactly according to his inner cravings and deeds, yet fail to grasp the justice. Jesus said that at Judgment Day, those in darkness will complain of their reward (Luke 13:28, Matt. 25:30, Matt. 24:51, Matt. 22:13). No one who loves the light will be in darkness. No one who loves darkness will be in light! God is just. Life is a proving ground for what kind of heart you possess.

All those who call upon the name of the Lord (Jehovah) shall be saved (Joel 2:32). In the Old Testament, this was acceptable because the people had no knowledge of the Lord Jesus Christ except in a shadow. Today, if a man does not have Jesus, he does not have the Father (1 John 2:23). It is a matter of embracing the truth. We cannot claim to be in the light if we reject the truth. Truth is light. Jesus is the incarnate truth of the Father, therefore, He is the Light of God. If anyone hates Jesus, then he hates the light. Salvation for that person is not possible, nor does he have a taste for it.

Jabez is a man mentioned only briefly in the scripture. He demonstrates a person who desires to have his life filled with God on every side. With such a desire, God is delighted. You can be assured that all such people will find an open ear to their prayers. God desires to dwell with us in intimacy. When we have the same desire, who can prevent its fulfillment? Notice what Jabez prayed: 1 Chr. 4:9 *And Jabez was more honourable than his brethren: and his mother called his name Jabez, saying, Because I bare him with sorrow.* 1 Chr. 4:10 *And Jabez called on the God of Israel, saying, Oh that thou wouldest bless me indeed, and enlarge my coast, and that thine hand might be with me, and that thou wouldest keep me from evil, that it may not grieve me! And God granted him that which he requested...*

"And God granted him that which he requested..." Jabez loved God's fellowship because of his heart's desire. The scripture says of him that he "was more honorable than his brethren [countrymen]." In the midst of darkness, light will shine.

It is not necessary for a person to be in a perfect environment to discover the desires of his heart. In many instances, the opposite is true. Although righteous attitudes are contagious, they can be unappreciated by those who lack understanding or a heart to love them. Thus, it is also possible to bring out one's innermost loves by an exposure to upright (not uptight) people. If the heart of this individual is not appreciative of this fellowship, this person will seek out other fellowship more to his liking. How can this person expect happiness in heaven with an entire nation of those with whom they do not enjoy? Yet at judgment, there will be weeping, wailing, and gnashing of teeth by those who have in their hearts not received a love for the truth. What can we say against the righteous judgment of God? Only that it is right and just.

I Form Light and Create Darkness

Is. 45:7 *I form the light, and create darkness: I make peace and create evil: I the Lord do all these things.* . . . If there were no darkness, there would be no manifestation of what is the substance of light. Darkness is set in order for the manifestation of light. How would we know what light is if we never saw darkness? How could we appreciate light if we never had to contend with darkness? We do not need to concern ourselves with this problem because Jehovah had determined that darkness is necessary for our development. It is obvious that the angels are yet developing in that there is a future judgment of those angels who followed Lucifer into darkness. If their development were complete, then their judgment would also have been completed as is Lucifer's. Lucifer, in his judgment, received the new name "Satan." This new name reflects his fully formed nature.[3] The name means hater or adversary, an opposing spirit. He is the only angel already judged. Why? Because his development is complete. We also shall receive a new name when we have proceeded further along our development in the Lord Jesus Christ. This new name will be consistent with the final nature and purpose into which the Lord has formed us.

This is exactly what is transpiring. God is forming us into spiritual light. Is. 45:7 *"I form the light.* . . . The Father is forming us. We are "light in the Lord." The apostle Paul speaks of this in his epistles. Eph. 5:8 *for you were formerly darkness but now you are light in the Lord; walk as children of light.* . . . The rest of Is. 45:7 states that He "creates darkness" and "creates evil." I have no desire to explain away this scripture but wish to bring our attention to the truth contained within it.

---

[3]Young, Robert. *Analytical Concordance to the Bible.* Copyright 1964, 1969, 1970.

But not all are being formed into light. Some are being created into darkness. Those who are being created into darkness will eventually have nothing to do with those who are light. Light and darkness are destined to be separate and cannot dwell together. Darkness cannot dwell in light and light cannot dwell in darkness. Light always dispels darkness. Those who are in darkness cannot dwell in the light. Those of the Kingdom of Darkness cannot live in "heaven" unless the very nature of "heaven" were changed.

Darkness is being created just as light is being formed. The decree of the Father in the beginning "let us make man in our own image" is this process of us being formed into light. With Lucifer's opposition to the light, God separated him from the light and thus created darkness. All those born in Adam who joined with Lucifer's (Satan) opposition are raised under the spiritual influence and nature of his idealizations. Ps. 58:3 *The wicked are estranged from the womb: they go astray as soon as they be born speaking lies.* But the influence of the light of God is also in the earth in the Lord Jesus Christ. We are exposed to this light that we may respond. The apostle John puts it this way: John 1:9 *There was the true light which, coming into the world, enlightens every man.*

The whole thing is a process. Light is light and darkness is the absence of light. Those being formed into light will go from one glory to another glory as they are fully transformed into the glorious image of God through the Lord Jesus Christ. These people will become pure light with no darkness within them at all. Those created into darkness also face a similar process, but in reverse. Matt. 13:12 *"For whoever has to him shall more be given and he shall have an abundance; but whoever does not have even what he has shall be taken away from him. . .* People in this world possess a certain amount of the knowledge and ways of Christ. His influence is a light which shines in the darkness. This knowledge of the nature of Christ is not destined to become a permanent part of their lives. Knowledge of the ways of Christ is not to be part of the natures of those destined to darkness. Any understanding those in darkness have of the life in Christ Jesus will leak away and be discarded by them. They have not received a love for the truth, therefore it will be taken from them in exchange for something else. Eventually, they are destined to become absolute darkness with not a trace of light within them. This is the fate for everyone outside of the Lord Jesus Christ.

Jesus said for us to fear Jehovah because of His awesome power. Luke 12:5 *"But I will warn you whom to fear: fear the One who after He has killed has authority to cast into hell; yes, I tell you fear Him!"* Do not let anyone water down this fear or try to explain it away. If you have the proper fear, it will translate into respect; it will keep you safe and save your life. When the Father speaks on your behalf, there is not one who can raise his voice with any significance or consequence except the Lord Jesus Christ.

Remember what we have been discussing in Isaiah. Is. 45:7 *I form the light and create darkness: I make peace and create evil: I the Lord do all these things. . .* God rules now and always.

Others, Turning Away or Toward the Light

There are many other examples of people in darkness turning toward the light at God's revelation. There are also numerous examples of those with some understanding turning away from the light to darkness, preferring it over life in Christ. I will briefly mention one example of each.

Jeroboam, Solomon's servant, was destined to be king. He serves an example of one chosen for greatness by the unction of God. Instead of Jeroboam seeking the fellowship of Jehovah, he instead chooses the riches of this life as his chief love. Jeroboam preferred to be popular through association with idols rather than putting his faith and alliance in God.

Abimelech is initially seen by Abraham as a wicked gentile king with no fear of God in his heart. This man becomes wondrously converted to worship and fear the God of Abraham. This man does not seek solace of protection from other gods, but seeks covenant relationship and terms to avoid any offense. This man, with his limited understanding, demonstrates a reverence for the truth. With such an attitude displayed by this man's actions, he demonstrates his desire for alliance. God does not reject such people as this, but nourishes them.

Quality of Choice

There is one basic quality we possess that helps us define life. It is the ability to choose. With this ability, we interact with our own development. We play a part in our own creation based upon what brings us satisfaction. Even our animals were given certain freedoms of choice. Many of these freedoms of choice are made on the basis of instinctual drives and conditioned by rewards. This behavior is also present in men and angels. Inevitably, it is God Who gives rewards for behavior. Thus, God can either block or encourage one's direction on the basis of the rewards He allows to flow. In this way, our behavior is conditioned. If He chooses to oppose our actions, we are discouraged. If He withholds correction and allows the reward of success, then we may proceed in the direction of our desires unchecked.

In the pursuit of our choices, we discover one of two things. We will enjoy the fruits of our pursuits or discover that what we had imagined was not fulfilling. In either case, we will have developed as a result of our choices. If we are blocked in our pursuits or allowed to apprehend them, it is all a part of the predestination of all things in history scheduled to occur. Nothing will ever occur outside of the Father's permission. Thus, His will also contains what He permits to occur. I hope that you can see that this is absolutely necessary in our own development and in the development of all things.

There is but one possible future. Many people entertain themselves with the notion that there are multiple possible futures. This is pure fantasy. The future is not left to the determination of man or angel. No angel can change the future, no matter what his exalted position. Satan learned this at the crucifixion of our Lord Jesus Christ. He thought that he could change the future to one of his choice by his actions. The future is as Jehovah has planned. People think that they, by their choices, can change the future. I say, as does prophecy, that history can only be fulfilled. The question is, Where do you fit into the entire scheme of things? When all is fulfilled, will you be in covenant relationship with the Father through the Lord Jesus Christ?

Man and angel were created unique in all of the works of God. We were each given the inner substance that could develop into the image of God. With this substance came the reality that other gods were possible from the one true God Jehovah. It is possible to have gods of different natures. To be granted the ability to develop into the image of Father God carried the power to develop into something else; a god of different character, a god far different than the image we see in the Lord Jesus Christ. This is what occurred at the fall near the time of the revelation of the Father about His intention to form man into His own image (Gen. 1 :2 6).

Satan, at that time, Lucifer, chose to take the authority contained in that commission to mold man into the creation of his choosing. He was to be the image of the god he would mold into man. Jesus put it this way: John 8:44 *Ye are of your father the Devil and the lusts of your father ye will do. He was a murderer from the beginning and abode not in the truth because there is no truth in him. When he speaketh a lie, he speaketh of his own: for he is a liar and the father of it...* Without the ability to develop into anything, even a different image than God, we could not, in reality, develop into His image. What is implied by this development is that we are destined to enter into the power and authority of the God head through the Lord Jesus Christ. We are given a choice in this matter based upon the substance of our heart. Some will be of the same heart substance as Lucifer, who became Satan. Others will receive a love for the truth and be changed from one glory to another as we are formed into the express image of Christ – the image of God.

Free will is a big issue in the minds of people whenever predestination is discussed. Let me assure you that each and every person will be given an opportunity to choose or reject the Lord Jesus Christ. This exercise of free will will be on the basis of the issues within their hearts. Attitude is a principal ingredient in the reception of mercy. Since we will make this choice on the basis of the love of our hearts, we need to pray that our hearts be watched over by God Himself. Solomon put it this way: Prov. 4:23 *Keep thy heart with all diligence; for out of it are the issues of life...* I encourage you to go one step beyond this by asking and resting in God to keep your heart and mind firmly in the Lord Jesus Christ. He cannot fail us if we are willing to rest in the confidence that it is He that works in us to do His pleasure. We put no confidence in the flesh. We acknowledge that it is God Who saves us and not our own efforts. Where is our boasting? We have none except in what He has done for us. It is God Who makes us and not we ourselves.

Other Sheep I Have Not of This Fold

John 10:16 *And other sheep I have which are not of this fold: them also I must bring and they shall hear my voice; and there shall be one fold and one shepherd...* Jesus is speaking of gentile lovers of the light. But who are these people who have not heard Him speak? Certainly He is speaking of gentile believers who will believe in Him for their salvation in the ages to come. The Lord Jesus is speaking of far more than those who will hear the gospel through His disciples.

At the crucifixion, prior to Jesus' ascension into glory, He descended into the spiritual netherworld to preach His message to all those who had died who harbored a love for God but had not heard the word of salvation. Eph. 4:9 *Now that he ascended what is it but that he also descended first into the lower parts of the earth?* The message of the Father has always been hope to anyone who has a heart to receive it. That hope does not end at death; it is alive at that time. The cry of the hopeful heart is always heard when it is directed to God in sincerity.

The apostle Peter discussed the issue of Jesus preaching His gospel to those already dead but who had a heart that could be directed to Him. (It is pure fantasy to claim to love Father God and dislike the Lord Jesus. If you love Jesus, you will be loved by the Father and accepted by Him.) Let's look at what Peter wrote of the preaching of Jesus at His death: 1 Pet. 3:18 *For Christ also hath once suffered for sins, the just for the unjust, that he might bring us to God, being put to death in the flesh, but quickened by the Spirit:*

1 Pet. 3:19 *By which also he went and preached unto the spirits in prison;* 1 Pet. 3:20 *Which sometime were disobedient, when once the longsuffering of God waited in the days of Noah, while the ark was a preparing, wherein few, that is, eight souls were saved by water...*

We are examining an area of doctrine avoided by most, but very important. It is an area where we see the impartiality of God. As I have stated earlier and say again, everyone who has a love for the truth will be presented with an opportunity for salvation. John 3:21 *"But he who practices the truth comes to the light that his deeds may be manifested as having been wrought in God."* This scripture does not speak only to Jews, but also to Gentiles. There is no exception, man or woman. You may rightly ask, How can they come to the light unless given an opportunity? They must be given an opportunity, because "he who practices the truth comes to the light." It is statement of fact! And Who is in the light? God is in the light; God is light. Jesus Christ is the manifestation of the light of God. The only way given to man to come to the light is through the Lord Jesus Christ (Acts 4:12). There is no other way!

This leaves us with a perplexing conclusion. If God is just (we know this to be true), what about all the people who have died never to hear the gospel? Surely some of these would have chosen Jesus. Yes, they would. All people born were given the substance within themselves to choose good or evil, right or wrong, light or darkness. Even the philosophies of the pagan nations reveal a search for the truth. The philosophy itself may be vain; however, it speaks volumes of the desire to practice the truth. Opportunity to hear the gospel of salvation is a very great privilege. It is the difference between eternal life and eternal judgment. Without the Lord Jesus Christ, no person can be saved, because the righteous of mankind is seen as unclean.

Note what it says in Isaiah about our own best efforts at self-righteousness: Is. 64:6 *But we are all as an unclean thing, and all our righteousness are as filthy rags; and we all do fade as a leaf; and our iniquities, like the wind, have taken us away...* The "filthy rags" with which self-righteous people clothe themselves is referring to menstrual cloth. This fact is revealed in the sole definition given for this word "filthy" in the Hebrew dictionary: 5713ch. "iddah" from an unused word; menstruation;. . . It is a socially unacceptable picture to think of a person clothed in menstrual rags. Then, imagine such a person demanding that such clothing should be acceptable for a wedding feast or all social gatherings. Would anyone be welcome wearing menstrual rags for clothing? This is what the self-righteous look like spiritually. These blood stained garments are the best the natural man has to offer. Thus even their best efforts are terribly soiled with blood.

God is not unjust. God is love. He will not abandon any who have a love for the truth and desire to practice it. Jesus, at His death, preached to the spirits in darkness who died in the judgment of the Flood at the time of Noah. When the flood came, many of these people realized that what Noah had been preaching was the word of God and they cried out in repentance. These people still drowned because they were outside of the ark. God, though, honored their repentance and sent Jesus to preach to them the gospel of salvation made possible through His own blood. Thus He (Jesus) offered the word of salvation through His name (Eph. 4:8). But what of those who died without the knowledge of Jesus since His resurrection or were not part of the repentance at the time of the Flood?

My Own Thoughts

Up to this point, I have limited my discussion only to those things which I had strong scriptural support. I feel compelled to discuss a concern of many regarding those who die in ignorance without the knowledge of Christ, through no fault of their own. God is just and wishes that none will perish into eternal darkness. Thus it is His will that all men and angels be given a choice. Note what our Lord Jesus says of damnation: John 3:19 *"And this is the condemnation that light is come into the world and men loved darkness rather than light because their deeds were evil. . ."* But what if a person did not like darkness? Why should they be condemned if they were never given a chance to be exposed to the light? They should be given an opportunity to choose Jesus.

In this section, I will discuss my thoughts on this subject. I ask you, the reader, to consider my arguments prayerfully. I think I have the mind of Christ on this subject; however, I wish there were more scripture from which to draw upon to cast light.

First, we see Jesus at His death before His resurrection to preach to spirits in prison. These spirits were those who had died without the knowledge of salvation. We read about this in the Epistle of Peter. 1 Pet. 3:18 *For Christ also died for sins once for all just for unjust, in order that He might bring us to God, having been put to death in the flesh, but made alive in the spirit;* 1 Pet. 3:19 *in which also He went and made proclamation to the spirits in prison,* 1 Pet. 3:20 *who once were disobedient, when the patience of God kept waiting in the days of Noah, during the construction of the ark, in which a few, that is, eight persons, were brought safely through the water...*

Was this preaching available to all people who had died before Jesus or only to a select few who died at the time of the Flood? Let me answer this with another question. Why would Jesus want to reject anyone or keep them from the opportunity to love and embrace Him? Would He tell some that they were not allowed to hear His message? Those who do not know Him would admit that this is unlikely; those who know Him would say that He would allow all to hear and respond. Jesus said this: John 6:37 *"All that the Father gives Me shall come to Me and the one who comes to Me, I will certainly not cast out..."* Jesus also said that He had others who were not of the Jewish sheep fold (John 10:16); meaning that others who were not Jewish belong, and would belong, to Him. Some of these others were "spirits in prison."

Who else might be someone who died without the knowledge of salvation? Many in Israel had the opportunity to hear the stories, be exposed to the teaching, and participate in the worship of Jehovah. These people would have some understanding of what He required of them They would also understand that, even with their best effort to follow the Law given by Moses, they would fail miserably to live up to the standard set before them. This failure, in itself, would bring those who cared about practicing the truth to the place of faith. They would have to rely upon the mercy of God because of their failures. This faith in the mercy of Jehovah was their justification and their salvation. This was true for the enlightened Jews. They knew God would save them because they loved Him. He was their God. Not everyone who was a Jew shared this love and devotion. Some took the birthright for granted and did not care because they had not a love for the truth; even that which they had would be taken from them (Matt. 13: 12). This is not a group that would have likely embraced the preaching of the Lord Jesus in the netherworld.

Many people around the world died, having been in darkness their entire lives. Many of these people devoted their lives to worshiping idols and false gods of their imagination or fantasy. In their belief in higher powers, some of them may have even worshipped demonic manifestations. All this, they did in ignorance. The deep faith and devotion of many Christians today is evidence that many of these people, if exposed to the light of the truth, would embrace God with a tenacity as great as any of the most noteworthy Jewish followers. Is this understanding apparent only to you and I? Was this not understood from the beginning by our Maker? Do you think He would be short sighted? Of course He knew all things from the foundation of the world and before. It is unthinkable to imagine that He would not have made provisions to save all who had the desire.

Jesus told us what was the main issue in judgment: John 3:19 *And this is the condemnation, that light is come into the world, and men loved darkness rather than light, because their deeds were evil. . .* If someone did not like the darkness, then there is no condemnation. God takes no pleasure in the spiritual death of anyone, as it is written: Ezek. 18:32 *"For I have no pleasure in the death of anyone who dies," declares the Lord God. "Therefore, repent and live."* It does not say the death of anyone, but "the death of anyone who dies." This significant difference declares that Jehovah is referring to spiritual death. Physical death is no problem because the relationship between us and God continues. But with spiritual death, the relationship has no future. God has no pleasure in the thought of no relationship.

It is only logical for the Father to make every effort to bring Himself pleasure in all the creatures He has made. Note what He says in Genesis in the account of creation: Gen. 1:10, Gen. 1:12, Gen. 1:18, Gen. 1:21, Gen. 1:25 . . .*and God saw that it was good.* . . It was good because it brought Him pleasure. God will expend every effort to bring people to the valley of decision and to choose light over darkness. With some people, it takes a lifetime of pain and suffering, such as the repentant "thief on the cross" dying next to the Lord Jesus. Others, like the other "thief on the cross," will not turn to the light because they have developed a contempt for it. The loss is theirs, but the Father has no pleasure in it. God's graciousness is demonstrated in the example of the thieves on the crosses being extended to the last minute.

With others, as we have demonstrated, this graciousness was extended beyond the grave. This is a very special group of people who died in darkness, never having had the opportunity to turn toward the light. Matt. 4:16 *The people which sat in darkness saw great light; and to them which sat in the region and shadow of death, light is sprung.*

Why were they sitting? Because their life was over; these people died and were still part of the Kingdom of Darkness. Isaiah states the following: Is. 42:6 *I the Lord have called thee in righteousness and will hold thine hand and will keep thee and give thee for a covenant of the people for a light of the Gentiles;* Is. 42:7 *To open the blind eyes to bring out the prisoners from the prison and them that sit in darkness out of the prison house.* . . Hell is the prison house for all disobedient and rebellious spirits. It is a place to restrict the activities of those who would, by their actions, disrupt the Kingdom of God. It is also the holding place of all spirits who do not know the ways of God. Those who die in darkness remain in darkness unless they choose the light. The Lord Jesus Christ is the light of God. To reject Jesus is to reject the light. Any spirit who rejects Jesus remains in the "prison house."

This wonderful and just opportunity presented to all people

who died in darkness prior to the revelation and death of the Lord Jesus Christ did not end with His resurrection. The gospel of salvation, although being heard by many, was and is yet to be heard by all the people in the world. This would seem to create some problems. God is just and is not willing that any be lost who have a desire to have relationship with Him. But what of those who have died since the resurrection of Jesus, having never heard the gospel? God has already shown us a pattern of His intentions to reach them.

Jehovah is not partial to any. He sent Jesus to preach to those who "sat in darkness" in the "prison house," leading them out whosoever believed and accepted the Lord Jesus Christ. He would repeat this pattern until all have the opportunity to accept or reject Jesus. None will be able to declare that God was unjust with them; that they did not get an opportunity to accept Jesus. The power of the scripture, Is. 42:6 *I the Lord... give thee [Jesus] for a covenant of the people, for a light of the Gentiles;* Is. 42:7 *To open the blind eyes, to bring out the prisoners from the prison, and them that sit in darkness out of the prison house,* did not end with the resurrection of Jesus. His preaching to all in darkness to present to them the gospel of salvation, became firmly established.

Today, as we speak, people are dying around the world having never heard the truth about Jesus. Do you think that God would give an opportunity of salvation to those who died in the Flood in Noah's day and not give the same opportunity to others? He does give them the opportunity to choose the light. The scripture clearly states: John 3:21 *"But he who practices the truth comes to the light, that his deeds may be manifested as having been wrought in God."* This scripture does not say that this person first comes to the light, then practices the truth. This is referring to any person living the truth to the best of his conscience and understanding, a person attempting to do what is right on a daily basis. This is a person who has a heart to "practice the truth." This person is outside the covenant of God, but has an appreciation for righteousness.

How will this person "come to the light" unless he is presented with the opportunity? The scripture (John 3:27) cannot be broken.

He will be presented with the opportunity, and so, come to the light! The apostle Paul put it this way: Rom. 2:14 *For when the Gentiles, which have not the law, do by nature the things contained in the law, these, having not the law, are a law unto themselves:* Rom. 2:15 *Which show the work of the law written in their hearts, their conscience also bearing witness, and their thoughts the mean while accusing or else excusing one another. . .* Thus, you can see that a caring person can practice the truth diligently by following the conscripts of his conscience. This is not salvation, but a demonstration of a love for the truth. Our conscience, like the Laws of God, are followed as a result of us appreciating what is right or rejecting it. Those who hate the truth will not come to the light. John 3:20 *For every one that doeth evil hateth the light neither cometh to the light, lest his deeds should be reproved.*

At their death, all people who have lived by the direction of their conscience, not knowing the salvation of God which comes through the Lord Jesus Christ, will be given an opportunity to choose or reject Him. Who does this? It may be our Lord Jesus or one of His angels. Those who have heard the gospel and rejected it may not be given another chance. Although a preacher named Kenneth Hagon claims to have had a second chance. He died from an illness as a young man, having been raised in a church but not embracing the doctrine. He recounts being escorted into hell. He began to cry out to God for mercy. The voice of God thundered to the dark spirits escorting him, who then released their grip. He then came back from death and repented, asking for the Lord Jesus Christ to accept him. This story is a matter of current history.

My position is very straightforward. The love and concern Jehovah showed for the ignorant people, who died at the time of Noah, was not an exception but the rule. God will not let you go unless you hate the light. We present the gospel when we have opportunity to those who have an open ear. Our best efforts are but a very small part of God's outreach to those in darkness. Yes, there will be a judgment. But those who have accepted the Lord Jesus Christ need not be concerned because God has already laid upon our Lord Jesus the judgment that would have been ours. Can any of us not love Him for that?

The Final Word

Having said this, one thing is all important. Relationship. Relationship is everything. It is not so much what you know but Who you know. Knowledge is important and strengthens you, but is vain without relationship. The most ignorant, if they have a relationship with the Father through the Lord Jesus Christ, are infinitely better off than the most knowledgeable if they live in darkness. If you love the darkness, you will disagree. I say this from the vantage point of one who strongly and faithfully loves the light.

ABOUT THE AUTHOR

Raymond H. DuRussel, born in 1948, grew up on a farm in Michigan. During that time, he faced a difficult childhood filled with turmoil and lost all faith in the existence of God. As a young man, he volunteered for the draft at the height of the Viet Nam war in an effort to find some stability in his life as well as some answers.

While in Army basic training, he often meditated, seeking the meaning of life and the source of his own identity. One evening, while he meditated in the barracks, his life was irrevocably changed when he was given three visions. In the first vision, he was taken to a corridor-like room. He was in darkness, yet he could see. There was a row of doors representing opportunities for fulfillment in life, yet all were closed to him. At the end, one door was open and light poured through it like he had never seen before. Where this light shined, there was no darkness.

As he sat meditating the next night, seeking the "light", he became paralyzed from head to toe. He could not even think, but only listen. The Lord said to him, "Get up and follow Me." For five days, he thought about the vision continuously. During this time, he decided again to seek the "light", which he found, and give the reply that he would follow.

Dr. DuRussel felt compelled to write this book and was inspired moment by moment as he wrote. It is his hope that your faith will be enormously deepened, and that you discover a new-found peace as a result of reading what he has written.

He currently lives in Harrison, Michigan.